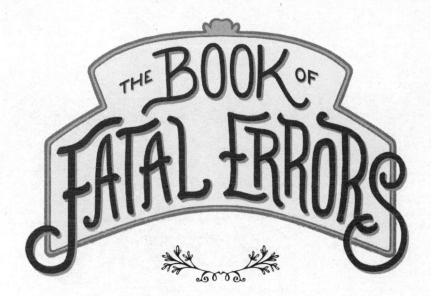

DASHKA SLATER

FARRAR STRAUS GIROUX
NEW YORK

Farrar Straus Giroux Books for Young Readers
An imprint of Macmillan Publishing Group, LLC
120 Broadway, New York, NY 10271

Printed in the United States of America
Designed by Carol Ly
First edition, 2020
1   3   5   7   9   10   8   6   4   2

mackids.com

Library of Congress Cataloging-in-Publication Data

Names: Slater, Dashka, author.
Title: The book of fatal errors / Dashka Slater.
Description: First edition. | New York : Farrar Straus Giroux, 2020. | Summary: Twelve-
year-old Rufus Takada Collins discovers feylings on his grandfather's farm and it is up to
him and his cousin Abigail to find the magical train cars that will carry them safely home.
Identifiers: LCCN 2019021283 | ISBN 978-0-374-30119-4 (hardcover : alk. paper)
Subjects: | CYAC: Fairies—Fiction. | Magic—Fiction. | Imaginary creatures—Fiction. | Lost
and found possessions—Fiction. | Cousins—Fiction. | Adventure and adventurers—Fiction.
Classification: LCC PZ7.S62897 Bq 2020 | DDC [Fic]—dc23
LC record available at https://lccn.loc.gov/2019021283

Our books may be purchased in bulk for promotional, educational, or business use. Please
contact your local bookseller or the Macmillan Corporate and Premium Sales Department
at (800) 221-7945 ext. 5442 or by email at MacmillanSpecialMarkets@macmillan.com.

In memory of my father, Philip Slater

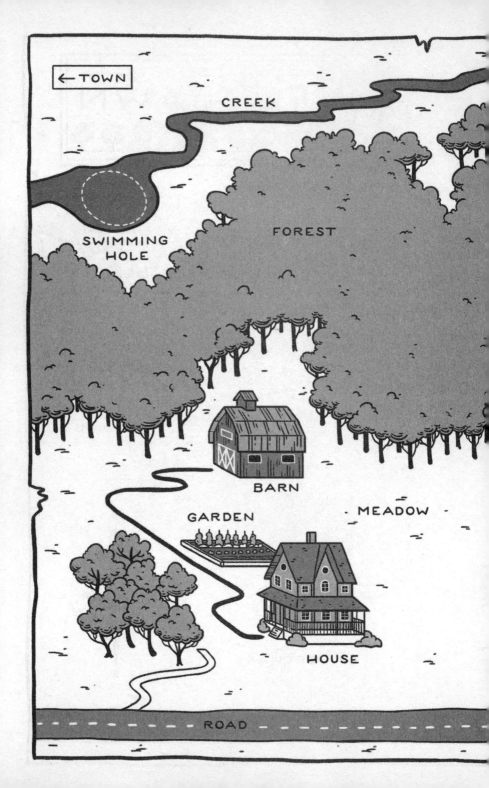

CONTENTS

HOW IT BEGAN

It was the last day of school and everything was singing. The birds were peeping and trilling and cooing. The bugs were buzzing and humming and chirping. The leaves rustled in the trees, the seeds rattled in the grass, and twelve-year-old Rufus Takada Collins, walking home with nothing in his backpack but the sweatshirt he'd found at the bottom of his locker, sang to himself: *Summer, summer, summer.* Of course Rufus knew better than to actually sing out loud, because people already thought he was weird, and also, the song didn't have much of a tune. But even if his lips weren't moving, even if he managed, through sheer force of will, to stay completely silent, his heart was singing, his bones were singing, his skin, warm in the sunshine, was singing: *Goodbye, sixth grade. Hello, summer, summer, summer.*

Rufus did not hate school, he just hated who he was when he was there. Which was, basically, nobody. He was not brainy like his father or athletic like his mother, and while he liked talking to people when he had the opportunity, he never knew exactly how to get the conversation started. He had one friend, Xander, who had spent all of sixth grade trying—without much success—to get him interested in an obscure collectible-card game called Marshannyx. Most of the other kids at Galosh Middle School ignored Rufus. The few that didn't found as many ways as possible to remind him of the three fatal errors he had made during his sixth-grade year.

Fatal Error Number One: In September, on a field trip to Crescent Cove, he had noticed an unusual shorebird and said—maybe a little too loudly—"That's a masked booby!" Which might not have been Fatal if he hadn't tried to explain how rare it was to see one on this side of the Pacific and if Aidan Renks hadn't stared right at him and said in a high, too-enthusiastic voice, "I know! It's crazy! I can't believe I'm looking at one now!"

Fatal Error Number Two: In October, during recess, he had stopped in the middle of a basketball game because there was a salamander under the hoop. Which might not have been Fatal if he hadn't then taken off his left shoe and put the salamander inside so it wouldn't get squashed. And even that might not have been Fatal, except that Aidan Renks had yelled, "Oh my God, look! It's a barefooted booby!" and suddenly the whole booby thing from September was back in play.

Fatal Error Number Three: In November, he forgot to clean out his pockets before coming to school, and when he sat down at his desk, a clump of unusual berries he'd collected in the woods had gotten squished and left a purplish-brown stain on the seat of his pants. Which might not have been Fatal if Tyler Zamboski, who sat behind him in Math, hadn't yelled, "Barefooted *poopy*!" And at that moment, Rufus had understood that his best choice—his *only* choice—was to become invisible and stay that way.

But now it was June and the school year was over. The rains, which fell in Galosh with little interruption from October to May, were done. Summer days could be spent at Feylawn, the rambling family property across town where his grandpa Jack lived. Galosh was small as cities went, with not too many high-rises and quite a few parks. But Feylawn was better than a park. It had a forest, and a meadow, and an orchard, and a cold trout-filled creek. The days there were long and bright and aimless, just the way Rufus liked them, and there were seventy-five of them before school started again in the fall. *Hello, summer, summer, summer!*

As Rufus opened his front door, he squared his shoulders a little, tucking his summer song deeper into his chest. His mother, Emi, would have already left for her shift at the hospital. His father, Adam, would be sitting at the kitchen table scrolling through job listings on his laptop. His dad never meant to ruin Rufus's mood, but lately he couldn't seem to help it. His gloom was so huge and dark and cloudy that it seemed to suck everything into it, like a black hole.

But today his father wasn't in the kitchen. He was in the hallway, waiting for Rufus.

"Grandpa Jack's hurt," he said. "We need to get to Feylawn."

༺ଓ୕ଡ଼༻

"I don't understand," Rufus said during the drive across town. "How did he break his arm?"

"He fell." His dad ran a hand over the uncombed clumps of his wavy brown hair.

"But *how* did he fall?" Grandpa Jack wasn't the falling type. Rufus had never seen him lose his footing, not even when jumping from stone to stone while crossing the creek at Feylawn.

"According to Mom, he stepped through some rotting floorboards in the barn." His dad glanced over at Rufus and raised his eyebrows, as if to add italics to the statement. "And since phones don't work up there, he had to drive himself to the emergency room. If Mom hadn't showed up for her shift just as he was leaving the hospital, we might not even know."

"What rotting floorboards?" Rufus asked. "I was just in the barn last week. I didn't see any—"

"It's *Feylawn*, Rufus. Don't try to make sense of it."

➤ 4 ➤

But Rufus wanted to make sense of it. He knew Feylawn and Grandpa Jack about as well as he knew anything in the world, and nothing his father was saying jibed with his understanding of either of them. He was about to ask his dad another question when he saw that they had just sped past the road to Feylawn.

"*Dad*," he said. "That was the turn."

His father slammed on the brakes and squinted through the windshield. "I can't see it."

"Back up—it's behind us."

The streets of Galosh had been laid out in an orderly grid. It had no cul-de-sacs, back alleys, roundabouts, or other streetscape surprises, and hardly any roads with curves. But for reasons no one could quite explain, the dirt road that led to Feylawn was almost impossible to find, even if you knew exactly where it was. It was on the edge of downtown, sandwiched between a parking lot and a burrito shop, yet it always faded from sight just as you approached it, as if swallowed by a sudden fog. Rufus, however, had a knack for finding it.

"Not yet," he coached as his dad reversed down the street. "Not yet. *Now*."

His father made an abrupt Hail Mary turn and their old blue Toyota plunged into a blur of green and brown. A moment later the road came into focus again, bordered by tall trees on either side. It meandered uphill and then suddenly ended. Grandpa Jack's bottle-green pickup was parked in its usual spot, smack in the middle of the road, keys dangling in the ignition. No one outside of the family ever came this way, so there was no need to worry about thieves. The road dead-ended at a stand of seven oak trees. Beyond that, flanked by a meadow dappled with blue lupines and orange poppies, was Feylawn.

2

FEYLAWN

Grandpa Jack was sitting on the wraparound porch of the old blue-and-white farmhouse, looking out over his garden. He was a stocky man with a salt-and-pepper mustache, thick capable hands, and a shock of white hair topped by a khaki cap. He wore horn-rimmed spectacles held together at the nose by electrical tape, and his right arm was in a sling.

As soon as he saw Rufus and his dad, Grandpa Jack got to his feet and enfolded each in a one-armed hug. "Well, this is an unexpected pleasure!"

"Emi told me about the accident." Rufus's dad frowned at the sling. "I had to make sure you were okay. Since we can't call." He enunciated the last four words as if they had sharp edges that might cut his mouth if he said them too quickly.

"Is your arm really broken?" Rufus asked.

"Just a little." Grandpa Jack sank back into his wooden

rocking chair. "No need to make a big deal about it. Could have been worse. Could have been my head."

"My point exactly," Rufus's father said. "I see you broke your glasses again, too."

Grandpa Jack winked at Rufus. "I think the tape looks quite dashing," he said. "Roguish, even."

"Can I get you something?" Rufus asked. "Do you want tea?"

"An old man takes a seat in a rocking chair and next thing you know, people are trying to serve him tea." Grandpa Jack leaned back and rested his feet on the porch railing. "Just have a seat and keep me company. I've got a jar of pills and a cooler of ice packs from the hospital. I'm feeling fine."

"A cooler? Does that mean your refrigerator's not working?" Rufus's dad lowered himself onto the porch steps, his gangly knees splayed like a cricket's. Rufus leaned against the railing. He wished his dad would stop seeing the dark side of everything.

"Power's out at the moment," Grandpa Jack admitted, "but it'll come back on. Always does."

"It's no way to live, Pop."

"It's a fine way to live. I know you and your sister never liked it here, but you were at a contrary age when we moved in. Rufus and I, though, we appreciate the scenery." He gestured at the view, which encompassed both the vegetable garden at his feet and the vast and varied landscape of greens beyond.

"You still haven't tried the rope swing Grandpa Jack and I made," Rufus said to his father. "You can see all of Fey-lawn, practically. It's like flying."

His father was still watching Grandpa Jack's face. "I'd like to know what happened in the barn."

"Funny story, actually," Grandpa Jack said. "As you know, I've been trying to clean out the barn for lo these many years."

"I'm going to help you again this summer," Rufus interjected. "We can make another Museum of Interesting Things."

Last year's museum had included an old bowling pin, a pair of leather aviator goggles, a ceramic chicken, a pile of boxing magazines from the 1930s, and a brush for grooming horses.

"Museum of Useless Junk, you mean," Rufus's father said.

"Anyway," Grandpa Jack went on. "This morning when I was poking around in there, I uncovered an old icebox—the kind that uses actual ice to keep food cold. Thought to myself: that might be useful, what with the electricity going on and off the way it does. But here's the funny thing. When I went back to measure it to see if it would fit in the kitchen, I noticed a honking big hole in the floorboards."

"And you *fell* in it?" The hair on Rufus's arms prickled. Below the main floor of the barn was the cellar, where Grandpa Jack kept firewood. It was a long way down.

"'Course not," Grandpa Jack said. "The hole I stepped in was the one I *didn't* notice. Itty-bitty one, just big enough for my foot—if I hadn't put out my hand to break my fall, it wouldn't have been any problem at all."

He gave a wheezing laugh, then stopped short when he saw Rufus's dad glaring at him.

"It's not funny, Pop."

"Sure it is. Feylawn has moods, always has. She's a bit cantankerous at the moment, but it'll pass. Never liked that footstool anyway."

He gestured at the charred chintz cushion of a three-legged footstool that normally sat in the living room.

"You had a *fire?*" Rufus's father leaped up to examine it.

"Just a small one. Could have been worse. Could have burned something I was fond of."

"Rufus," his dad said. "Grandpa Jack and I need to talk. Why don't you go take a look at that osprey nest you keep telling me about?"

"But I wanted to show it to *you*," Rufus said. Back when his dad worked in the accounting department at the Buckett Brand Windshield Wiper Company, before the Great Gloom descended, he used to let Rufus show him the things he'd discovered at Feylawn—fox dens and swimming holes and the cluster of tall granite stones that

Rufus called the Boulder Dude because if you squinted at them from just the right angle they looked kind of like a person.

"Maybe next time." His father stood beside the scorched footstool, his long arms folded, his shoulders hunched. Rufus sighed. He'd been trying to show him the skunk-striped osprey chicks for weeks. Now they were almost ready to fledge.

"Speaking of the Museum of Interesting Things!" Grandpa Jack boomed suddenly. "I found something I wanted to give you, Rufus. It's inside that icebox in the barn. What with all the excitement, I never went back to get it."

"I'll get it on my way to the nest," Rufus said.

His father shut his eyes and exhaled slowly. "Do not. Go in. The barn," he said to Rufus. "For Pete's sake, Pop, what are you thinking?"

"Stop being such a worrywart," Grandpa Jack said. "What are the chances that two of us fall in a hole on the very same day?"

"No barn, Rufus," his father said. "Have I made myself clear?"

Rufus sighed. "Very."

3

THE BARN
AND THE BELL

Nothing seemed strange or out of place as Rufus walked along the path that led to the barn. Bees mumbled in the clover. Birds trilled from the wood. So what had Grandpa Jack meant when he said Feylawn was feeling *cantankerous*? It wasn't the first time he'd talked about the old property as if it were alive, but Rufus had never understood what he meant by it. How could a place have a mood, other than maybe *green*, or *windy*, or *wet*? Feylawn was hard to find, but it wasn't normally the kind of place where floorboard holes opened up of their own accord, no matter what Rufus's father said.

Rufus wanted to see what those holes looked like. And while he was in the barn, he could grab whatever Grandpa Jack had found in the icebox. He'd be in and out of there long before his father was done lecturing Grandpa Jack.

Having been on the receiving end of many of his father's lectures lately, Rufus knew they could go on awhile.

The barn door hung by one hinge and had to be lifted before it would swing open. Rufus stood on the threshold, letting his eyes adjust to the dim light. Then he pushed the toe of his sneaker against the floorboards, testing their strength. They *seemed* solid enough. He took a hesitant step forward and then another, threading between the furniture stacked on either side of the doorway: dressers, desks, tables, a wardrobe, a curio cabinet, a coatrack, a rabbit hutch, and about a dozen different kinds of chairs, with and without seats. To his left were a motorcycle and the remains of a horse-drawn cart, and in the back of the barn were tools and equipment, cans of paint, a plow, a butter churn, skis and snowshoes, fishing rods, easels, old computers, and a couple of saddles. To Rufus's right, behind the furniture, crates and boxes were piled in ten-foot stacks. The boxes were the usual sources of Interesting Stuff. You never knew what you'd find inside.

Rufus didn't see the hole until he had tiptoed past the piled-up furniture. When he did, he stopped short and stared. The floorboards were shattered. Pieces of splintered wood were strewn around them, as if something had burst through from underneath. Rufus drew closer, stepping gingerly, and squatted beside the hole, which was bisected by the thick crossbeams of the ceiling below. A dank smell wafted up. He knew firewood was stacked down there—that's where he and Grandpa Jack went in winter to get logs for the stove. But peering through the hole now, he couldn't see anything at all—just shadows.

He stood up, heart pounding inexplicably, and looked around for the icebox. It wasn't hard to find—a wooden cabinet with three metal doors; it had been dragged into the middle of the floor and left there. There was a small hole beside it.

The door of the largest compartment hung open. Inside was a dusty burlap sack. Rufus had just picked it up when he heard a scraping noise, like a sled being dragged over an icy snowbank. It came from the cellar.

He took a step backward, then whirled around, remembering the hole in the floor. Below him, something flapped like a flag in the wind. Then it slammed against the boards under his feet.

Heart now galloping in his chest, Rufus tightened his grip on the burlap sack and bolted for the door.

⁓⁓⁓⁓

Once he was out in the sunshine, Rufus immediately felt foolish. So something had been moving down in the wood cellar—big deal. It was a possum or a raccoon or a wood rat. He'd tell Grandpa Jack about it later, when his dad wasn't around. They'd trap it, set it free out in the woods. Nothing to get spooked about.

He sat down in the grass and opened the burlap sack.

Inside was an old-fashioned locomotive, bright green, and much bigger than any toy steam engine he'd ever seen. It was about the size of a loaf of sandwich bread, and it shimmered in the sunlight. Painted in gold capitals on its side were the words ROVING TREES RAILWAY, LTD.

Most of the things Grandpa Jack found in the barn were old and rusted, but this didn't even look dusty. The inside of the cab contained an impressive array of miniature brass gauges and levers, and it had a boiler that seemed as if it might actually open if Rufus could fit his fingers around its little handle. Mounted on the top of the engine was a shiny bell the size of a gumball. Rufus flicked it with his finger.

The peal rippled around him, far too loud for something so tiny. A dizzying pins-and-needles sensation jittered over his skin. It wasn't a comfortable feeling but it was a thrilling one, like when you jump off a high dive and know both that you never want to do it again and that you want to do it again immediately. The world seemed to turn silver and for a moment Rufus felt silver, too, every particle in his body buzzing as if electrified.

Then the chime died away. Once again Rufus was exactly as he had been—a twelve-year-old boy sitting in the grass beside an old barn.

Well, maybe not *exactly* as he had been. He studied the steam engine, a little dazed. Something was different. But what?

Rufus had always known himself to be a very ordinary person. He got Bs and Cs in school, played passable but not particularly inspired trumpet in the school band, and was neither awful nor amazing at soccer and basketball. He didn't whip up gourmet desserts in his spare time or win spelling bees or rack up high video game scores or know any impressive skateboard tricks. But just then, he somehow felt extraordinary. He got to his feet and jumped in place to see if he'd acquired the ability to fly or leap over the barn in a single bound. He scanned the trees to see if he suddenly had X-ray vision. As far as he could tell, he still didn't have any superpowers, or even any above-average powers.

All the same, something felt different.

He sat down in the grass again and turned the steam engine over in his hands, amazed at how light it was given its size. A Steller's jay landed in the grass beside him and stared at him with its black crest cocked forward inquisitively.

"Hello there," Rufus said. "Do you like my train?" Carefully, he returned the train to the burlap sack. Time to get back to the house. His dad never wanted to stay at Feylawn for very long.

The jay was still watching him. It hopped along in the grass, its indigo chest puffed out. Then, with a harsh squawk, it grabbed the burlap sack in its beak and spread its wings.

"Hey," Rufus cried as the bird flapped into the air. But

while the Steller's jay was clearly an avian of unusual ambition, it seemed unprepared for the weight of a burlap sack containing a large toy locomotive. For a brief time it rose and sank and rose again, like an airplane caught in a squall. Then bird and bag parted company. The jay flew over the trees, screeching in frustration. The bag tumbled down into the grass.

As it hit the ground, the steam engine's bell rang out a second time, loud and bright and shivery-silver. Rufus felt the chime strike him like a wave. As it did, a cry rent the air, keening and anguished, like a heart being broken. It was the single saddest sound Rufus had ever heard.

He picked up the bag and drew out the engine. Miraculously, it wasn't even dented.

"Time to go!"

Rufus looked up to see his dad striding toward him on his long legs. He eyed the train in Rufus's hands. "Where'd that come from?"

"I found it in the barn," Rufus said, still reeling from the strangeness of the shivery bell, the heartbroken cry, the oddly behaving bird.

His father's face darkened. "The *barn*?"

It was only then that Rufus realized what he'd said.

TURNAROUND SUMMER

For the whole drive home, Rufus waited to be lectured about Feylawn's dangers and his own disobedience. But his dad said nothing. He just tapped his thumbs against the steering wheel and occasionally blew air out of his nose like a surfacing whale.

It wasn't until after dinner, when Rufus was sitting on the floor of his room organizing his collection of unusual seeds, that both of his parents came in and sat on his bed. His mom was still in her scrubs. She balanced a plate on her knees, eating the pasta and broccoli they'd saved for her.

"Your seed collection's getting pretty big," she said, gesturing at the tackle box where Rufus kept it. Each kind of seed had its own little drawer and there were dozens of drawers. Rufus liked to pull them open and pour the seeds into his palm. He liked the feel of them in his hands, their different sizes and shapes. It was almost as if they had voices, each one murmuring its own tiny song.

Rufus held out a papery lantern-shaped pod containing three jet-black seeds. "Look at these."

"They're like cut glass!" His mom traced the beveled edge of one of the seeds with the tip of her finger. "Did you find this at Feylawn?"

"If I could make a suggestion," his dad interjected before Rufus could answer. "Perhaps you should look up each seed's scientific name and put labels on those drawers?"

"I've tried—but I can't find them in any books," Rufus said.

"Try more books. Try online," his dad said. He drummed his fingers on his knees. "Grit. Determination. That's what makes people successful."

Rufus felt a prickle of unease. His father looked even more unhappy than usual. He put the seed pod back in its drawer.

"You should come seed hunting with me this summer," he said to his dad. "We can bring a field guide. Identify things. Remember how we used to do that with birds?"

His dad cleared his throat. "That's what we want to talk to you about, actually. There are going to be some changes this summer."

"I know: Mom's going to be gone and I'm going to need to help out more. We've talked about it." Rufus's chest tightened, thinking about his mom's absence. On Monday she would leave for Phoenix, where emergency room nurses could make more money than at the hospital in Galosh.

She'd be gone for three months. Rufus had been trying not to think about it.

He looked around the room for something he could use to distract his father from wherever the conversation was headed. The green steam engine sat on the floor beside him, its paint gleaming. Rufus picked it up.

"You have to admit—it's pretty cool." He placed the engine on the bed next to his dad. "A Steller's jay tried to steal it from me today."

His mom laughed as she speared a piece of broccoli with her fork. "Rotten birds," she said. "Your grandmother used to make me and your uncles throw rocks at them so they wouldn't ruin the fruit in her garden."

"Stealing toys isn't the same as stealing fruit." Rufus's father took out his phone. "What kind of bird did you say?"

"Steller's jay. They're blue, with a black crest."

"Look at that." His father held up his phone so they could see the picture. "Says here that jays, like other members of the corvid family, have an affinity for shiny objects. I guess you know your birds." He looked over at Rufus's mom as if hoping she might say something, but she was focused on her plate.

"Speaking of knowledge," he said after a moment. "A lot of kids do educational activities in the summer. Stay sharp for school. Find, uh, ways to excel. And with Mom away, you're going to need some structure."

"I'll be fine at Feylawn," Rufus said. "I can help Grandpa Jack. It's hard to do stuff with a broken arm."

His dad shook his head. "You can't spend your whole summer taking care of an old man."

"We haven't seen much of Xander lately," Rufus's mom said. She gave him a reassuring smile. "I thought you guys were best buds."

This was one of those things that was hard to explain to parents—the difference between a school friend and a *friend* friend. Xander was fine to have lunch with and sit next to in class, but once they left school, they quickly ran out of things to say. Xander didn't like basketball or riding bikes or visiting Feylawn. In fact, the only thing he really liked was playing Marshannyx. Or talking about playing Marshannyx. Or watching videos of other people talking about playing Marshannyx.

"Xander's okay," Rufus said. "We're not really *best buds* though."

Rufus's dad pulled a square of folded pages from his back pocket with a flourish, as if performing a magic trick. "Then you're in luck. Because summer camp is a *great* way to make new friends."

"*Summer camp?*" Rufus repeated. He swallowed, picturing a summer spent surrounded by Tyler Zamboskis and Aidan Renkses. "No. I don't want to go."

"Of course you do," his dad said. "Summer camp is an opportunity to *excel*."

Uh-oh. *Excel* was a favorite word of Rufus's aunt Chrissy, who had just moved back into town with her daughter, Abigail. Abigail was always excelling—winning trophies and starring in shows and being named student of the year. The only trophies Rufus had were the ones you got for just being on the team.

"I'm not really an *exceller*, Dad." The memories of the year's Fatal Errors tightened his chest. He looked to his mom for help, but she was still wearing her reassuring smile. Rufus suspected it was the same one she gave to patients who came into the emergency room with gaping wounds or missing limbs.

"Sure you are," Rufus's dad said, unfolding the pages and fanning them out like a deck of cards. "And I found quite a few camps that still have openings. Take a look."

Rufus flipped through the papers. "Chess Camp? What kind of horrible idea is that?"

"I loved chess when I was your age," his dad said. "I went to the finals in a national tournament."

"I'm not a boy genius like you were," Rufus said irritably. "I stink at chess."

"There are other options," his mother said. "Your dad spent a long time looking."

Rufus scanned the rest of the pages. Healthy Eating Camp (*Learn about good nutrition and cook up some tasty sugar-free desserts!*). Plumbing Camp (*Bring your plunger and prepare to get wet!*). Puritan Camp (*Experience the simple, uncluttered life of early Americans!*). Banking Camp (*We're* banking *on fun!*).

"No way." He tried to hand the pages back to his dad, but his dad wouldn't take them.

"This is what's available," his dad said. "You need to do *something*, Rufus. It's a tough world out there. People are competing for jobs. *Fighting* for them."

"I'm not looking for a job though," Rufus said. "I'm only twelve."

His mother cocked her head at him. "I had a job when I was twelve. Working in the Takada Nursery with my brother—after school *and* during the summer. Camp's a better option."

"Abigail goes to camp every summer and she's learning to speak Mandarin," Rufus's dad added.

"Good for Abigail. Now she can annoy a billion people in their native tongue."

His dad sighed heavily. "You can't just lollygag around staring at the birds. You need to apply yourself, find something you're passionate about—a project!"

Ever since he'd lost his accounting job eight months ear lier, Rufus's father had been obsessed with projects. Rufus had learned to be careful about what he expressed an interest in, because his dad was apt to turn any topic into a *project*, thus rendering it deeply and irrevocably boring. When Rufus had asked about the difference between a star and a planet, his dad bought a book of astronomical charts and a telescope and started waking him up in the middle of the night to look at distant blurs through the lens. When Rufus suggested going to a baseball game, his dad had sat him down to watch a nine-part documentary on the history of the sport.

"Can't we just do things for fun like we used to?" Rufus asked. He turned to his mom for support. "Why does it have to be a *project*?"

His mom picked up her plate and got to her feet. She looked from Rufus to his father and back again. "You two are going to have to work this one out. Starting on Monday, I'm not going to be here to mediate." She squeezed Rufus's shoulder on her way to the door. "Like it or not, we're all going to have to make some changes this summer."

"Dad," Rufus said when she was gone. He tried to keep the panic out of his voice. "I'll be fine. I'm almost in seventh grade. I don't need a lot of supervision."

His father ignored him. "When I was a kid, do you know what I wanted to be?" he asked.

"The next Steve Wozniak?" Rufus asked. He'd heard this story before.

"That's right. An inventor or a mathematician or a computer whiz, somebody who solved an important problem, made his mark. But I didn't get into Harvard like I expected. I went to an ordinary college and got a dead-end job and I never even left Galosh. I'm not going to let *you* be ordinary, Rufus. You're going to excel. This is going to be a *turnaround* summer." He got up and went to the door. "Choose the camps you want and we'll get you registered." He shut the door behind him, then opened it again and stuck his head back into the room. "And for now—no Feylawn."

"What?" Rufus said. "Why not?"

But the door had already closed.

5

THE INFESTATION

Rufus came awake all at once. He checked the wrist-watch he kept by the bed: five o'clock. The sky through his window was still a deep, sleepy blue, but Rufus felt as shivery and wide-awake as if he had just emerged from Feylawn's swimming hole. He rolled over to look at the steam engine, which he'd left on the floor. Its green paint shimmered, like sunlight on leaves or wind on water. But how? The room was dark and still. He sat up and lifted the engine. There was something peculiar about it—something that had made a bird want to steal it. Something that cried out from inside the chime of the bell.

Grandpa Jack could explain—he was the one who'd found it. Rufus looked at his watch again. His parents wouldn't be awake for another couple of hours, but Grandpa Jack was always up at dawn. If Rufus rode his bike to Feylawn now, he could talk to Grandpa Jack and be back before anyone noticed. If he was really banned from Feylawn, this might be his only chance.

Grandpa Jack stood on the porch swinging a broom over his head with one hand.

"Good morning!" he called when he saw Rufus approach. "Don't mind the moths—they don't bite!"

He waved the broom wildly. "Shoo! Go on! Go *away*!"

Rufus stopped halfway up the porch steps, mouth gaping.

Circling Grandpa Jack's head were half a dozen tiny winged *people*.

Rufus closed his eyes and opened them again. He blinked rapidly. Any moment, the flying creatures would reveal themselves to be something ordinary that just happened to resemble miniature winged humans.

"Don't be scared!" Grandpa Jack called out. "It's a small infestation, but they're not dangerous." He swatted at one of the little people fluttering over his head, then brought the broom down to sweep furiously at one scurrying across the floor of the porch.

"Wait!" Rufus shouted as the creature dove for cover under the rocking chair. "Grandpa Jack—don't! They're not moths!"

"Flies, you think?" Grandpa Jack said, slashing the broom before him like a sword as he strode through the front door into the farmhouse. "Well, I'm no bug scientist, but it's an infestation either way. Are you hungry for breakfast?"

Rufus followed him, his legs wobbly. The creatures covered every surface in the small living room—they perched on the fireplace mantel, roamed over the pine floor, and congregated on the saggy brown couch and the overstuffed chairs. Roughly four inches tall, they had leathery, leaf-shaped wings and a scrawny, wild look. Rufus suppressed a shriek as one scampered over his left foot. "Grandpa," he whispered. "Are you seeing what I'm seeing?"

"I see 'em all right—I just can't figure out where they're coming from." Grandpa Jack looked around the room in dismay. "After breakfast we'll shake out the sofa cushions."

Rufus was having trouble finding his voice. As wild and haggard as the creatures looked, they clearly weren't bugs. They wore clothes made of fabric scraps and candy wrappers, and some carried bundles and boxes as if they were on their way somewhere. A small group played double Dutch with two shoelace jump ropes at one end of the sofa. Another cluster seemed to be building a fire in a candy dish in the center of the coffee table. As one of them struggled to light an oversize match, Rufus suddenly understood what might have singed Grandpa's footstool. He snatched up the kindling-filled candy dish. There was a chorus of groans as he emptied it into the fireplace and set it on the mantel.

"Stupid glomper," one said.

"I really don't think they're bugs, Grandpa," Rufus said. His heart was hammering in time to the rhythm of the tiny people's game of double Dutch. "They're *talking*."

"Buzz, buzz, buzz!" Grandpa Jack chuckled, sweeping

the entire group off the coffee table with his broom. "I suppose you could call that talking." He sighed. "I've tried putting up flypaper, but for every one I catch, there's another dozen more."

He pointed to three strips of sticky paper dangling from the ceiling. A small and very irritated-looking man in a brown suit struggled to detach himself from one of them.

"How long has this been going on?" Rufus asked, staring at the thrashing man. Could his grandfather really not hear the long and inventive string of curse words issuing from the man's tiny mouth?

"Well, as I said, Feylawn's been in a bit of a mood all week. Then yesterday afternoon it started to get bad. Now it's a full-scale infestation." Grandpa Jack smiled at Rufus. "Could be worse, I suppose. Could be snakes. I'll put on the kettle."

As soon as he was sure Grandpa Jack was busy in the kitchen, Rufus tiptoed closer to the man in the brown suit, which appeared to have been made from Hershey's candy wrappers and mouse fur. The little man was stuck to the flypaper by one wing. His feet egg beatered the air as he tried to pull himself free. A small crowd fluttered around him, offering advice. Their voices should have been as tiny as they were, but they seemed to Rufus to be just as loud and clear as if they were full-size.

"Just let me give you a tug—I'll get you free," offered a burly man with large wings shaped like ivy leaves. His own suit seemed to have originated as a striped necktie. He yanked the legs of the unfortunate gentleman in the brown suit, but only managed to detach the flypaper from the ceiling. Paper and man both tumbled to the floor.

"Oh, dear!" someone in the crowd said. "That's not good."

The little man thrashed wildly, but each contortion only served to get another part of his body stuck to the paper.

"Stop!" Rufus hissed at him. "Stop, you're making it worse!" Swallowing hard, he squatted down and lifted the sticky mass of man and flypaper to eye level. "Hold still and I'll help you," he whispered in the soothing voice he used with birds he wanted to get closer to.

There was a sudden silence.

"Clear-eyed," a woman in a sky-blue dress said. "That's something new."

"No, he isn't," said the burly man with the ivy-leaf wings. "I've seen him out by the creek. He never so much as glanced at me."

The man in the brown suit peered at Rufus from inside the ball of flypaper, trembling with fear or frustration, it was hard to say which. "Well, which is it, glomper? Can you see us or not?"

Rufus nodded, not trusting himself to speak. "Can't everyone?" he whispered.

"If by *everyone* you mean other glompers, the answer's no," said a woman with wispy white hair. "And those that *can*, keep quiet. If they're smart." She tapped her lips with an index finger.

"Why?"

The man in the brown suit kicked impatiently and then gave a rattling cough. "Hey, glomper, I thought you said you were going to help!"

"Sorry," said Rufus. "I've just never seen—"

He glanced over at a series of framed pictures that hung on the wall next to the fireplace. The pictures had been drawn by Grandpa Jack's mother, the famous children's book author Carson Sweete Collins. They showed tiny golden-haired fairies with sheer dragonfly wings perched on the edges of pink blossoms. Those willowy creatures looked nothing like the ragtag bunch in front of him, with their sinewy wings and knobby limbs, and yet—what else was he supposed to call them?

"Feylings," said the white-haired woman. "We're green-blooded American feylings." She grinned slyly. "We don't look much like the pictures, do we? Not pretty enough for storybooks, I guess."

"Ooooh!" the man in the brown suit trilled in a high voice. "Look at me, I'm a fairy with gossamer wings! Here I am sprinkling sparkles and happiness!" He made a prancing motion as best he could, given that most of him was stuck to the flypaper. Then he spat. "How about letting me go, glomper?"

"Sorry, I'm not sure how—"

"Scissors," barked the white-haired woman. "Quick, before he's overcome."

Too astonished to reply, Rufus found a pair of scissors in an end-table drawer and used them to trim the sticky paper away from the feyling's clothes and wings.

"About time," the little man grumbled as he flew off. A moment later, he dropped to the ground in a dead faint.

Rufus gasped and went to pick him up, but the white-haired feyling got there first.

"That's what comes of getting overexcited!" She tutted. She pulled a folded leaf from the pouch she wore at her waist and used it to cover the man in the brown suit. "There you go," she cooed. "You'll be all right in a moment." She looked up at Rufus. "Run along, glomper. You've done your bit."

Rufus started toward the kitchen, but the feyling in the sky-blue dress stood in his path. She had both hands wrapped around the handle of a suitcase nearly twice her size and was bent double as she dragged it forward, her breath coming in gasps.

"Can I help you with that?" Rufus said, keeping his voice low so that Grandpa Jack wouldn't hear.

The feyling smiled up at him. "Would you?" She sat on the floor, her pale green wings drooping. Rufus bent down and picked up the suitcase with his thumb and forefinger. It was surprisingly heavy.

"Whoa, what's in here?"

"Souvenirs. Ephemera," the feyling said. She coughed into her fist. "A few artifacts I've collected during my time among the glompers. And, of course, my manuscript—*A Lexicon of Common Glomper Expressions and Their Meanings, with Examples from Everyday Life.*"

Rufus wasn't entirely sure what she had just said, but he nodded as if he understood. "What are you all *doing* here?" he asked. "Why does everyone have suitcases?"

"We heard the bell," the feyling said. "The train is coming. At long last."

Rufus frowned. "What train?" He suspected he already knew the answer.

"*The train to the Green World,*" the feyling said, her tone suggesting that this should have been obvious. She heaved herself to her feet, then flew to Rufus's shoulder. "You can drop my suitcase on the baggage rack by the back door. I'm Iris Birchbattle, by the way."

"Rufus Collins."

"A descendant of Carson Sweete Collins, I presume? Well, I won't pinch you just now since you're helping me with my suitcase. But don't expect me to hold off once we're done. Remind me if I forget."

"I don't think I will, actually," Rufus said.

Iris sighed. "Have it your way," she said, and pinched him on the earlobe.

Rufus winced, amazed that such a tiny creature could be so strong. "What was *that* for?"

"Carson Collins and I have a score to settle," Iris said. "Stop complaining. If you'd been cooperative, I could've waited."

⟷⟜⟞⟐

When Rufus entered the kitchen, Iris fluttered from his shoulder toward the back door, where a low shelf containing several oversize pots seemed to be serving as a baggage check.

"Stow my suitcase over here," she ordered. Rufus dropped her suitcase on the shelf and collapsed into a seat at the kitchen table, which Grandpa Jack had laid with a pot of tea, a basket of muffins, and two settings of plates and mugs.

"Everything all right?" Grandpa Jack asked, pulling up a chair beside him. "You look a little shaky."

Rufus glanced at two feylings perched on a shelf of cookbooks above the table. "I just— Can you—?" he stammered. "Those bugs . . . Do they look at all . . . like . . . *people* to you?"

"You're wasting your time, clear-eyes," one of the feylings on the shelf called. "He's gonna think you're nuts."

Sure enough, Grandpa Jack was looking at him with concern. "People? Can't say I've looked that closely. But I suppose if some people have bug eyes, some bugs must have people eyes, right?" He bugged out his own eyes and chuckled.

Rufus decided to take a different approach. The feyling called Iris had said the train was coming. Maybe if he could get Grandpa Jack to tell him something about the train he'd found, this whole strange morning would start to make sense. He just wished he could ask without the feylings overhearing.

"I was wondering about that . . . Interesting Thing," he said cautiously. "The one you found in the icebox."

"Beautiful, isn't it? Did you show your dad?" Grandpa Jack dropped a muffin on each plate.

"He didn't really look at it." Rufus bit into his muffin. "He was in the middle of banning me from Feylawn, actually," he continued, the muffin lumping in his throat. "What does he have against Feylawn, anyway?"

"He didn't grow up with it, like you did," Grandpa Jack said. "Remember, there were years and years when Feylawn was empty—abandoned. So when Grandma Lulu and I decided to move back here, it didn't go over that well with your father and Aunt Chrissy. After living in Seattle, they found Feylawn a bit remote. And being teenagers, they made a big deal about the little inconveniences."

"You mean it being so hard to find?" Rufus asked.

Grandpa Jack nodded. "Chrissy missed prom because her date couldn't find the house. And your dad was always complaining about the mail not being delivered."

Using his uninjured hand, Grandpa Jack poured tea into two cups, ladled a few teaspoons of sugar into each of them, and slid one to Rufus. Then he took a sip of his own, the steam clouding his eyeglasses.

"Do you remember how you said yesterday that Feylawn was in a mood?" Rufus asked. He looked up at the two creatures on the shelf. One made a face at him.

"Cantankerous," Grandpa Jack said. He took off his steam-clouded eyeglasses and rested them on the table. "It's not the first time. Fact is, if Feylawn hadn't been cantankerous, the previous owner might not have been so willing to sell it to my grandfather."

Rufus knew the story. His great-great-grandfather Avery Sweete had stumbled onto Feylawn while selling encyclopedias and had ended up buying the property in exchange for volumes A through R. According to family legend, it had taken him the better part of a month to find it again and another five years to tame it.

"Now, *that* was a mood," Grandpa Jack said. "Pop Avery told me he'd never been so badly vexed in his life. Tools broke. Horses bolted. Cows went dry. Every time he tried to build a house, it would get disassembled in the middle of the night and he'd have to start fresh the next morning."

"But what was causing it?" Rufus didn't know why he'd never wondered this before. He'd always just accepted Feylawn's peculiarities the way other people accepted their homes' squeaky floorboards or running toilets. But now? This was not an ordinary kind of peculiar.

Grandpa Jack added another spoonful of sugar to his

tea and stirred it thoughtfully. "Weather? Magnetic fields? Termites? Pop Avery always said the place was cantankerous, and that seemed as good an explanation as any."

"But the name," Rufus persisted. "Feylawn. Where did that come from?" The little people had called themselves *feylings*. Were they named for Feylawn or the other way around?

"That's just local folklore. *Fey* means fairy, you know. In the olden days, people in town used to say the place was filled with fairies doing mischief with their little wands or what have you. That was the inspiration for my mother's books."

"But then the mood passed," Rufus said. He eyed the feylings on the cookbook shelf again.

"In time. Pop Avery and Feylawn found a way to get along. Place never stopped being quirky, mind you, but—"

At that moment, a large cookbook fell from the shelf over their heads and landed on Grandpa Jack's glasses. The impact sent the teapot skidding off the table. Pottery shards and hot tea flew in all directions.

"Nice shot!" shouted a feyling from the kitchen counter.

Grandpa Jack didn't seem to notice. "Oh well, could have been worse," he said, mopping his tea-spattered legs with his napkin. "Could have been the *good* china. Looks like that's the end of my specs though. Grab me a new pair from the drawer, will you?"

As Grandpa Jack went to get a towel to clean up the tea,

Rufus stepped gingerly over the remains of the teapot and opened the top-right drawer of the yellow-and-red hutch next to the pantry. The drawer was filled with an assortment of eyeglasses that Grandpa Jack had picked up at garage sales and thrift stores. He was always needing new ones—no pair of glasses seemed to last him more than a day or two—and he claimed the prescription mattered less than people said. Rufus picked out a pair of gold-rimmed granny glasses and put them on.

"How do I look?" he asked.

Grandpa Jack grinned. "Like an old lady. Now hand them here. I can't see what I'm mopping up."

Rufus took them off, then put them on again. It was the strangest thing, but when he looked through the lenses, the feylings disappeared. Crawling on the counter and circling the table were nothing but large brown moths.

"You can't stay clear-eyed with those things on your face," said Iris, settling on his right shoulder. Fearing another pinch, Rufus brushed her off. She circled around to his left shoulder and coughed. "What I find curious is that you didn't used to be clear-eyed," she continued. "What happened?"

He ignored her and went to get the broom. As he swept the remains of the shattered teapot into a dustpan, the feylings fluttered around him, chattering among themselves.

"I don't see the point in causing so much trouble," one said. "We've lived peaceably till now."

"Too peaceably," said another. "Rest-in-peaceably."

"The long wait's over, that's the important thing," said a man in a red-checkered coat that looked remarkably similar to the dish towel Grandpa Jack was using to mop up the spilled tea. He slumped in a corner, his wings brown and curling at the edges, like withered leaves. "We're going home at last."

"So we thought," Iris said from Rufus's shoulder. "But where's our train?" Then she flew off, disappearing through a hole in the window screen.

Grandpa Jack came back to the table and sat down. "Now, what were we talking about?" he asked.

Rufus looked at his watch. It was almost seven o'clock. "I should get home before Mom and Dad wake up," Rufus said. "Technically, I'm not supposed to be here."

He looked around the kitchen, trying to fix it in his mind. Was his father really going to keep him away from Feylawn all summer? Now, when it was more interesting than ever?

As Grandpa Jack walked him to the door, Rufus remembered that he still hadn't asked his question. "That toy steam engine," he said quietly. "Do you know where it came from?"

"Must have been my mother's," Grandpa Jack said. "She loved toys. Children's book writers are basically just children, she always said." He ruffled Rufus's hair. "At any rate, it's yours now."

THE SUMMER PROJECT

Rufus's parents had plans for him that day. First his mom, who had been a college track star, took him running. She wasn't a talkative person, but when she had something to say, she didn't beat around the bush.

"I know you went to Feylawn this morning," she said as they jogged through their leafy neighborhood. "But you can't keep doing that. If Dad says you can't go, you can't go. End of story."

"But it's not *fair*!" Rufus panted, trying to keep pace with his mom's effortless stride. "Just because *he's* in a bad mood all the time doesn't mean *I* have to be."

His mom slowed a notch so that Rufus could catch up. "He's having a tough time," she said. "Not having a job. Me having to spend the summer working in Phoenix. Don't take it personally."

"But it *is* personal," Rufus said. "Feylawn's my favorite place in the whole world."

"You're going to have to be flexible," his mom said. "We all are. You and Dad need to get along this summer." And then she accelerated, knees lifting, until neither of them had any breath left for conversation.

Rufus's dad was waiting at the front door when they got back, holding a pad of lined paper and a pen. "Turnaround summers don't happen by themselves," he said. "It's time to make lists!"

And so they did. A list of camps to sign up for. A list of goals for the summer. And, of course, a list of potential summer projects. It wasn't until late afternoon that Rufus was able to go to his room, shut the door, and take another look at the steam engine. There had to be a label or a mark or a switch or something that would tell him why the feylings were so interested in it. He turned it over in his hands, stilling the bell with his fingers, and examined the underside.

His fingers brushed something crinkly.

A folded scrap of paper was tucked into the under-carriage, just behind the small wheels at the front of the engine. He pulled it out. The yellowed page was so brittle that the edges crumbled as he unfolded it.

If you find this, don't jump to conclusions. I'm ahead of you by leaps and bounds.

—*Carson*

He read the note three or four times, then tossed it aside. "What's *that* supposed to mean?" He groaned.

"That's what I always say when I read her books," said a voice behind him. "Which I try not to do very often."

The feyling in the sky-blue dress flew to the steam engine in his lap, landing on its roof.

Rufus half leaped, half tumbled off the bed, landing on the floor with the train still on his lap and the feyling still on the train. This couldn't be right. Seeing weird stuff at Feylawn was one thing. But seeing weird stuff here? In his bedroom? With his parents downstairs?

"Stop staring at me like I'm a talking radish." Iris had her arms folded over her chest and she looked as severe as a four-inch person could. "I hitched a ride in the basket of your bike this morning. I had a hunch I needed to follow up on. A good one, as it turned out." She tapped her toe on the roof of the train. "Maybe you'd like to tell me what you're doing with our train?"

Rufus opened his mouth and shut it again. "I didn't know it was yours until this morning," he said after a moment. "Why are all of you so obsessed with it, anyway?"

Iris surveyed him with her head to one side, a tangle of black hair falling over one eye. "That's none of your business," she said. "Just return it to Feylawn and we'll be on our way."

"On your way *where*?" Rufus realized his voice was getting a little too loud. His parents were downstairs and he could only imagine his dad's reaction if he caught Rufus talking to an invisible person or giant moth or however Iris would look to him. "What did you mean when you said you were going to the Green World?" he said more quietly.

The feyling tossed her hair out of her face. "You've never read your great-grandmother's books?"

"The books about Glistening Glen?" Rufus thought of the pictures of golden-haired fairies hanging on the walls of Grandpa Jack's living room. "I tried to read them when I was younger but . . . they were kind of boring."

"Nine-tenths of what she wrote was lies," said Iris. "But she got a few things right. Like the fact that we rove between the Blue World—that's this one—and the Green one, where we live."

"But how did she know that stuff?" He didn't know much about Grandpa Jack's mother—she had died long before he was born. But nobody had ever said that anything in her books was actually *true*.

"Carson Sweete Collins was the first clear-eyed glomper we ever met. Clear-eyed from the moment she was born. She made quite a stir. We couldn't get enough of her at first." Iris stared off into space for a moment, as if remembering something.

"At first?"

"Well, you know what they say—*Clear-eyes, clear lies.* Once you start talking with glompers, they'll start lying to you. Sort of like you did when you offered to carry my suitcase and didn't mention that the train I was waiting for was sitting in your room. Where did you find it, anyway?"

"In the barn."

"It's been in the barn the whole time?" Iris put her face in her hands. "We looked there, I know we did. We looked *everywhere*."

"It was in the icebox," Rufus said.

"I don't know what that is," Iris said. "But I suppose it doesn't matter. Where's the rest of it?"

"What do you mean?"

Iris coughed. "The train has a tender for carrying fuel," she said. "And two coaches for carrying passengers. Plus a caboose at the end."

"Passenger trains don't have cabooses," Rufus said. He'd been fascinated with trains when he was little, so he knew that cabooses were only for freight trains.

"This one does," Iris said. "And we need it. We need all five pieces for the train to work."

"I didn't find any cars," Rufus said. He set the steam engine on the floor and stood. "I wish you would just explain what's going on. I don't get why you feylings are suddenly all over Feylawn or why I can see you when no one else can, or how you knew the steam engine was here or why the bell on it made me feel like . . ." He trailed off, not sure how exactly to explain how the bell had made him feel.

Iris looked at him coolly. "The only thing you need to understand is that we need those cars. Are you sure you don't know where they are?"

Rufus shook his head.

"Think hard."

"I told you: I don't know."

Iris slumped, her wings drooping. "Then we're no better off than we were before."

Rufus had never seen anyone pass so quickly from bossy to dejected. "Look," he said, taking a seat on the bed. "Maybe if you explained, I could help you. I know Feylawn pretty well."

Iris snorted. "You don't even know what Feylawn is."

Rufus didn't answer. He'd spent enough time watching birds to know that if you were quiet, sometimes the bird came to you.

"It's a sanctuary," Iris said. "A safe place for unusual plants and irregular creatures. That's why we keep it hidden."

"You mean you're the reason it's so hard to find?"

Iris nodded. "We smuckled the boundary. Otherwise you glompers would pave over it, like you pave over everything else."

"Wait—" Rufus interrupted. "What do you mean *smuckled*?"

Iris blew her hair out of her eyes impatiently. "I thought you knew Feylawn *pretty well*," she said. "Smuckling's a way to hide something by making it so that no one notices it. It isn't invisible, it just isn't obvious."

Rufus thought about the way the road to Feylawn

seemed to fade into fog. "But why have I never seen you before? I'm at Feylawn all the time."

Iris stared into his face, scrutinizing him. "That's how I knew you had the train," she said. "Carson Collins was born clear-eyed, but not you. I've seen you around for years. You were cloud-eyed and then suddenly you were clear-eyed and the only thing that can turn a cloud-eyed child into a clear-eyed one is the peal of a calling bell. And the only calling bell I know of is on this engine."

Rufus could see the bell mounted on the boiler. The memory of its peal passed through his body like a shudder. He had felt it changing him. And he had felt something else—that cry, the saddest sound he'd ever heard. "What's a calling bell?" he said. "And how did it make me clear-eyed? And why—?"

Iris coughed again, her wings shaking. "Enough questions," she croaked. "I've decided to tell you the whole story. Once I've finished, I think you'll understand what you need to do."

"What *I* need—?" Rufus protested.

"*Shhh,*" Iris said. "Listen. Every creature has its own kind of road. Ants make theirs with scent. Goblins with tunnels. Glompers with asphalt. We make ours with a kind of tree we call a Roving Tree. If there are Roving Trees in two different places, there's a road between them."

"Like stretching a rope between two posts," Rufus said.

"If you say so. The point is, there was a road between the

Roving Tree at Feylawn and the Roving Tree in the Green World. And we traveled that road frequently, because we have work to do in both worlds. But then Carson Sweete Collins chopped down Feylawn's Roving Tree."

"Why would she do that?" He thought about the note he'd found. *I'm ahead of you by leaps and bounds.* For someone who had made a career of writing books about feylings, his great-grandmother didn't seem to have liked them very much.

"I don't know," Iris said. "We tried to stop her but . . ." She took a rose petal from the pouch she wore at her waist, wiped her eyes, then blew her nose. "Then, after she cut it down, we thought we had a solution. Our queen made a deal with the goblins, which shows how desperate we were."

"Hold up," Rufus said. "Queen? Goblins?"

Iris shut her eyes for a long moment, then opened them. "It must be tiring being so ignorant," she said. "I know *I'm* getting tired of explaining things to you. Goblins are hideous, destructive creatures from the Sunless World. They're good at digging, tunneling, and metalwork, and we spend far too much of our time trying to keep them from entering Feylawn and turning it into a slag heap. But they have metal-craft and we don't, so our queen convinced them to build us a train that could make its own track, connecting the dead Roving Tree stump at Feylawn to the live Roving Tree back home. We paid a steep price for it, but afterwards we were able to rove between the worlds just as we always had. But by train."

With her fingers, she traced the gold lettering on the train's side: ROVING TREES RAILWAY, LTD. "It was an odd kind of craft that made it—a mix of their abilities and ours—but it wasn't meant to last forever," she said. "The Roving Tree back home drops a seed every seventy years or so. We figured that as soon as it did, we could plant ourselves a new tree at Feylawn and then we wouldn't need the train. It was just supposed to buy us some time."

"So what happened?"

"Our train vanished," Iris said. "Just a few months after we got it. And we've been stuck here ever since, unable to go home. Meanwhile, the feylings in the Green World can't come here."

Rufus was silent, trying to make sense of all he'd just heard. "The stump of the Roving Tree—it's by the back door of Grandpa Jack's house, isn't it? That big reddish one—like a tabletop."

Iris nodded. "That's where we gather when the calling bell rings. We thought, when we heard it . . ." She dabbed her eyes with the rose petal.

"I'm sorry I don't have the rest of the train," Rufus said. "I'd give it to you if I did."

Iris looked at him as if considering what he'd said. Then she flew over and kicked him in the ear.

"Ow!" Rufus cried. "What was that for?"

"Don't give me *sorry*," Iris screamed. "What am I supposed to do with *sorry*?"

Rufus rubbed his ear. "What do you want me to say?"

"Say you'll help us find the train cars," Iris said, landing on the floor at his feet. "You said you know Feylawn *pretty well*. So find them."

"I can't," Rufus said. "I'm not even allowed at Feylawn anymore. My dad's making me go to summer camp."

Iris slumped.

"I know you don't want to hear it, but I really am sorry," Rufus said.

Iris looked up. "They say there are two sighs to every sorry," she said. "But I'm far too angry to sit around and *sigh* every time you say it."

She lifted from the ground and swooped toward Rufus's other ear. But he was ready for her this time. He waited until she was close, then swatted her away with the back of his hand. There was a squeal and a soft thud as Iris ricocheted off his fingers and landed on the floor.

"The expression is two *sides to* every *story*," Rufus said. "Are you okay?"

Iris didn't move. She lay sprawled on her back with her eyes closed, her wings twisted beneath her.

"Iris?" Rufus bent over the four-inch feyling, his heart thumping. In an instant, she grabbed a fistful of his bangs and pulled, hard, until his nose was nearly touching hers.

"Don't trifle with me, Collins," she said. "This is life or death for us."

"It is?"

Iris let go of Rufus's hair and sat up, wrapping her arms around her knees. "We're dying, actually. Not to be overly dramatic, but there it is."

"Dying?" The word caught in Rufus's throat. "*All* of you?"

Iris nodded. "Your world—it's killing us. Back when we could roam between the worlds, we lived forever. We just needed to go home to the Green World occasionally, to recover. But we've been here for sixty-five years now and I guess that's as long as we can go without—" She fixed him with her large brown eyes. "Without going home. Half of us have died already. The rest will be dead within a few weeks." She put her head on her knees, her hair curtaining her face. "Please?" she said quietly. "Please help us?"

Rufus put his hand on the train. He had the feeling he was about to make yet another Fatal Error.

"Okay," he said. "I'll help you."

7

ORCHARD MEADOWS

"Morning, sleepyhead."

Rufus opened his eyes. His mom was sitting on the edge of his bed. Instead of her usual running shorts and T-shirt, she wore a flowered skirt and a short-sleeved white blouse.

"Why are you dressed up?" he asked.

His mom smoothed her skirt. "I'm not dressed *up*. I'm dressed *nicely*. We're going to visit Great-Aunt Biggy today, remember? Aunt Chrissy and Abigail are going to be here in half an hour."

Rufus sat up and looked around the room for Iris. He'd promised he'd take her back to Feylawn in the morning so they could start hunting for train cars. "I'm going to Feylawn today," he told his mother. "Grandpa Jack needs my help."

His mom laughed. "Nice try." She got up to open the curtains. "Pack your swimsuit. You and Abigail can play in the Orchard Meadows pool while the grown-ups talk with Great-Aunt Biggy."

"Abigail doesn't *play*," Rufus objected. Abigail, Aunt Chrissy, and Uncle Victor used to visit from Houston every Christmas. Whenever Rufus suggested they play a game or watch a movie, Abigail looked at him as if he had suggested catching measles or eating Styrofoam.

"That's not true," his mom said. "The two of you used to love playing together."

"When we were little. She doesn't even talk to me now."

"Just make an effort. She left her dad and all her friends behind in Houston. She's probably lonely." His mom returned to Rufus's bed and tugged at the blankets. "Now get dressed—breakfast is on the table."

As soon as his mom left the room, Iris swooped onto Rufus's shoulder. "Well, that's a lucky break."

"Lucky?" Rufus dug through the clothes on his floor in search of a clean T-shirt. "You haven't met my cousin. And we're certainly not going to find any train cars at Orchard Meadows. It's just a bunch of buildings with lawns you can't walk on and a gazillion old people."

Iris shrugged. "I don't care about Orchard Meadows; I care about Biggy. She's Jack's sister. Carson Collins's *daughter.*"

"I know who she is," Rufus said. He pulled on a T-shirt that didn't have any visible stains. "We visit her once a month."

"Then you should know that she grew up at Feylawn.

She was there when the train disappeared. You can ask her where the other cars are."

"I can ask her, but she won't remember. Most of the time she doesn't even remember who *I* am."

"Forgive me, but it's not like you're all that memorable," Iris said. She coughed into her fist. "She might remember *important* things."

✑ᘓᘚᘓᢓᘓᢓ✑

Abigail smiled at Rufus as he climbed into Aunt Chrissy's enormous red SUV.

"How nice to see you, Rufus," Abigail said, and immediately scooted to the far side of the farthest-back back seat and put her headphones on. She was a little taller than Rufus, with a round face and thick eyebrows. She wore her black hair in two neat braids.

"Go sit next to her," his mom whispered, climbing into the row of seats closer to the front. Rufus ignored her. He sat next to his mom with his backpack beside him. Iris was inside. He'd left the zipper partly open so she could get air.

"Tell me, Rufus, what are you going to do this summer?" Aunt Chrissy called back to him. Her voice was very loud and bright. Everything about Aunt Chrissy was very loud and bright, in fact, from her bright blond hair to her hot-pink polo shirt to her white-and-gold rhinestone-encrusted sunglasses.

"I don't know," Rufus said. "My dad wants me to go to summer camp."

Aunt Chrissy turned to Rufus's father, who was sitting in the passenger seat. "Glad you're seeing the light, Adam! You've gotta pack kids full of knowledge while their brains are still spongy. Give 'em a chance to excel! Abigail hasn't had a free minute since she was five years old. By the end of every summer, she's learned five or six new skills—computers, Mandarin, horseback riding, Latin American cooking, ballroom dancing. Last summer she was so busy, she barely even noticed her father and I had gotten"—she lowered her voice to a whisper—"*divorced.*"

She turned back to Rufus. "What about swimming? Are you on a team? Abigail's on a team. She won the two-hundred-meter backstroke in her last meet. Are you a good swimmer?"

Rufus shrugged. "I'm okay."

"Abigail!" Aunt Chrissy shouted. "Tell Rufus about your swim team! He wants to join!"

Abigail took out one of her earbuds. "The season hasn't started yet, but if the Galosh team works like my team in Houston, we practice three afternoons a week and race on Saturdays." She spoke as if giving a book report to an audience of preschoolers. "Do you like to race, Rufus?"

"I like to swim," Rufus said. "At Feylawn, the creek has a perfect swimming hole."

Abigail gave Rufus a long look, then put her earbud back in. "He's not a racer, Mom."

Aunt Chrissy turned to Rufus's dad. "I won't lie to you, Adam, hanging around Feylawn makes you weird. Even Abigail was showing signs of it when we left town. Luckily, it wasn't permanent."

Rufus's mom made a small noise in her throat. His dad ran a hand over his hair.

"Rufus is fine," he said. "He just marches to the beat of a different drummer." He laughed uncomfortably. "He's quite the accomplished bird-watcher, actually."

"Then send him to bird-watching camp!" Aunt Chrissy said, slowing for a red light. "Send him to drumming camp! They have camps for everything now!"

"I'm not an *accomplished bird-watcher*, Dad," Rufus said. "I just like watching birds sometimes." He hated when his father used the "different drummer" line. It was just a fancy way of saying that he marched to a song nobody else liked or had even heard of. Which was exactly what Aunt Chrissy meant by *weird*.

"Don't sell yourself short," his father said. He turned to Aunt Chrissy. "He can identify hundreds of birds. What's this one called, Rufus?"

He pointed through the windshield at a bird that had just landed on the hood of the SUV.

The bird fixed Rufus with a beady glare. Rufus swallowed.

"It's a Steller's jay," he said. "Like the one I was telling you about."

"Here's something interesting," Rufus's father announced. "The Steller's jay is attracted to shiny objects. I learned that from Rufus."

"Don't let it poop on my car!" Aunt Chrissy shouted. She turned on the windshield wipers, then tapped the horn. "I just washed this car! Adam, get the bird off my car before it poops."

Rufus's father rapped on the windshield with his knuckles. The jay cocked its head without taking its eyes from Rufus. Rufus narrowed his own eyes, determined not to be intimidated. Maybe he was an accomplished bird-watcher after all.

The light turned green and Aunt Chrissy accelerated sharply. The bird lost its footing and lifted off, leaving a large green-and-white splotch on the hood.

"I knew it was going to poop!" Aunt Chrissy said. "I *hate* birds. You need a new hobby, Rufus."

"Do you like going to camp, Abigail?" Rufus's mom asked. She gave Rufus's hand a stealthy squeeze, as if to signal that she was on his side.

Abigail was looking out the window. Tinny musical notes spilled from her earbuds.

"ABIGAIL!" Aunt Chrissy hollered from the front seat. "AUNT EMI IS ASKING YOU A QUESTION! SHE WANTS TO KNOW WHICH CAMPS YOU LIKE BEST!"

Abigail removed one earbud. "I'm going to Gymnastics Camp, Soccer Camp, Mandarin Camp, Music Camp, Swing Camp, Science Camp, Swimming Camp, Mandarin Camp again, Gymnastics camp again, and then I'm going with my father to visit relatives in Mexico," she said. "I can't tell you which camp I like best, because I haven't gone to any of them yet, and last summer I was in Houston and the camps were different. But I'm sure all of them will be educational and a good experience." She smiled at Rufus's mother in a way that reminded Rufus of politicians he'd seen on television. "What was your favorite camp when you were my age, Aunt Emi?"

Aunt Chrissy beamed. "Abigail went to Manners Camp last summer," she said to Rufus's father in a perfectly audible whisper. "Worth every penny."

"I didn't go to camp," Rufus's mom said. "I worked. My family had a plant nursery. I helped out from the time I could hold a trowel."

"That's what kids did before they invented summer camps!" Aunt Chrissy said. "They either worked or they were bored! Remember how bored we used to be?" She turned to Rufus's father. "Stuck at boring old Feylawn all summer?" Before Rufus's father could answer she looked back at Rufus. "You're bored right now!" she said. "Go sit next to Abigail and she'll put on a movie!"

Rufus didn't want to watch a movie, but it was better than being grilled by Aunt Chrissy. He settled into the wayback beside Abigail, who dutifully loaded a film on the tablet she pulled out of her bag. He tried to focus on the movie she'd chosen—a documentary about desert tortoises—but his thoughts kept straying to the problem of finding the feylings' missing train cars. Feylawn was so big. If they were buried in the woods or something, they'd be almost impossible to find.

Suddenly he saw movement. Iris had crawled onto the back of the seat in front of him, looking bedraggled and somewhat green. "What a horrible way to travel," she said. "I feel awful."

Rufus was silent, acutely aware of Abigail's presence at his side. His cousin glanced at him, eyes narrowing, then went back to watching a tortoise slowly lumber across the desert.

"I never felt like this on the train!" Iris continued. She fluttered over their heads and landed by the window. "I think I'm going to vomit," she murmured.

Rufus tried to keep his eyes on the screen, but it was hard to do with Iris flying around the car. Suddenly Abigail shrieked. "Ow!" She swatted at Iris, who dove for cover under the seat, then turned to Rufus accusingly. "There's a bee in here—and it stung me!"

⚬⚭⚬

"What is *wrong* with you?" Rufus whispered as the family walked from the parking lot to Great-Aunt Biggy's apartment carrying shopping bags full of food. He had hung back behind Abigail and the adults, but he was still worried someone would overhear.

"What?" Iris said innocently.

"You can't go around *pinching* people. You promised you would keep a low profile."

"I only pinched her once."

"I don't care. Just lay low, all right?"

They were approaching the entrance to Orchard Meadows, a series of white stucco buildings with Spanish-tile roofs, surrounded by acres of thick grass. Great-Aunt Biggy's apartment was on the fourth floor of the main building, at the end of a carpeted corridor that smelled of French onion soup and air freshener. When they got there, Aunt Chrissy rapped at the door.

There was no answer.

"Aunt Biggy?" Aunt Chrissy called. "Are you in there?"

Silence. Aunt Chrissy pounded on the door a few more times and then began punching numbers into her cell phone. A moment later she was shouting into Great-Aunt Biggy's answering machine: "Aunt Biggy? It's Chrissy. We're outside your door."

Rufus's father jiggled the doorknob. "She can't have gone far—she knows we're coming," he said. "Let's go down to the lobby and check the clubhouse and the dining room. The kids can stay here with the food in case she gets back before we do."

Abigail watched the grown-ups disappear into the elevator. As soon as the doors closed, she whirled to face Rufus.

"There's something on your shoulder," she said.

"I'm not a some*thing*; I'm a some*one*," Iris retorted before Rufus could open his mouth.

Abigail's eyes flicked to Rufus's face.

"That's Iris," he said, then flushed. Now she'd really think he was weird.

Abigail seized him by the forearms. "You're telling me *you* can see her? And hear her? Even though our parents can't?"

Rufus nodded. "And you can, too?" He felt a rush of relief.

Abigail nodded wordlessly. She turned to Iris. "You *pinched* me."

"Had to be done," Iris said. "I needed to find out if you were clear-eyed."

"She's sorry," Rufus said.

"Are *you*?" Abigail narrowed her eyes at Rufus. "You totally lied to me."

"*Me*? When?"

"You told me you couldn't see them. Remember? When we were little?"

"I remember you used to play a game about chasing fairies around Feylawn," Rufus said slowly.

"It wasn't a *game*," Abigail said. "But then *you* pretended you couldn't see them and *I* got taken to see a psychiatrist."

"I wasn't pretending," Rufus protested. "I really couldn't see them."

"Speaking of seeing," Iris said. "How about we go inside and see your Great-Aunt Biggy? Much as I'm enjoying this trip down memory lane, I do have a few urgent questions for her."

"She's not home," Abigail said. "That's why we're standing here."

"Wrong on both counts," Iris said. "She *is* home. And we're standing here because neither of you has the good sense to reach out and open the door."

8

RED HOTS

Rufus tried the door. Sure enough, it opened. He and Abigail gathered up the shopping bags and carried them in. The room was carpeted and dimly lit, the heavy gold drapes closed against the sun. Great-Aunt Biggy sat on a maroon sofa among a mountain of throw pillows, paging through a magazine. She was so tiny that her feet didn't quite touch the floor.

"Hello," she said, looking up. She gave them a puzzled smile. "You're my visitors, aren't you?"

"We're *some* of your visitors," Abigail said. She sat down on the couch and took Great-Aunt Biggy's hand. "I'm Abigail, your grandniece."

"*I'm* Abigail," Great-Aunt Biggy said petulantly. "Biggy for short."

"Now's your chance," Iris whispered in Rufus's ear. "Ask her about the train, before the adults get back."

Rufus sat down on the flowered chair across from them. "I was wondering—"

"Did you bring Red Hots?" Great-Aunt Biggy asked.

Abigail squeezed her hand. "*Yes!*" she said in a tone that implied that the very existence of Red Hots was cause for celebration. "The grown-ups have them!"

"I have a taste for spicy candy," Great-Aunt Biggy remarked. "I always have."

"Can we get on with it?" Iris said from Rufus's shoulder. "Or are we going to natter on about candy all day?"

Great-Aunt Biggy jumped. Her eyes flew to Rufus. "Get it out of here," she said in a low, urgent tone. "Young man, get it out. I will not have it in my apartment."

"Get what out, Great-Aunt Biggy?" Abigail said sweetly.

"That flying creature." Great-Aunt Biggy folded her magazine in half and handed it to Abigail. "Give it a good swat, would you? I don't know how it got here, but it can't stay."

"Stay?" Iris protested. "Why would I want to *stay*?"

"Ssssh," Abigail hissed. She stood in front of Rufus, blocking Great-Aunt Biggy's view. "Play dead," she whispered to Iris, and then swatted Rufus's shoulder with the magazine, a little harder than was strictly necessary. Rufus winced. Iris opened her mouth to speak.

"Play *dead*," Abigail whispered again. "Now."

To Rufus's astonishment, Iris closed her mouth and keeled over onto her back.

"Hold on a sec—" he objected, but Abigail had already picked up Iris by one foot and was holding her out to Great-Aunt Biggy.

"Good girl!" Great-Aunt Biggy cried. "Flush it down the toilet, please. The bathroom's that way."

Rufus grabbed Abigail's arm, but Abigail shrugged him off with a withering look and carried the limp feyling in the direction Great-Aunt Biggy had pointed toward. After a minute the toilet flushed and Abigail returned, brushing off her hands in a showy good-riddance-to-bad-rubbish kind of way. Rufus waited for her to wink or give some other sign that Iris was safe, but she just gave him a blank smile and returned to her spot on the couch. The pocket of her shorts, he saw with relief, bulged slightly. He glanced at the apartment door. The adults would be back at any moment.

"Great-Aunt Biggy," he said. "I wanted to ask—"

The old lady looked at him with surprise. "Hello, young man," she said. "Do you have my Red Hots?"

"My mother has them in her purse. But I was wondering—"

"I do love Red Hots," Great-Aunt Biggy said dreamily. "Would you like some?"

"Do you have any?" Rufus asked.

"No, I don't, do you?"

"Soon," Rufus said, feeling slightly dizzy. "The grown-ups—"

"I know *that!* I asked if you'd *like* some. I know I would."

Abigail had been listening to this exchange with growing impatience. "Great-Aunt Biggy," she said suddenly. "I want to know about the thing Rufus had on his shoulder, the feyling. Have you always been able to see them?"

Great-Aunt Biggy looked nervous. "I don't know what you mean," she said. "See what?"

"A *feyling*," Abigail said. "A little person with wings. Like the one I just flushed down the toilet."

Great-Aunt Biggy stared at her for a moment, as if trying to decide what to say. "You saw it?"

"Of course I did," Abigail said. "We all saw it. But my mother can't see them. And my father can't. Until ten minutes ago, I thought I was the only one who could."

"My parents can't see them either," Rufus added. "Just us."

"You don't want to see them," Great-Aunt Biggy said. "They're dirty, nasty things. My mother knew. She made them sound pretty in her books, but she knew what they were really like." A frightened look passed over her face. "You won't tell anyone though, will you?" She twirled her fingers through her hair like a nervous child. "She said never tell. She said if I told people what I saw, they might lock me up in an insane asylum."

"We won't tell anyone," Abigail said. "Believe me. My mother will frog-march me to a psychiatrist if she hears I've been seeing them again."

"That's what they did to my mama," Great-Aunt Biggy said. "Took her away and locked her up! She had the last laugh though, didn't she? After she got out, she wrote her books and made buckets of money. Those were nice times. Just Mama and Pop Avery and Jack and me."

"Oh yes," Abigail said, as if she knew exactly what Great-Aunt Biggy was talking about. "Those were great times."

"Great-Aunt Biggy?" Rufus said after a moment. "Did you ever see—"

"What was it doing here? What did it want?" Great-Aunt Biggy burst out. "There are no feylings at Orchard Meadows; I made sure of that before I came. No feylings, no orchard, no meadows. Just a nice lawn, a dining room, and a clubhouse with activities. Do you like activities?"

"I like trains," Rufus said. "Toy trains. Which reminds me—"

"We have very nice activities at Orchard Meadows," Great-Aunt Biggy continued. "We have karaoke, poker, Zumba, and ballroom dancing." She reached into the sleeve of her sweater for a tissue and wiped her nose. "Feylings don't like activities, the lazy creatures. How did it get in here? I need to call the manager and ask him to spray."

"Maybe Rufus picked it up at Feylawn," Abigail interjected. "Like fleas."

"But Feylawn doesn't have feylings anymore! They all died!" Great-Aunt Biggy exclaimed. Then she hesitated. "Didn't they all die? They die in the story." She gazed off into space as if trying to remember something.

"Speaking of Feylawn," Rufus said. "I was wondering about a toy steam engine that Grandpa Jack found there."

"Your brother," Abigail added helpfully.

Great-Aunt Biggy's eyes narrowed. "I don't know anything about trains."

"The engine's green," Rufus prompted. "Do you know where the passenger cars are?"

"Tell them I don't know anything," Great-Aunt Biggy said. She clutched Abigail's hand. "Tell them to leave me alone."

"Tell who?" Rufus asked.

But at that moment, there was a very loud knock.

◈◈◈

"Where have you been?" Aunt Chrissy shouted when Abigail opened the door. "We looked everywhere for you! Why didn't you answer the door? We've been pounding for ages."

Rufus and Abigail exchanged glances. "We didn't hear you knock until just now," Rufus said.

"How could you not hear?" Aunt Chrissy said crossly. She collapsed onto the sofa next to Great-Aunt Biggy. "We thought you had been kidnapped. We banged at the door. We looked in the lobby. We banged at the door again. We probably went up and down the elevator twenty times."

"Twice," Rufus's father said. "Anyway, it doesn't matter.

We're all here now. Hello, Aunt Biggy." He kissed her cheek.

"I brought you a present." Rufus's mom placed a box on Great-Aunt Biggy's lap.

Great-Aunt Biggy opened it. "Red Hots," she said. "It's about time."

⚬⚭⚬

The shopping bags the adults had brought were filled with loaves of bread and containers of food: sliced turkey and roast beef, potato salad, fruit salad, noodle salad. Now they all crowded around the glass-topped dining table for lunch. Aunt Chrissy dominated the conversation, asking Great-Aunt Biggy for news of Orchard Meadows in the same tiresome way that grown-ups always ask kids about school. Except instead of saying *Do you like your teacher?* and *What's your favorite subject?*, Aunt Chrissy asked, "Do you like the girl who comes in to help you?" and "Have you been playing bingo?"

Rufus tried to catch Abigail's eye from across the table, but she refused to look at him. He was beginning to wonder if Iris was in her pocket after all. Surely she would have emerged by now if she was. He excused himself and went into the bathroom, checking for Iris behind the shower curtain, under the sink, and inside the medicine cabinet. There was no sign of her.

"Did you hear about Jack's fall, Aunt Biggy?" Rufus's

mom was saying when he returned to the table. "He fell through the floorboards in the barn."

Great-Aunt Biggy pursed her lips. "Feylawn's dangerous. I always said so."

"It does seem to be in bad repair," Aunt Chrissy said. "I worry about Pop being there by himself."

Rufus squirmed in his chair, feeling increasingly anxious. Was Iris okay? What if Abigail had actually flushed her down the toilet?

"I think Pop would like it here at Orchard Meadows," Aunt Chrissy announced. "There are so many interesting things to do."

Rufus looked at her in astonishment. "Grandpa Jack wouldn't like it here at all," he said. "He likes Feylawn."

Aunt Chrissy smiled at him in a way that suggested he hadn't the faintest idea what he was talking about. "Feylawn's a lot of work for an old man," she said. "For *you* it's a great big place to play, but that's because you don't have to take care of it."

"I *do* take care of it," Rufus said. "I help Grandpa Jack in the summer. Or I would, if I could spend more time there." He gave his dad a pointed look. "I'd *live* there if I could."

Rufus's father chuckled. "You only say that because you've never done it."

"Moving to Feylawn was the worst day of my life," Aunt Chrissy said. "We'd been living in the twentieth century and suddenly we're sent back to the 1800s."

Rufus studied the potato salad on his plate, unable to think of anything to say that wouldn't sound rude.

"Could Rufus and I be excused?" Abigail asked. "We want to play in the pool."

"Great idea!" Rufus's mom said. The grown-ups leaped to their feet like children who have just heard the recess bell. Rufus's mom went with Aunt Chrissy to the car to get the swimsuits and towels. Rufus's father began clearing the table, handing dishes to Rufus and Abigail to take into the kitchen. Even Great-Aunt Biggy got up and wandered into her bedroom. Rufus was just clearing the last of the plates when she returned, holding her hands behind her back.

"Little boy!" she hissed. "I have what you're looking for."

Rufus put down the plates and went to her, his heart thumping.

"I just have one," Great-Aunt Biggy said.

"That's okay," Rufus said. "One is great."

"Ta-da!" She drew her hands from behind her back and held out a very dingy and tattered jump rope.

Rufus made himself smile. "Thanks."

"You do know how to use it, don't you?" Great-Aunt Biggy asked. "It's not as hard as it looks. It's not as easy as it looks either. Here, I'll show you."

She took one end of the jump rope in each hand and began to jump, slowly and expertly, like an old coin-operated machine whose gears have been kept well-oiled.

"*Engine, engine, shiny green,*" she chanted. "*Prettiest one I've ever seen. If the train goes off the track, how do we get the engine back?*"

"Careful, Aunt Biggy!" Rufus's father said, coming out from the kitchen with Abigail behind him. He reached for Great-Aunt Biggy's arm, but she shook him off and kept jumping.

"*If you're bold, go where it's cold. Better do as you've been told.*"

"This isn't a good idea," Rufus's father warned. The rope whipped past his face and he took a step back, like a circus lion flinching from the whip.

"She's fine. She takes Zumba," Abigail said. She was watching Great-Aunt Biggy as if preparing to answer a quiz about her.

"*Even then you're no contender,*" Great-Aunt Biggy chanted. "*Trains can't run without a tender. One lies deep where fishes sleep. And goblins take what they can keep.*"

"That's enough, I think," Rufus's father said. He led Great-Aunt Biggy to the sofa. She sat down, breathing heavily, and held out the jump rope to Rufus.

"That's all I know about trains," she said.

Then she reached for the box of Red Hots on the coffee table and filled her mouth with spicy candy.

JUMPING TO CONCLUSIONS

As soon as they were in the elevator, Abigail and Rufus both started talking at once.

"Fill me in," Abigail began. "What's the deal with the train you keep asking about?"

"Where's Iris?" Rufus said at the same time. "Is she in your pocket?"

"My pocket?" Abigail pulled a wad of tissues from the pocket of her shorts. "I thought *you* had her."

"Then where is she? You didn't flush her, did you?"

"*Flush* her? I was trying to *save* her."

The elevator doors opened. Abigail picked up the bag that held their towels and stalked out ahead of him.

"Just tell me what you did with her," Rufus persisted. He followed Abigail across the lobby's white tile floor and through the automatic doors that led outside. He found

Abigail standing in front of a vast expanse of bright green lawn.

"I left her in the bathroom," she said. "I told her to wait for you there."

"She wasn't there. I looked."

"Well, I *didn't* flush her," Abigail said. "I can't believe that's what you think."

She turned down the path that looped around the edge of the lawn toward the pool, dodging a pair of elderly residents in bathrobes and sun hats. Rufus hurried after her, still carrying the jump rope he'd gotten from Great-Aunt Biggy.

"I need to know where she is," he said. "I'm supposed to be helping her."

Abigail didn't answer for a long minute. "It's so weird to be having this conversation," she said at last, slowing so Rufus could catch up. "I thought feylings were something I imagined when I was little." She turned to face him. "That's why we left Galosh, you know. My parents wanted to get me away from Feylawn and my *little delusions*."

Rufus could hear Aunt Chrissy's voice in his head, talking about how Feylawn made people weird. "Why didn't you just pretend not to see them?" he said.

"I was only six," Abigail said. "By the time I realized I should keep my mouth shut, we were already in Houston."

They had reached the white metal gate that separated the pool area from the rest of Orchard Meadows. Abigail unlocked it with Great-Aunt Biggy's key and led the way to an umbrella-shaded table tucked in a corner of the pool deck. All around them, old people in bathing suits reclined on lawn chairs and did slow-motion aerobics in the shallow end of the pool.

"Do you feel like swimming?" Rufus asked.

Abigail shook her head and plopped down in a chair. "I want some answers," she said. "Why did you keep asking Great-Aunt Biggy about a train? Why did you bring Iris to see her? And why couldn't we hear our parents when they knocked on the door?" She kicked off her sandals, stretched her legs across the seat of one of the other chairs, and stared at him as if preparing to grade him on his answer.

Rufus sat down on a chaise longue next to her and rummaged in the bag of suits and towels until he found the cookies his mother had packed. It was nice having Abigail interested in something he had to say. He didn't want to ruin it by revealing how little of the situation he actually understood. "It's complicated," he said, helping himself to a handful of cookies.

"I think I can handle it," Abigail retorted. "I have an IQ of 140."

Rufus offered her the bag of cookies, determined not to look impressed. He had no idea what his own IQ was, but he was pretty sure it was average, like the rest of him. "The feylings have asked me to find the missing parts of a toy train," he said. "It's not actually a toy though. They need it to travel between their world and ours."

"How's your search going so far?" Abigail asked.

Rufus sighed. Not well, obviously. He'd lost Iris, for one thing. And all he'd managed to get out of Great-Aunt Biggy was a frayed jump rope and some possibly-significant babble about trains, goblins, and fishes. "I've got some good leads," he said.

"Like that jump rope rhyme?" Abigail stuffed a cookie into her mouth, still watching him intently.

He nodded. "I also found a note yesterday. It was inside the locomotive. It's from Carson Sweete Collins—Grandpa Jack and Great-Aunt Biggy's mother."

"The author." Abigail ate half of the second cookie and crumbled the remainder onto the pavement for the benefit of a small brown sparrow that was pecking in the concrete cracks beneath the table.

"It said, *If you find this, don't jump to conclusions. I'm ahead of you by leaps and bounds.* I thought it was just a taunt, you know: *neener, neener, neener.* But then—"

"Then Great-Aunt Biggy starts hopping around like a kangaroo." Abigail helped herself to another cookie. "'Jump to con-*clue*-sions,'" she said thoughtfully.

A rustle came from the table. "Jump to contusions?" Iris said. "I don't think that one's in my book of glomper expressions."

Rufus looked around. The table was empty except for the bag of cookies. "Iris? Where are you?"

Slowly, as if emerging from a fog, Iris appeared on the table—first her tangled hair, then her brown eyes, and finally the rest of her. "Contusions are bruises, aren't they?" she said. "I suppose *jumping to contusions* means jumping so hard you hurt yourself."

"Where have you *been*?" Rufus said. "I looked everywhere for you!"

Perched on the glass table, Iris looked flushed and a little wilted. "I'm not a dog," she said. "I wasn't going to just sit there in the bathroom wagging my tail. I looked through Biggy's things to see if I could find any train cars and then I lifted the muffle and slipped out a window to get some fresh air."

"You were invisible," Abigail said. "How long have you been sitting there?"

"Not invisible—smuckled." Iris rubbed her temples. "It's a lot of work. Maybe not the best idea just now."

"What's *smuckled*? And what did you mean when you said you *lifted the muffle*?" Abigail asked.

"Well, if it isn't another clear-eyed glomper with a list of questions," Iris said. "Just my luck."

Abigail lifted her chin. "I do have a list of questions," she said. "A *long* list. My father says the only stupid questions are the ones you don't ask."

"Your father must have a lot of time on his hands," Iris said. "Which I don't."

"Was your *muffle* the reason Great-Aunt Biggy couldn't hear us knock?" Rufus asked. "And the reason we couldn't hear our parents knock?"

"And what about the door?" Abigail added. "First it was locked and then it wasn't."

Iris sighed. "Let's get this over with. One, feylings can talk to locks and make them do our bidding," she said. "Two, smuckling makes it so you don't notice things. Three, if you cast a muffle around a room, sound doesn't go in and sound doesn't come out. It's all basic seedcraft—latchthorn, fern seed, mufflewort." She patted the little pouch she wore at her waist, then held up one hand as Rufus opened his mouth. "Enough questions. I'm tired. I plan to sleep on a baby tonight."

"Sleep *like* a baby," Rufus corrected.

"No, sleep *on* a baby," Iris said irritably. "They're soft and plump and warm—the perfect place to lie down for a nap."

"But we don't have any babies in the house."

"Whatever—it's an expression. It just means you're going to have a good sleep." Iris shut her eyes for a long moment, then opened them. "Did you learn anything more from Biggy?"

"Yes," Abigail said. "She gave us a clue. A jump rope rhyme about a train."

"She gave it to *me*, actually," Rufus said.

Abigail picked up the jump rope from the ground next to Rufus's chair and began to skip in place. "*Engine, engine, shiny green,*" she recited. "*Prettiest one I've ever seen. If the train goes off the track, how do we get the engine back?*"

"No horseplay, young lady!" an elderly man scolded from the next table.

"I know that rhyme," Iris said. She unplugged the earbuds from Abigail's phone, which was tucked into the towel bag. Then she fluttered to the ground with a section of cord in each hand and began jumping in time with Abigail.

> "*If you're bold, go where it's cold.*
> *Better do as you've been told.*
> *Even then you're no contender.*
> *Trains can't run without a tender.*
> *One lies deep where fishes sleep.*
> *And goblins take what they can keep.*"

Iris leaned over and spat, still jumping. "That's part of the rhyme," she explained. "You have to spit when you say *goblin*." Then she continued.

> "*If you find it, you won't go far.*
> *Every train needs a passenger car.*
> *Find the key at BDNC.*
> *It's as easy as 1-2-3!*"

"You should write this down, Rufus," Abigail said. "There's a notebook and a pen in the swim bag. So I can work on my pen pal letters."

Rufus found the notebook just as Iris started the next verse. She was breathing heavily now, her voice coming in staccato bursts.

> *"You found the coach car—good for you.*
> *But every good train must have two.*
> *Waltz and fox-trot, twirl and prance!*
> *Wake the dancer! Make him dance!"*

Iris slowed until she was stepping over the rope more than jumping over it.

> *"Pack your bags, say au revoir,*
> *You're only missing one more car.*
> *But you cannot go vamoose.*
> *Someone has your train's caboose.*
> *The man you greet is very sweet,*
> *But here you'll meet your grave defeat."*

"Grave defeat?" Rufus repeated as he wrote down the words. "Is that where it ends?"

Iris coughed and the earbud cord fell slack at her feet.

"Is something wrong?" Abigail asked.

Iris sat down. "Just a bit woozy." She wiped her forehead

with the sleeve of her dress. "Biggy used to skip around the house chanting that rhyme day in and day out. We all learned it. For a while every feyling at Feylawn was crazy for jumping rope."

"And it never occurred to you to wonder what the rhyme *meant*?" Rufus said.

"Why would I wonder about that?"

"Because it's a *clue*," Abigail said. "Don't you see? The jump rope rhyme says where the parts of the train are hidden."

"*If you're bold, go where it's cold*," Rufus burst in. "That's talking about the icebox where the engine was."

"And you can find the tender somewhere deep, where the fishes sleep," Abigail added.

"Like the creek at Feylawn," Rufus said.

Iris stared at them in astonishment. "A clue," she repeated. "You mean, like a puzzle?" She ran her hands through her hair. "But we can't possibly . . ."

"Of course you can," Rufus said.

Iris shook her head. "No. We can't. Feylings can't do puzzles. They make our heads hurt."

"They make everyone's head hurt," Abigail said. "That doesn't mean you can't do them."

Iris put her head down on her knees. "Carson did it on purpose," she said. "She knew we couldn't figure it out. She must have relished the sight of us all jumping and chanting without having the faintest idea what we were saying."

"But what did she have against you?" Abigail said. "She wrote books about you, didn't she?"

Iris shrugged. "About some version of us. I guess she got tired of us after a while." She shut her eyes. "I need to rest for a few minutes. Rufus, you get your cousin up to speed."

So Rufus told Abigail about finding the locomotive, about its bell giving him the ability to see feylings, and about what he had learned from Iris afterward.

"You just need to be systematic," Abigail said when he was done. "First, write down the entire rhyme. Then list the possible solutions for each part of the clue."

She seemed to think he was completely without a clue himself. "Great idea," he said.

Abigail didn't seem to register the sarcasm. "I can help you. I'm extremely organized."

"That's okay," Rufus said. "You've got all your camps and stuff."

Abigail's face fell. She got up to retrieve her earbuds from where Iris had left them on the ground. "You're right," she said, rummaging in the swim bag for her phone. "I'm super-busy. I start Gymnastics Camp tomorrow and I have swim team and violin practice and I'm supposed to be writing my pen pal in Shanghai."

"And that cure for cancer you've been working on," Rufus said, hoping to make her laugh. Abigail wouldn't look at him. He suddenly felt like he'd made another Fatal Error, although he wasn't sure why.

"Don't you have camp next week as well?" Abigail said as she attached the earbuds to her phone. Her voice was prim and formal, the way it had been in the car.

"Everything's full next week," Rufus said. "I start the week after."

At that moment, Aunt Chrissy's blond mane appeared on the other side of the pool gate. "Time to go, kids!" she boomed.

"Abigail," Rufus said as Iris flew to his shoulder. "I was just being practical, about how busy you are. I didn't mean that I don't want your help—"

"Let's go, kids," Aunt Chrissy called again.

Abigail shrugged and gathered up the swim bag. She kept her earbuds in for the whole car ride home, and when Rufus turned to say goodbye to her, she seemed to be asleep.

10

MAYHEM

When Rufus came downstairs the next morning, he found a suitcase by the front door and his mom at the kitchen table.

"I was about to come wake you," she said. "I have to leave for the airport in half an hour."

A weight like a soggy towel wrapped itself around Rufus's heart. His mom was actually leaving. Today. For the whole entire summer. He was glad Iris was still upstairs. He didn't want her running commentary, distracting him from his last few minutes with his mom. He just wanted to sit with her, maybe discuss the bobbled baton transfer in the NCAA Track and Field finals they'd watched on tape delay the night before. Pretend it was a normal summer morning. But the moment he sat down, his mom sprang to her feet, as if they were on a seesaw.

"Let me make you breakfast," she said, going to the stove.

"It's fine—I'll eat cereal. Just keep me company."

His mom ignored him and cracked an egg into a skillet with one hand, pushing down the lever of the toaster with the other. He couldn't see her face, just her heavy black hair sliding out of its ponytail, the muscled calves visible below the cuffs of her cropped jeans, and the brisk movements of her hands. She looked over her shoulder at him, her smile bunched awkwardly at the corners. "I want to see you eat something nutritious before I go."

"I'm not going to starve. Dad's a good cook." Rufus went to the stove and wrapped his arms around his mom's waist, resting his head in the hollow between her shoulder blades. "Where is he anyway?"

His mom put her hands on his and squeezed. "He's helping Aunt Chrissy with something. He left you a note." She plucked a piece of notebook paper from a stack of books piled on the counter and handed it to Rufus.

Rufus—

I'll be home at 1. These will keep you occupied until I get back.

—Dad

Rufus examined the books. They had titles like *Chess Strategies for Young Masters* and *Extra-Chewy Number-Crunching Math Puzzles for Middle Schoolers.*

He groaned. "It's the first real day of summer vacation!"

"Sorry, dude," his mom said. She slid the egg onto a plate alongside the toast and set it on the table.

As he ate, Rufus could feel his mom watching him, her expression wistful.

"We'll Skype tonight," she said. "I'll show you where I'm staying."

"That'll be cool." He felt like he should reassure her that he'd be fine, but he didn't actually feel fine.

His mom leaned to the side and bumped his shoulder with hers. "Keep an open mind," she said. "Maybe this summer will surprise you. Maybe it'll surprise all of us."

⚬⚭⚬

An hour after his mom left, having failed to solve even one of the math puzzles, Rufus was on his bike and bound for Feylawn with Iris in the basket. He knew he was pushing his luck sneaking back there a second time, but Iris wanted him to show the locomotive to the other feylings and explain about the jump rope rhyme. If he explained the clues, maybe they could find the train cars without his help.

But when he got off his bike at the end of the dirt road that led to Feylawn, he found two cars parked beside Grandpa Jack's truck. One was Aunt Chrissy's red SUV. The other was his father's old blue Toyota.

He ducked behind the SUV and peered across the meadow.

"What are you waiting for?" Iris asked impatiently.

"My dad and Aunt Chrissy are here," he said. "If they see me, I'm toast."

Iris flew onto the rim of the basket. "I'd better keep an eye on them."

"Why?"

"There's a feyling faction that's pretty hostile to glompers at the moment. Get going on those train cars—I'll meet up with you when I can."

Rufus was still debating how best to avoid being seen when the door to Aunt Chrissy's SUV slid open and Abigail stepped out. "Hi." Her tone was carefully neutral.

"I thought you had camp." The words came out sounding ruder than he'd intended.

"It got canceled. The overhead fire sprinklers went off during our balance beam drills and flooded the gym—there's like two feet of water in there." Her two long braids dripped down the front of her shirt.

"Where's your mom?" Rufus said. It was odd for Aunt Chrissy to be there—she hated Feylawn even more than his dad did.

"She and Uncle Adam walked up to the house with Grandpa Jack. Except he said they couldn't go inside because he has a moth infestation, so they're going to sit in the garden."

"Why aren't you with them?"

"My mom thinks Feylawn will make me weird. I'm supposed to be watching a movie on my iPad."

Rufus nodded and wheeled his bike into the stand of seven oaks. If the adults were in the garden, they wouldn't see him come up to the house. "Look, I need to talk to some of the feylings," he said, once he'd hidden his bike behind a tree. "I'll be back in a few minutes. Don't tell our parents I was here."

Abigail lifted her chin and folded her arms over her chest. "No can do."

"You don't have to lie," Rufus pleaded. "Just don't mention you saw me."

"No," Abigail said again. "I'm coming with you."

⚬৩᷈৺৹⚬

Abigail's gaze swiveled in all directions as they walked across the meadow, as if she were trying to take a panoramic photo with her eyes. "They said they'd be talking for at least an hour," she said. "Plenty of time to show me around."

Rufus inwardly cursed her camp's malfunctioning sprinkler system. He didn't have time to play tour guide. "The thing is, I really need to talk to the feylings."

Abigail didn't answer. Rufus tried to think of something else to say. "Too bad about your camp," he ventured.

"I'm sure they'll have it cleaned up by tomorrow," Abigail said. She stopped and looked at the farmhouse. "Where's the Roving Tree?"

"By the back porch," Rufus said. "But that's really close to the garden—"

Abigail was already striding around the side of the

farmhouse. He followed, pressing his body close to the porch.

"Is this it?" Abigail squatted beside an immense tree stump half-hidden in the tall grass beside the farmhouse's wraparound porch.

"I think so." Rufus swished through the grass to join her. The stump was the size of Grandpa Jack's kitchen table, its surface etched with reddish rings.

Abigail put her palms on the stump. "I bet it took forever to chop down. Why'd she do it, do you think?"

"I guess she didn't like feylings." He glanced toward the garden. "We should go in the house before anyone sees us."

But as soon as Rufus pushed through the screen door into the living room, he stopped short. The place was a shambles. Broken knickknacks, shredded paper, and ripped pillows littered the floor. The fairy paintings over the mantel had been knocked askew. The candy dish was back on the coffee table and a fire raged inside it. Several feylings stoked the flames with pieces of a wooden picture frame and pages torn from a paperback book. Others slumped along the sofa and the mantel, staring into space and coughing intermittently.

Abigail circled the room, her eyes wide with astonishment. "This is absolutely bananas," she said. "*Look* at them all!"

"It's not usually like this here," Rufus said.

He went into the kitchen to look for Iris. Abigail followed.

The situation there was even worse than in the living room. A shattered bowl of peaches lay upturned on the floor, the contents squashed into a pulpy mass. Upended cookbooks, broken crockery, and tattered dish towels were strewn across the counters. The refrigerator door was wide open. On the top shelf, a milk carton lay on its side, dripping milk onto the floor. Feylings clustered around the resulting puddle, some lapping up milk, others splashing around in it like kids in a wading pool. Sick-looking feylings huddled on the stove, hacking and wheezing, cloth napkins wrapped around their shoulders.

"Excuse me," Rufus said, clearing his throat and looking around. "I need to talk to your leader."

"We have no leader," said a feyling in a dress made from a yellow washcloth. "Our queen's gone forever. Just like we will be." She lifted her skirt and sucked milk from its hem while squinting at him through shadowed eyes.

"We should clean up in here," Abigail said. She grabbed a dish towel and begin mopping up the spilled milk. Feylings flew into the air, shouting protests.

Abigail shook her head. "They're so *different* from the way I remember," she said. "I remember them being happy."

"What exactly do we have to be happy about?" one of the stovetop feylings called. "Our broken lives? Our dead friends?" She locked eyes with Abigail and pushed an egg timer off the stove. It hit the floor and shattered. The other feylings applauded.

Rufus picked up the pieces of broken egg timer and put them in the trash, then scooped the smashed peaches into the compost bin with a paper towel.

"I know you're all upset," he said, trying to make himself heard above the jeers and catcalls. "But I'm going to find your train for you and then you can all go home." He took off his backpack and set it on the floor. "In fact, I brought—"

"Don't talk to us, glomper!" A feyling stood on the kitchen table, clutching a sharpened pencil in his fist. He wore a green lizard-skin suit and his long hair was swept into a topknot that bobbed up and down as he spoke. There was something familiar about him. Something Rufus didn't like.

"We know what to expect from a Collins," he yelled. "*Clear-eyes, clear lies!*"

More feylings landed beside him, dressed in matching lizard-skin suits and armed with pencils and cutlery.

"But I have something to show you," Rufus said. A pencil whizzed past his ear, followed by a ladle and a set of measuring spoons. He raised his backpack as a shield. "Just listen for a sec—"

Two forks and a can opener bounced off the backpack.

"We're done listening, glomper!" the top-knotted feyling shouted.

More feylings in lizard-skin clothes flew in from the living room, hurling pencils, walnuts, and pennies. Rufus ducked beside the stove as objects rained down on him.

"Stop that!" Abigail cried. She stood in the center of the room, brandishing a colander. A walnut bounced off her shoulder. "*Ow!* We're trying to help!"

"We don't need glomper help," the top-knotted feyling yelled. "This is all-out war!"

"*All-out! All-out!*" chanted the feylings in lizard-skin clothes. They fired a volley of marbles and other small objects at Rufus and Abigail using a slingshot made from a pair of Grandpa Jack's white briefs.

"Why on earth do you want to help them?" Abigail said, crouching beside Rufus with her hands over her head. "They're jerks!"

"We're not *all* jerks," a feyling said indignantly as she landed beside them. She wore a pleated orange skirt that had once been a Reese's candy wrapper, and had a fat green caterpillar wrapped around her neck like a feather boa. "That's stereotyping."

"My sister is abundantly in favor of equality," explained a second feyling, alighting next to the first. He was pear-shaped, with disproportionately large green wings, and he wore a silver suit made from a discarded juice pouch. "But the main point," he added, "is: you should flee."

"Flee *where?*" Rufus asked. A handful of marbles pattered onto the backpack he held over his head.

"We'll show you," said the feyling in the orange skirt. "Follow us!"

11

WHERE
FISHES SLEEP

Marbles and pennies drummed the floor behind them as they skidded through the living room and burst out the front door.

"This way," urged the feyling in the orange skirt as she veered down the path that led to the barn. Rufus looped a backpack strap over one shoulder and sprinted after her. Abigail followed.

Suddenly the feylings swerved into the woods. "Come on, come on, come on!" squeaked the feyling in the silver suit.

At last, they burst into a clearing. Around them were gnarled oaks, their branches hung with shawls of Spanish moss. The two feylings came to rest on a branch.

"Did we lose them?" Rufus asked.

"Lose who?" asked the feyling in the silver suit.

"The feylings who were trying to kill us," Abigail said, still gasping for breath. "The ones wearing those scaly green suits."

"Oh, we weren't running from *them*," said the feyling in the orange skirt. She did a somersault into the air and landed on a twig that was closer to eye level, still clutching her green caterpillar. "I mean, we were at the beginning, but then we started running to the creek. Isn't that where you want to go?"

Rufus stared at her. "How did you know?"

"Iris told us you found a clue," explained the feyling in the silver suit. "She's our aunt. I'm Quercus and the one who can't stop moving is my sister, Trillium."

"And this is Smacker," added Trillium, holding out the caterpillar. "Iris told us to point you in the right direction. She's got her hands full keeping your parents safe from Nettle and his troop of goons."

"Is Nettle the one with the man-bun?" Abigail asked.

Trillium nodded, a full-body gesture that sent the twig bobbing up and down. "Nettle Pampaspatch. He and his followers call themselves the All-Outers."

"Because they're fighting an all-out war against the glompers, pardon the expression," Quercus said, hitching up his silver pants.

"The creek is that way," Trillium said. She tucked Smacker around her neck, did a backflip, and landed on her hands, pointing through the trees with her feet. Her orange skirt bucketed over her head, revealing a pair of matching leggings.

Abigail turned to Rufus. "What time is it?"

Rufus consulted his watch. "Eleven forty-five."

"My mother said she'd be done talking to Grandpa Jack at twelve thirty. She'd better find me in the car."

"Go back, then," Rufus said. "I'm going to the creek." He was cutting it close, he knew, given that his dad had said he'd be home at one o'clock. But when would he get another chance?

Abigail folded her arms over her chest. "I told you: I want to see more of Feylawn. We just have to watch the time."

Rufus sighed. There was no point in arguing. He turned to the two young feylings. "Are you coming?"

"Can't," Quercus said. He patted the pouch he wore at his waist. "Gotta clean up Nettle's mess, then go on goblin patrol."

"We're the youngest," Trillium said. "Which means we have to do all the worst chores."

"What do you mean, *goblin patrol*?" Abigail asked.

But the two feylings had already flown off.

⚬⚬⚬

Rufus led the way among the trees, following the sound of moving water. Soon the dense canopy of oaks and madrones gave way to yellow-green willows. The air filled with the murmur of the creek as it meandered through a jumble of boulders into a deep pool.

"*One lies deep where fishes sleep*," Abigail quoted as she stood at the edge of the creek. A fallen tree, bleached white by the sun, laddered across the pool. Its submerged limbs trailed sheets of green slime.

"I don't even know what I'm looking for," she added, peering into the water. "What *is* a tender anyway?"

"It's like a little wagon that carries the fuel and water for a steam engine," Rufus said. "It's green, like the engine. Here—I'll show you."

He sat down in the grass and unzipped his pack. As he set the locomotive on the ground, light swirled over its green surface like ripples on a lake.

Abigail reached out a tentative finger to touch the gold letters that read ROVING TREES RAILWAY, LTD. "It's a lot bigger than I expected," she said softly. "It's not like a toy at all. It almost looks *alive*."

As if in response, the engine began to buzz like a summer cicada. Then it began to move. Rufus scrambled after it. It picked up speed, bumping over dirt and rocks.

"Stop!" Rufus cried. He dove onto his stomach, clapping his hands around the locomotive's metal sides just as the front wheels spilled over the bank of the creek. "Gotcha!"

The engine strained toward the water, pistons churning.

"Turn it off!" Abigail instructed. "Flip the switch or whatever."

"There *is* no switch!" Rufus panted. The train pushed against his fingers. Its surface was warm, almost hot. "Just help me hold it."

Abigail tumbled down the creek bank and caught the engine just as it burst out of Rufus's hands. The wheels whirred in the air, buzzing like an angry bee.

"Hold tight," Rufus said. "I'm going to try to get it into my backpack."

He started back to the grass, then turned. A noise was coming from the pool, a burbling rumble like someone slurping the last bit of a milkshake through a straw.

"What the—?"

There was a loud pop, followed by the kind of swirling glug you hear after the toilet flushes. A basketball-size clump of mud flew out of the water, slammed into the locomotive, and stuck there.

"Yikes!" Abigail shrieked. The engine in her hands shivered into stillness. She sat back on her heels. "Ew. What is it?"

Rufus poked the mud clump with his finger. "There's metal underneath. Hold on."

He used the hem of his T-shirt to wipe away some of the mud. A glint of green. A silver wheel. "Oh, wow," Rufus said. "Wow-oh-wow. I think it's the tender."

"It *is*?" Abigail grinned at him. "We found it?"

"It was so easy!" Rufus felt giddy with triumph. He

detached the tender from the train and squatted by the creek to rinse away the rest of the mud.

"I guess it's lucky for you my camp was canceled," Abigail said.

Rufus had no idea why she thought she deserved credit for a ball of mud flying out of the creek on its own, but there was no point in arguing. He held up the tender for her to see. "Look how shiny it is. It hasn't rusted or anything."

Then something grabbed his ankles and yanked his feet out from under him.

"Hey!" Rufus yelled.

A head surfaced between the two hands. It was muddy and dripping, with tent-shaped ears and a flat, bristled nose. Two prominent teeth protruded from its lower jaw.

"Mine," the creature said, and tugged harder on Rufus's legs, dragging him into the pool. "Shiny mine!"

Rufus kicked out, trying to loosen the creature's grasp. "Abigail! Do something!" He twisted one ankle free and tried to scoot backward. But the hand landed again—this time on the tender. "Choochk!" it wailed. "*Mine!*"

Abigail charged to Rufus's side, wielding a dead branch. "Let *go!*" she yelled, and thwacked the creature on the head.

"Owie!" The creature dropped Rufus's ankle and rubbed its head, one hand still tugging on the tender. "Choochk!" it said earnestly. "Shiny, shiny, shiny *mine!*"

"It's *not* yours," Abigail retorted. "It belongs to the fey-lings." She brandished the stick at the creature, which gazed at her with large, dirty tears in its eyes.

"Lady gave it," it said, pulling at the tender with both hands. "Gave it, save it, mine!"

"It's stolen property," Rufus said. He dug his heels into the creek bank and yanked at the tender with all his might.

"It's no use reasoning with him," said a voice. "He's got mud for brains."

They looked up. A small, furry woman leaned against a willow tree near the edge of the creek. She had the same large, pointed ears as the creature from the pool and the same fangy underbite. But instead of being wrinkle-skinned and mud-colored, her face and body were covered with a patchwork of bristly hair in brown, orange, green, and pink. Over her fur, she wore a large turquoise cardigan. She looked like a very plump and very ugly guinea pig that had been stuffed into doll clothes and set free in the woods. Rufus couldn't imagine how they had failed to notice her before.

"It's like dealing with a child," she continued. "And not a smart child either."

"But what *is* he?" Abigail demanded. "And how do we make him let go?"

"His name's Mump and he's a water goblin," the hairy woman said. "I'm his aunt Garnet, although as you can see we're only distantly related." She smoothed her fur with one hairy hand. "Let go now, Mump. Give the choochk back to the nice humans."

"No," the water goblin said. He shook his head vigorously, sending drops of mud flying in every direction. "Mine."

"You see what I mean." Garnet shrugged. "You can't reason with him."

Alone on the grass, the locomotive began to vibrate again. Abigail snatched it up in both hands just as it began to move. "Look," she said holding the engine in front of the water goblin. "They're both ours. They fit together." She tapped the end of the engine against the tender. "See? Like this—choo-choo!"

"Choochk!" Mump burbled happily. He released his hold on the tender. "Shiny!" he exclaimed, stroking the engine with one finger. "Mine!" he added, and snatched the locomotive out of Abigail's hands. In an instant, he had disappeared with it into the depths of the pool.

"*No!*" Rufus yelled. "Come back!" He turned to Abigail. "Great job." He felt like crying.

Abigail began taking off her shoes.

"It's not a problem. I'll swim down and get it from him. I'm an excellent swimmer."

"Sit down, missy. You won't have to go in," Garnet said. "The train wants to be with the tender. It'll pull Mump up in a minute. Unless he has both of them, he can't go all the way down."

"How do *you* know?" Rufus asked. It didn't look like Mump would be surfacing anytime soon.

"I think I know a bit about goblin workmanship," Garnet said. "My brother made that silly thing in the first place."

"Your *brother*?" Rufus said. He tried to remember what Iris had said about goblins. It hadn't been complimentary, he knew that.

Abigail's face lit up. "Do you know where the rest of it is?" she asked. She smiled at Garnet and tucked a loose strand of hair behind her ear. "Some of the pieces of this one were lost, you see. If we could just find them—"

Garnet chuckled. "We don't find things, dear. Anything we make is built to last to the end of time—you can't dent it, rust it, or break it. But if you can't keep track of it—well, that's not our problem."

Rufus looked at his watch. "We have half an hour to get our engine back and get back to the car. Any ideas?"

"I'm going in," Abigail said. "It's the only way." She walked to the edge of the pool.

"Wait!" Rufus said.

The pool gurgled, churned. Then Mump surfaced, whimpering with frustration as the engine slammed into the tender in Rufus's hands. "CHOOOOCHK!" he wailed. "SHINY SHINY SHINY MINE!"

"He's not going to let go," Garnet said. "If you want that engine, you're going to have to find him a new toy."

"Thanks, that's very helpful," Abigail said. "We'll just

run over to the toy store now and look in the Water Goblin aisle."

"The barn," Rufus said. His arms ached from holding the tender. "I bet I can find a toy in there." He wiped a splash of muddy water from his chin with his shoulder. "I just better not get caught."

"I'll go," Abigail said. She stuck her feet back in her shoes. "I never get in trouble."

Rufus took a deep breath. Now was not the moment to push his cousin into the creek, much as he wanted to. "You don't know the way," he pointed out. "And there's a huge hole in the floor."

Abigail looked unexpectedly relieved. She reached for the tender, which was still attached to the locomotive. "Okay. I'll wait here."

"Hold on tight," Rufus said. "Don't lose it."

"I. Have. It. Under. Control," Abigail said through gritted teeth. She sat down on her haunches, locked eyes with Mump, and gripped the tender with both hands. "Just hurry."

12

BARTERING

A dank smell hit Rufus's nostrils as he stepped into the barn and pulled the door closed behind him. All at once, he remembered the scrapes and thumps he'd heard under the floorboards the day he found the train. Something had been down there, in the wood cellar. *Just a raccoon*, he told himself. *Or a skunk. It's probably dug its way out by now.*

He flipped the overhead light switch. Nothing happened. The bulb had burned out—or maybe the power was out again. No matter. A dim light came through the cobwebby windows. Good enough.

Moving cautiously, he dragged a chair to the stack of cartons near the back, skirting the holes in the floorboards. There were more holes than he remembered—half a dozen splintery openings, at least. He swallowed and looked around. Had the All-Outers been in here? Were they waiting to ambush him? *Quit freaking out,* he ordered himself. There wasn't much time to find a toy for Mump.

He climbed onto the chair and stood on his tiptoes to wrap his arms around the topmost carton in the stack. As he did, something scraped the underside of the floorboards below him.

A long slow rasp, like a toboggan whisking over snow.

He froze, the carton teetering over his head.

Thwack! The floor shook as something hit it from below. The stack of cartons, already unbalanced by Rufus's efforts, teetered, then toppled, spilling books, tools, cookware, and clothes. A noisy hail of golf balls bounced in all directions. Rufus stood paralyzed on the chair for a long minute as they rolled into stillness. *It must be a bird trapped down there,* he told himself. *A large bird.* He jumped from the chair to dig among the wreckage of the toppled cartons. Sweat trickled down the back of his neck. What would Mump like? Not books. Not saucepans. Golf balls?

Below him, the large bird-or-whatever-it-was shifted, flapped. Rufus stuffed a few items from the cartons into his backpack—a hat, a small tin box with an enamel lid, three golf balls, two balls of yarn—and bolted for the door.

He had his hand on the latch when he heard a scream— shrill and cold, as if it had burst from a throat made of ice. He turned around. An enormous dark shape spilled from the hole in the floorboards, screeching horribly. At first it was a long thin tube. Then it unrolled itself like a scroll of paper, becoming a flat indigo cape with a long pointed tail. It was about the size and shape of a manta ray and it hovered just above the ground, its undulating body scattering gusts of musty air. Rufus sucked in a breath. The dark shape watched him through two wide-set white eyes. Then it shrieked and sailed toward Rufus.

"Go away!" Rufus shouted.

The creature inflated like a balloon. A jet of smoke spurted from its body, wreathing Rufus in a violet-black cloud that smelled of mildew, marsh, and morning breath. He choked, his eyes watering, and yanked at the handle of the barn door. The smoke was in his nose, in his eyes. Nimble fingers of smoke poked into the drawers of his mind, pulling out memories like folded clothes.

A jumble of images: *That time in third grade when he accidentally walked into the girls' bathroom . . . Being left standing during a game of musical chairs at a kindergarten birthday party . . . A fifth-grade math quiz with all eight questions marked wrong . . .*

And then the smoke seemed to find a memory it liked. Rufus felt himself on a shoreline path looking out at the water. *Don't say it*, he told himself. But there it was, a white bird taking flight—the sharp elbows of its black-edged wings, the dark mask of its face. The words were already out of his mouth, "That's a masked booby!" Why did he have to say it so loud? Why did he think anyone else would care? But now Aidan Renks was grinning, nudging Tyler Zamboski, and Rufus was trying to explain, "They live in Australia—you *never* see them here . . ."

In the barn, Rufus cringed, cheeks flaming. *What an idiot,* the smoke whispered in his ear. *No wonder people think you're weird.*

He tugged at the door, desperate to get away from the smoky voice, the marshy smell, the burning shame. The smoke swirled around him. *Forget,* it whispered. *Forget any of this ever happened.* And with a grateful sigh, Rufus did.

Wiping his stinging eyes, he stumbled into the sunlight and dragged the door closed behind him. Then he shouldered his backpack and ran into the woods.

⟡

When he reached the creek, he found Garnet asleep in the grass and Abigail kneeling at the edge of the pool. She was still gripping the tender as fiercely as Mump gripped the engine. Together they rolled the train back and forth along the creek bank.

"Thank God you're back," Abigail said. Her face and clothes were spattered with mud. "What took you so long?"

Rufus glanced at his watch but it seemed to have stopped. How long had he been gone? A memory pricked at the back of his mind, but he couldn't bring it into focus. "It wasn't easy to find stuff," he said.

"Well, it hasn't exactly been a picnic here either,"

Abigail said. "Mump has tried to drag me down into the pool about fifteen times. The only way to make him stop is to roll the train around screaming *choo-choo!* like a cuckoo bird."

"Choochk!" Mump echoed earnestly. "Choochk!"

"I thought I heard something thwacking around in the barn," Rufus said. He rubbed a hand over his forehead, oddly disoriented.

"Fascinating." Abigail blew a strand of hair out of her eyes. "Did you find a toy for Mump?"

"I think so." His backpack seemed to have stuff in it, although Rufus couldn't remember putting it there. He held up a pillbox hat topped with a veil and flowers. "Look at my cool hat, Mump! It has flowers!"

"Violets, I believe," Garnet said, taking the hat from Rufus. She put it on her head and trundled to the edge of the pool to look at her reflection. "Definitely violets."

"Hatchk," Mump said. He reached out one hand. "Pretty."

"No, no, Mump," Garnet said. "Not for you. This is Auntie Garnet's hat."

"No, it isn't," Abigail said. "Rufus got it so we could trade with Mump for the train."

"Oh, I don't think it's his type of thing," Garnet said. "Shall we see?" She turned to Mump. "Do you want to trade your train for Auntie Garnet's hat, Mumpsy?"

Mump looked at her. "Hatchk?"

"That's right. You give Auntie Garnet your bright, shiny

choo-choo to keep forever and she'll let you wear this dusty old hat for a minute."

Mump shook his head. *"Mine."* He nudged Abigail. "Playchk!"

"Not his style, I guess." Garnet adjusted the hat and peered at her reflection from a different angle.

"Rufus," Abigail said from between clenched teeth. "My mother is going to be looking for me. Find something else."

Rufus extracted an enamel box from his backpack and shook it.

Mump looked up. Rufus shook the box again. Mump drew a little closer, dragging Abigail and the train with him. Rufus lifted the lid. The box was filled with buttons.

"Shiny!" Mump exclaimed. "Shiny-mine!"

Rufus poured some of the buttons into his palm.

"Okay," he said. "Let Abigail have the choochk and I'll give you the shinies."

Mump extended one arm toward Rufus. His grip on the train loosened. Abigail put one hand on the locomotive, while holding the tender with the other. Rufus held out the buttons.

"Buttons!" said Garnet. "Just what I need!" She snatched the buttons out of Rufus's palm. "Not for you, Mump," she said. "You'd only lose them."

Mump wailed with disappointment. His hand landed on the locomotive again and he gave it a sharp tug. "Shiny-miiiiiine!"

"That's not *fair*," Rufus protested. "Give them back!"

Garnet smiled pleasantly. "I don't have buttons for my cardigan," she said, holding out the sweater so that they could see.

"I don't care about your stupid cardigan!" Abigail was shaking with frustration—or maybe it was from the strain of holding on to the tender. She yanked it away from the locomotive and sat down on the creek bank. "You can't just take everything Mump wants!" she shouted at Garnet. "It's cheating."

Garnet blinked at her mildly, the pillbox hat still perched between her large hairless ears. "Goblins don't cheat," she said. "We always honor a bargain. What else do you have in that bag of yours?"

Rufus pulled out two balls of yarn and three golf balls.

"Yellow yarn!" Garnet said. "I'll take that, if you don't mind."

"We *do* mind," Abigail said. "Don't give it to her, Rufus."

Garnet shrugged. "Did you have plans for it? I was going to make myself a nice scarf. Cable knit, with fringe at the ends. You can keep the red yarn—it doesn't go with my coloring."

"We want our train back," Rufus said. "We don't care about yarn."

"Then you might as well let me have the yellow." Garnet waddled over and put her paw on the ball of yarn. "Now, take two of those golf balls and throw them into the creek. Go on. Don't be so suspicious."

Rufus hesitated, then lobbed the golf balls into the center of the pool. As they sailed toward the water, Mump reached up and caught one in each hand. The engine splashed into the pool with a cartoonish kerplunk.

"Where is it?" Abigail cried. She stared into the pool, still holding the tender. A second later the train surfaced and sluiced through the water. It hit the tender hard enough to send Abigail reeling backward. In a moment she was next to Rufus, even muddier than she had been before, but with both the tender and the engine clutched in her arms.

Mump was still in the middle of the creek, tossing the golf balls in the air. "Ballchk!" he murmured. "Mine!"

"Nice to have met you," Garnet said as they stuffed the engine and tender into Rufus's pack. "Hang on to that ball of red yarn. If there's anything I can help you with, you'll find me at the other end of it."

She met Rufus's eyes and smiled, her grin exposing each of her pointed yellow teeth.

∽༄⁊༄∾

"We got the tender," Abigail said as they trotted through the woods. She held out her fist. "We *got* it."

Rufus bumped his knuckles against hers. He grinned at Abigail. One of her braids was half unraveled and her polo and shorts were streaked with mud. She looked so different from the well-groomed girl with the polished smile who'd been sitting in the SUV that it was almost hard to believe it was the same person.

"You should fix your hair before we get back to the car," Rufus said. He pulled a black-and-green seedpod from the end of her undone braid and stuffed it in his pocket.

Abigail eyed him curiously as she replaited her braid. "What did you just take from my hair?"

"Nothing. Just a seed pod."

"Why did you put it in your pocket?"

Rufus felt his face grow hot. "I kind of collect them."

"You have a *seed* collection? Like a stamp collection?" She seemed to be adding this fact to her mental list of Weird Things About My Cousin Rufus. "Is that your hobby?"

"Not really. I mean, it's not like it has a name or anything. There's just a lot of interesting-looking ones at Feylawn, so if I find one I haven't seen before, I put it in a box I keep in my room."

Abigail studied him for a moment. "Don't you birdwatch, too?"

"Sort of." Rufus examined the leaf litter next to his shoe.

Abigail made several sharp chirps, like an opera singer trying to hit a series of high notes and failing.

Rufus laughed. "That's an osprey call."

"Birdcalling Camp," Abigail said. "Pretty much the worst camp ever."

Just then, Aunt Chrissy's booming voice drifted their way. "There's no reason for you to live like this!"

Abigail gripped Rufus's arm. "What do we do now?" she whispered.

Rufus peeked through the trees. His dad, Grandpa Jack, and Aunt Chrissy were just passing. The lenses of Grandpa Jack's glasses were a spiderweb of cracks. Aunt Chrissy was limping—it appeared that one of her shoes had lost its heel. His father had a large, greenish smear on his shirt. Nobody looked happy.

"Let's just recap what's happened in the past hour," Rufus's father was saying. "Stung by bugs, pooped on by birds, pelted by falling rocks, sprayed with a busted hose . . ."

"That's country living for you," Grandpa Jack countered amiably. "Could be worse. Could be traffic jams and parking tickets." He tried to balance his busted glasses on the bridge of his nose. They were new ones, Rufus saw. Aviators.

Rufus waited until they were well past, then led Abigail through the garden and behind the house. "There's no way to get to your car without crossing the meadow," he said. "Just go as fast as you can and hope they don't see you."

Abigail nodded and took off. Rufus edged around the side of the house until he could see the front steps. The three adults stood at the base of the porch, still talking. Or at least his father and Aunt Chrissy were talking. Grandpa Jack was standing with his hands in his pockets, looking as if he had heard just about enough.

Iris landed on a rock beside Rufus. "Well?"

"We found the tender!" Rufus whispered, kneeling in the tall grass. "I'll show you when we get home." He couldn't wait to ask her about everything that had happened.

But Iris shook her head. "I need to stay here and calm things down." She moved gingerly. A gash on her leg leaked green liquid.

"What happened to you?"

Iris lifted off, coughing. "Find the rest of those train cars, will you? Nettle Pampaspatch needs a one-way ticket back to the Green World."

"Wait, I need to ask you something!" Rufus called after her.

All three adults turned to stare in his direction.

"Rufus?" His dad strode over to where Rufus crouched in the grass. "What are you doing here? Didn't I tell you to stay away from Feylawn?"

Rufus stood. "I—I—I wanted to check on Grandpa Jack," he stammered. He tried not to look toward the meadow, where Abigail was presumably sprinting toward her mom's car.

"Grandpa Jack is not your responsibility." Rufus's father ran a hand over his hair, then grimaced and examined his palm with disgust. It was streaked with bird poop. "This cockamamie place!" he groaned, wiping his hand on his pants.

"You should go wash up," Rufus said, happy for the distraction. "I'll meet you at home."

His father folded his arms over his chest. "You're coming with me. Do you know why? Because I can't trust you." His jaw muscles clenched, as if he was biting back something he wanted to say. "Your mom hasn't even been gone a full day," he said at last. "I expected better from you."

"I wasn't going to stay long—" Rufus protested.

His father cut him off. "I've had enough of your romance with Feylawn," he said. "I don't like the choices you make when you're here."

"I'm sorry." Rufus hated the way his father was looking at him. "I promise I won't come here again without telling you."

"No, you won't," his father said. "You will not set foot on this property again until you've proven to me that you've made this a turnaround summer."

GRUEN'S TRAINS AND HOBBIES

Rufus woke the next morning with his stomach in knots. His dad was furious with him, Feylawn was in chaos, and he still had three more pieces of train to find. He went to the sheet of paper on his desk where he'd written down the jump rope rhyme.

> *If you find it, you won't go far.*
> *Every train needs a passenger car.*
> *Find the key at BDNC.*
> *It's as easy as 1-2-3!*

What on earth was BDNC? And what kind of key was he supposed to find there? An actual key or a metaphorical key, like when his dad said, *Strategy is the key to success*?

He groaned. Trying to decipher the jump rope rhyme

felt a lot like doing one of his dad's extra-chewy number-crunching math puzzles.

Focus, he told himself. *Think about what BDNC might stand for.*

Big Drama. No Clue.

Something poked his leg from inside the pocket of his shorts—the green-and-black seedpod he'd picked out of Abigail's hair. He sat on the floor and opened the tackle box that held his seed collection. He liked the feel of the pods between his fingers, papery-thin purses, spilling seeds like coins. It helped him think. Sometimes it seemed like the seeds were singing very softly, a soothing hum, like drizzle on the roof. Was BDNC a place? An organization?

Bewildering, Difficult, Needlessly Confusing.

He wished he had someone to talk it over with. Iris or even Abigail. But Iris was at Feylawn and Abigail would be back at Gymnastics Camp.

Boy Doesn't Need Cousin.

Like it or not, he was going to have to figure this out on his own.

⁂

When Rufus went down for breakfast, his dad was sitting in his usual spot in the kitchen, scrolling through job listings on his laptop.

"Morning," his dad said brusquely. "After you eat, we'll get started on that summer project."

Rufus took a bowl from the cabinet and filled it with cereal. "Do you happen to know what BDNC stands for?"

His dad opened a new browser window and typed in the letters, forgetting for the moment to be angry at Rufus. "Belly Dancing National Convention," he said after a moment. "Why?"

"I just heard it somewhere," Rufus said as he got milk from the fridge. "Could it be anything else?"

His dad scrolled down. "Are you sure you have the letters right?"

"It might not be on the Internet," Rufus said. He started in on the bowl of cereal. "It's from a long time ago."

As he said it, he saw how hopeless the task was. The clue was more than sixty years old. BDNC might not even exist anymore. And he wasn't exactly a genius at puzzles. He watched his dad clacking the keys of his laptop. Too bad he couldn't just go to a website and order a new set of cars for the train and be done with it.

A sudden thought occurred to him. "When a train's pulling cars, it's the engine that does the work, right?"

His dad looked up. "That's right. The locomotive provides the power. But each car adds momentum once the train gets going. It's basic physics, really. A body in motion tends to stay—"

"And steam engines work the same way, right?" Rufus interrupted.

"Sure," his dad said, typing something else into his

browser's search bar. "It says here the concept was first used in Ancient Greece, with horse-drawn wagons running in grooves cut in limestone."

"Wow," Rufus said, but not because of the Ancient Greeks. A surge of excitement dazzled through his body. He had the engine and the tender. What did it matter what kind of cars they pulled? All he needed was something the right size.

"About that summer project," he said. "What if we build a model railroad?"

⸎

"Math," Rufus's father said as they drove into downtown Galosh. "A model railroad is great for developing math skills—you'll need to calculate scale and ratio. And there's electricity, which is science. Plus physics, engineering, historical research, architecture, and design. There's a lot we can do with this, Ru."

Rufus grinned. His father's superpower, he decided, was taking something that should be fun and making it sound incredibly boring. But that was okay, really. It was *all* going to be okay. His dad wasn't mad at him anymore. Iris and the feylings would be able to take the train back to the Green World right away, instead of waiting for Rufus to solve all the clues. If things went well, his dad might even let Rufus go to Feylawn again. All this for the price of two passenger cars from a model train store. He was, he had to admit, brilliant.

"There it is," he said. "Gruen's Trains and Hobbies." They were in the shabbiest part of downtown. The shop was crammed between a brick warehouse and a boarded-up wig store.

"Hey, there's that jay you told me about," his dad said as he got out of the car. "Now that you've pointed one out to me, I keep seeing them."

Rufus froze. A Steller's jay perched on a fire hydrant. It swiveled its crested head and locked eyes with him.

"They're pretty common," Rufus said, trying to feel as casual as he sounded. He gripped the strap of the backpack on his shoulder. It probably wasn't the same bird, he told himself. No reason to be alarmed.

⚜

The blast of air that hit them as they opened the shop door felt as if it had escaped from an oven, one in which someone was baking a cake made of dust and machine parts. The shop was crammed with rows of shelves holding tracks and train cars. Near the front, glass cases displayed a hodgepodge of locomotives—old-fashioned steam engines jutting smokestacks and cowcatchers, sleek and streamlined diesel engines. At the back of the shop, two men bent over an elaborate miniature scene.

"Look at that!" his dad said, nudging Rufus.

They moved closer. A small black steam engine crossed a bridge over a lake, then disappeared into a tunnel through a granite mountain. When it reappeared, it huffed along a rocky riverbed, past a bear frolicking with her cubs, past a carnival with a Ferris wheel and a carousel, until it came to a fork in the track. The right fork led to the town, where there was a movie theater and a diner and even an ornate train station that was a replica of Galosh's own—although the real one was now derelict and abandoned. But the train chose the other fork, following the tracks into a train yard, where miniature figures gathered around a tiny campfire.

"Still wobbles on the turn," one of the two men said. He was tall and thin, with skin so white it was almost translucent. He wore a gray wool overcoat buttoned up to his chin. Rufus couldn't understand why he wasn't suffocating. The other man's T-shirt was damp with sweat. He wore striped overalls and a red bandanna, like a theme park engineer.

A cell phone jangled, sounding absurdly loud in the quiet of the shop. Rufus's father felt for his pocket.

"Take it outside," the man in the overcoat snapped. He pointed to a sign that hung above his head: PLEASE SILENCE PHONES AND CHILDREN.

"I'll be right back," Rufus's dad whispered. He slunk toward the door, putting the phone to his ear.

"No unattended kids!" barked the man in the overcoat. He had a thin, almost invisible mustache and blond hair slicked back in a shiny wave. "I'm not running a day care."

Rufus's father stopped halfway out the door. "I'll be back in just a minute."

"It takes less than a minute to break a twelve-hundred-dollar train," the man called as the door closed. He turned to Rufus. "These are not toys," he said severely. "They are models. Expensive models. Look with your eyes, not with your hands."

Rufus thought about retorting that he wasn't a baby or an idiot, but he couldn't find words that wouldn't make him sound like both. The man in the overcoat picked up the black steam engine and brushed past him, retreating through a door labeled REPAIRS. Rufus stepped closer to the layout. It all looked marvelously real, even close up.

"I could stare at it for hours," the man in the overalls said. "Never seen another one even half as good." He was the physical opposite of the man in the overcoat—stocky and brown-skinned, with his hair cut in a boxy hi-top fade. He pulled a bandanna from his pocket and wiped the sweat from his face.

"Don't mind the boss," he said. "Normally we try to keep him away from the customers. I'm Ray."

"Rufus." Rufus let his hand be engulfed by Ray's large, calloused one.

"Can I help you find something, Rufus? Or are you just looking around?"

"I have a train," Rufus said. "But it's just an engine and a tender. I wanted to find some coaches for it."

Ray nodded. "Easy enough. What scale is your train?"

"What *scale*?"

"Model trains come in different scales," Ray explained. He led Rufus to one of the display shelves. "See those ones up there, the big ones? Those are O-scale trains. But that layout you were looking at is HO, which is half the size. Those huge ones there are G scale—mostly used outside, for garden railways. And then some hobbyists like the little-bitty ones—N scale, or even Z. Not me though—I got these big fingers I can barely pick my nose with." He held out his hand for Rufus to see.

"My train's pretty big," Rufus said. He unzipped his backpack and took out the locomotive, unswaddling it from the T-shirt he'd wrapped it in. Surrounded by ordinary model trains, it seemed more otherworldly than ever. It shimmered beneath his hand, shadows and light swirling over the surface.

Ray reached out to touch it. "That's a beautiful engine," he said in a low voice. "The level of detail here—I've never seen anyone make a cab interior like this, with actual knobs and levers." He slid behind the counter and put a magnifying glass to one eye, the kind a jeweler might use to examine a diamond. "Every last detail. And mint condition. Where'd you get this train, Rufus?"

"My grandfather gave it to me."

"And you don't have any coaches for it?"

"Just the tender."

"Did you bring that with you, too?"

Rufus hesitated, remembering how he'd nearly lost the

engine the day before. But Ray seemed like a nice person, and if Rufus was going to find passenger cars for the train, he'd have to make sure they could connect to the tender. He unrolled a second T-shirt bundle.

"Dang," Ray said. He took out some pieces of track from below the counter and tried fitting the engine into them. "Too big for O. But just a little shy of G." He drummed his fingers on the counter thoughtfully. "It's not a standard gauge. So what is it?" He turned the engine upside down to scan for a manufacturer's mark. As he did, the train's silver bell chimed.

The peal echoed throughout the store. Rufus's skin dimpled as if he'd been thrust into a pool of ice. Dried leaves seemed to swirl around him, yellow and brown. Someone sang, someone whispered, and then came that keening, sorrowful cry.

The man in the wool overcoat burst out of the repair room.

"What is that racket?" he demanded. "This isn't a belfry!" Then he caught sight of the engine and stopped. Each of his features seemed to have a different idea about which expression to adopt, and for a moment his face was chaos. But at last his lips gained the upper hand, stretching into a reasonable approximation of a smile.

"Did that big sound come from such a little train?" he inquired in an altogether different voice. "How unusual!"

14

BARGAINING

The man in the overcoat drew close to Ray and nudged him out of the way.

"I'm Alastair Gruen Jr.," he said to Rufus in the high, singsong voice certain adults use to address children, old people, and dogs. "I own this store because I like trains. May I see yours?"

He took the eyepiece from Ray and examined both the tender and the locomotive. "Very nice. Where did you find them?"

Rufus shifted his weight from one foot to the other. He didn't like the way Mr. Gruen was looking at him.

"My grandfather gave them to me," he said. It was half true, anyway.

"What a coincidence—*my* grandfather founded this store. Do you, or your grandfather, have any other pieces?" Mr. Gruen folded one hand under his chin and stared at Rufus expectantly.

"No," Rufus said. His cheeks flushed, but it was hard to say whether it was from the heat or Mr. Gruen's unblinking stare.

"That's why he came here," Ray explained. "He wants cars for it."

"How I wish we could help." Mr. Gruen coupled the train and tender and rolled them back and forth. They were so large they took up almost the entire length of the counter. "Sadly, this isn't a real model train. It's merely decorative—meant to go up on your mantel, like a porcelain figurine." He smiled at Rufus again, more convincingly this time. "When I was a boy, I liked a train I could run along a track. I'm sure you feel the same."

"I don't need a track," Rufus said. "I just need passenger cars."

"It's not standard gauge," Ray said. "But maybe we could find *something*—"

"Not possible, I'm afraid," interrupted Mr. Gruen. His grip on the locomotive was so tight, his knuckles were white against the green paint.

The shop door opened.

"Sorry!" Rufus's father said, tucking his phone into his pocket. "That took a little longer than I expected. Find anything for your train?"

Mr. Gruen spoke before Rufus could form an answer. "I was just telling your son that what he has is not a real model train at all." He paused long enough for Rufus's father to look disappointed. "But *perhaps* we can work out a solution. I have a very nice HO set in the store. Diesel engine, two boxcars, a caboose, plus a figure-8 track. Ray, show this young man and his father the Märklin starter set."

Ray looked surprised, but he slid out from behind the counter and went to the shelves.

"Go have a look, son," Mr. Gruen said to Rufus. "I'll hold on to your train for you."

Rufus stayed where he was, his eyes glued to the engine in Mr. Gruen's grip. It was clear to him now that coming to the train store had been yet another Fatal Error.

"I don't usually barter," Mr. Gruen said to Rufus's dad as Ray pulled a large box off the shelf. "But your son is such a nice boy and he was *so* disappointed that there aren't any cars or tracks for that old train of his."

"I'm fine, actually," Rufus said. Mr. Gruen ignored him.

"I learned about model railroading from my own father, Alastair Gruen Sr. What a beautiful hobby for a father to share with his son." He directed a hasty smile at Rufus. "For that reason, I would be willing to let your boy trade his ornamental train for this top of the line set. Show them, Ray."

Ray rested the box on a nearby display case and raised the lid. "It's a beautiful set," he said, but his forehead crinkled as if something were worrying him.

Rufus's father cast an eye at the price on the box. "That's quite an offer," he said. "What do you think, Rufus? Trade in Grandpa Jack's piece of junk for a brand-new train? We certainly couldn't afford a train like this on our own."

"It's not junk," Rufus said. "Let's just come up with another summer project."

His dad looked crestfallen. "Don't tell me you're losing interest in trains already. You have to stick to things, Rufus. You can't just give up at the first sign of trouble."

"I'm not *giving up*," Rufus said. "I just want to keep the train I have." He wished his father didn't look so disappointed. "I'll come up with a different summer project," he promised, touching his father's arm with his fingertips. "Something else educational."

"Don't be hasty," Mr. Gruen said. "How about you try running the Märklin engine over our layout?"

"Come on, let's take her for a spin," Rufus's father said. He put his arm around Rufus and guided him over to the miniature town at the back of the room.

Rufus craned his neck, trying to keep an eye on his train. Ray placed the starter set's gray locomotive on the layout and handed him a set of controls. "This dial makes it go forward," he explained. "The more you turn it, the faster it goes. Just take it slow around the curves."

There was a sudden scrabbling sound—as if a small dog or large rat were moving between the shelves. Rufus swiveled and saw that a man had joined Mr. Gruen behind the counter. He was very short and wore an orange-and-brown-checkered suit that was quite possibly the ugliest piece of clothing Rufus had ever seen. There was something odd about him. Rufus turned away, not wanting to stare.

"Don't be nervous," Ray said. "Start slow. It's okay, you won't break it."

Rufus turned the dial. The small gray diesel engine began moving along the track.

"A little more juice," Ray said. "There you go. Easy does it."

Rufus snuck another glance at the little man behind the counter. He had climbed onto a stool beside Gruen and was bending forward to examine Rufus's train. As he did, his ears came into view. Large pointed ones like the ears of a pig. Rufus started, jerking the dial forward. The little gray engine went careening around the track.

"Whoa there," Ray said. "Slow her down some."

Rufus fumbled with the controls, still watching the little man who wasn't a man at all. He was a goblin; there was no mistaking it. A goblin who was bending over his train with a small gold screwdriver.

"Hey!" Rufus yelled. "What are you doing?"

"Pay attention, Ru," his dad said. "You're going too fast."

"Turn the knob counterclockwise," Ray instructed.

Rufus turned the knob—which way was counterclockwise?—and the little gray engine surged forward, lurched around a curve, and then leaped off the track and into the miniature train yard, landing on its side on top of the campfire.

"Sorry!" Rufus yelped. His dad tugged away the controls

while Ray scrambled to replace the little engine on the track. Rufus's own engine still shimmered on the counter, pinned in place by Mr. Gruen while the goblin twisted his screwdriver. "What are you *doing*?" Rufus asked again.

"Minor adjustment," the goblin said without looking up. Rufus looked to his dad and Ray for help, but they were both occupied with the Märklin engine.

"I always wanted a train set," Rufus's father said as he eased the gray diesel engine forward again. "It's incredible how real this layout looks."

Ray nodded. "It's pretty unusual—built back in the thirties. The gentleman who built it was actually the father of Mr. Diggs, who runs our repair shop." He gestured toward the goblin behind the counter. "The Diggses are model-making masters. Isn't that right, Mr. D.?"

The goblin grunted and stepped out from behind the counter. "We pay attention to the details," he rasped.

Once he was in full view, it was impossible to mistake him for human. He was only about three feet tall, with a long, beaklike nose and two prominent fangs jutting from his lower jaw. The legs that protruded from his orange-and-brown suit pants were thin and scaly like those of a large bird, with talons instead of feet. As he came to join them by the layout, his talons clicked and scrabbled on the floor.

Rufus waited for his dad to show some sign of surprise at the sight of a bird-legged goblin, but Rufus's father just nodded and smiled as if he were looking at a perfectly ordinary man. "That mountain looks like it's carved out of genuine rock," he said, guiding the gray engine into a tunnel.

"We only work with real materials," Mr. Diggs said. "Real stone. Real wood. Real metal." He turned to Rufus and stared at him without blinking. "It takes patience. But I am a very patient man."

The hairs on the back of Rufus's neck stood up. He looked back at the counter. His train was gone.

"Where's my train?" He darted across the store to the counter. "Where is it?"

Mr. Gruen winced and put a hand to his temple. "No need to shout. Your locomotive and tender need a few repairs." He gestured to a shelf behind him where the engine and tender now sat. Each of them had a large white tag attached to one wheel. "Mr. Diggs noticed the wheels aren't rotating properly. He'll fix them for you, free of charge."

"No!" Rufus said. "Give them back."

"Rufus," his dad said. "Be polite. He's been very kind."

Rufus held Mr. Gruen's gaze. He enunciated the words slowly: "I'd like my train back. Please."

Mr. Gruen didn't move. "It'll be ready next week."

Ray appeared at Rufus's side. "Youngster wants his train," he said, resting one of his thick-fingered hands on Rufus's shoulder. "Doesn't sound like he can wait."

For a moment no one spoke. Then Mr. Diggs cleared

his throat. "Go ahead, Mr. Gruen," he said. "The boy must make his own choices."

Gruen took the engine and tender from the shelf and placed them on the counter. Rufus grabbed them one at a time and stuffed them in his backpack.

Mr. Gruen handed a clipboard to Rufus's father. "Perhaps you'll sign up for our mailing list. We'll be having a big sale next month." He shook his head as Rufus's dad wrote down his email address. "Your *street* address, actually," he said. "I'm afraid I don't use computers."

"We should just go," Rufus said to his dad. "You always say we get too much junk mail."

But Rufus's father was already filling in their address. Mr. Diggs clicked closer to Rufus and handed him a business card.

"Call me," he said in a low voice, "when you're ready to make a deal."

THE GLISTENERS

Rufus bolted up the stairs to his room and dove under his bed, shoving the engine and tender ahead of him. Mr. Gruen and Mr. Diggs wanted that train. Now that they had his address, they'd be coming for it. He wedged the train against the wall and barricaded it behind a wall of shoeboxes containing his long-abandoned collections of Pokémon and basketball cards.

The door squeaked open. He froze, heart pinballing around in his chest. A pair of pink sneakers came into view. "Rufus?"

He slid from under the bed.

"Either you've been under your bed long enough to grow a long white beard," Abigail said, "or you have a dust bunny on your chin."

Rufus wiped his face with the heel of his palm. "Don't you have camp?"

"I guess the flood ruined the equipment. Camp's

canceled all week. My mom had to meet with a client, so she dropped me off here. We haven't even unpacked yet and her real estate business is already booming." She tugged at one of her braids. "Can I sit down somewhere?"

Rufus gestured to his bed. Abigail took a seat, her gaze sweeping the room as if she were planning to redecorate but hadn't settled on the color scheme.

"What were you doing under the bed?" she asked.

"Hiding the train."

"Why?"

He shook his head. "Because I thought I had a good idea for how I could save the feylings and make my dad happy at the same time, but I was completely and totally wrong."

He explained about his dad's summer-project obsession, and his own not-so-brilliant idea of buying passenger cars at Gruen's Trains and Hobbies.

"You were thinking outside the box," Abigail said. "That's good."

Rufus shook his head. *Thinking outside the box* was like *marching to the beat of a different drummer*. Just another way of saying *weird*.

"Mr. Gruen's eyes lit up as soon as he saw the train," he said. "It was like he already knew what it was. And then this other guy came out from a back room to look at it, but he wasn't a guy, he was a goblin."

Abigail had been absently twirling one of her braids as she listened. Now she let it fall. "What do you mean, a goblin?"

"Like Garnet—three feet tall, big ears, underbite. But instead of fur, this guy had legs like a bird—with talons on them instead of feet."

"And everyone could see him?"

"That was the weird part. Everyone just acted as if he was a regular human."

Abigail gave him a familiar look. It was the look a smart person gives to a stupid one.

"Think about it logically," she said. "Why would there be a goblin in the middle of downtown Galosh? And if there *was* a goblin, wouldn't he be invisible to people who aren't clear-eyed? And if other people *could* see him, wouldn't they scream or something?"

"Well, they didn't." He met Abigail's eyes. "I know what I saw, okay?"

"What you *think* you saw," Abigail said. "I'm not saying he didn't try to take the train from you, but that doesn't mean he was a goblin. He could just be a really short, ugly man who thought he could sell the train for a lot of money."

"So *you*, of all people, don't believe me."

Abigail looked stung. "Fine. If you say it was a goblin, it was a goblin." She got up and went to Rufus's bookcase. "Do you have Carson Sweete Collins's books? *The Fair Folk of Glistening Glen* and whatever the other ones are called?"

"My dad does," Rufus said. "He read some of them to me when I was little."

"Perfect." Abigail went to the door. "Let's go talk to him."

∽⚬⚬∽

Rufus's dad was making ham-and-cheese sandwiches in the kitchen with his laptop open on the counter in front of him.

"Say hi to Mom." He swiveled the screen toward Rufus. His mom's round face grinned at him. She was in her scrubs, sitting in some kind of cafeteria.

"Hi," Rufus said. "How's Phoenix?"

"Hot," his mom said. "How's Galosh? Your dad tells me you're spending the day with Abigail."

"Hi, Aunt Emi." Abigail waved enthusiastically at the screen. "Are you going to join us for lunch?" She sat down at the table and helped herself to a sandwich.

"I've got my lunch right here," Rufus's mother said, holding up a plate of salad. "Put the laptop on the table so I can see everyone."

"So Abigail," Rufus's dad said when they were all seated. "You're pretty good at finding a hobby and sticking to it. Any ideas for a good summer project for Rufus? He seems kind of at a loss."

"I'll figure it out," Rufus said. "It's only the first week of summer."

"How about studying Carson Collins?" Abigail suggested.

"She's a famous writer, yet nobody knows anything about her."

"Famous?" Rufus's father laughed. "I wouldn't go that far. I doubt anyone even remembers her now."

"Sure they do," Abigail said. "She has a fan club called the Glisteners. I saw it online."

"Really?" Rufus's father took his phone from his pocket and tapped at it. "Well, look at that. *Carson Collins, forgotten luminary of children's literature.* Emi, you should google this!"

Rufus leaned across the table to look at the image on his father's phone. A woman with a sharp, discontented face sat at the base of a cluster of granite stones, her chin resting on her hands.

"That's the Boulder Dude!" he said. "Mom, there's a photo of Carson Collins in front of the Boulder Dude at Feylawn!" He read the caption aloud: "*Carson Collins at her beloved family estate (exact location unknown).*"

"*Beloved family estate,*" his mom repeated. "Didn't she abandon it?"

"That's right," his dad said. "After her father died, she took Grandpa Jack and Great-Aunt Biggy to Seattle. She never went back to Feylawn again." There was a note of triumph in his tone, as if he'd just scored a point.

"But I thought Grandpa Jack grew up at Feylawn," Abigail said.

"Only until he was twelve," Rufus's dad said. "Then they all moved away. The place stayed empty until Chrissy and I were teenagers, when Grandpa Jack had the bright idea to move our family into an abandoned old farmhouse in the middle of nowhere. I can't believe my mother agreed to it."

"Grandma Lulu loved Feylawn," Rufus said. "You just never gave it a chance."

His father shrugged. "I was thirteen. I didn't want to leave my friends."

"Or your computer," Rufus said. He turned to Abigail to explain. "He had one of the first home computers, but it didn't work at Feylawn."

"Froze up four days after we moved there," Rufus's father said. He pressed his lips together. "Power surge or something. Never worked again."

Abigail widened her eyes. "That's *terrible*!" she said. "I couldn't *live* without a computer. I learned web design last summer—it's really interesting."

Rufus was beginning to be able to tell the difference between Normal Abigail and Fake Abigail—Fake Abigail was the one who smiled and widened her eyes all the time. But why was she suddenly pretending to love designing websites? Or maybe she *did* love designing websites. It was so hard to tell with her. He looked over at his mom's face on the screen. She was still smiling, but there was a tiny crease between her eyebrows as if she was having trouble following all the back-and-forth.

"You know what would be fun?" Abigail said. "Making our *own* Carson Collins website. Rufus and I could do it together—we could read her books, and research her life, and take photographs of her favorite places. It would be a cool project for when we're not in camp."

Rufus stared at her. Build a website? Was she nuts? He only had five days before Chess Camp started and he had a train to find. He opened his mouth, trying to think of a plausible objection, but it was too late. His father was sitting up in his chair, looking like a cat who had just heard the sound of a can opener.

"Making a web page about Carson Collins would be a *great* summer project," he said, ticking off the educational benefits on his fingers: "Research, writing, design, history, technology . . . ."

"We'd need to interview Grandpa Jack. And take some photos at Feylawn—like of those boulders." Abigail smiled at Rufus, a real smile, not the politician's grin she directed at adults.

"I'm not so sure about that, actually." Rufus's father ran a hand over the clumps of his hair. Behind his forehead, an epic battle seemed to be raging—Summer Project vs. Feylawn Ban.

"What do you think, Aunt Emi?" Abigail said, turning her wide-eyed glance to the image of Rufus's mom on the screen. "I can teach Rufus about taking pictures—I went to Photography Camp last summer."

The crease between Rufus's mother's eyebrows vanished. "It would be great for you kids to spend some time together."

Rufus's father shook his head. "They can spend time together over here."

Abigail's mouth tugged down and her eyes seemed to fill up with tears. "That's fine," she said in a tone of false cheer. "It was probably a bad idea. I was just hoping to get to know my family a little better. I haven't lived here for so long—I never really had the chance."

Rufus tried not to roll his eyes. She'd had plenty of chances. They saw each other every Christmas. She'd just never been *interested* before.

But his mom's face had moved closer to the screen, as if she was hoping to climb right through and emerge onto the kitchen table.

"Adam," she said. "I think it's important to make Abigail feel at home here. Cousin relationships are important for only children."

"We'd just have to go to Feylawn once or twice, Uncle Adam," Abigail said. "I'll make sure Rufus doesn't get into trouble."

Rufus opened his mouth to protest that he didn't need her supervision, but Abigail grabbed his forearm under the table and squeezed it hard.

Rufus's father took a bite of sandwich and chewed it

slowly. "Fine," he said at last. "A couple of hours to do research. That's it."

Rufus gave a small squeak of surprise. Had his dad just said *Fine*?

Abigail smirked at him. "We'll start by taking notes on Carson Collins's books," she said, getting up to clear the plates. "May Rufus and I be excused? We'd like to get started."

⟿⟾

"You could have *asked* me if I wanted Carson Collins to be my summer project," Rufus said when they were back in his room.

"But I already knew it was a great idea," Abigail said. "Carson Collins hid the train and wrote the clues. If we want to figure them out, we need to know more about her." She tossed Rufus two of the Glistening Glen books Rufus's dad had brought them. "You read two and I'll read two. If we see anything about BDNC or keys or 1-2-3, we'll write it down." She opened his notebook to a fresh page.

Rufus sighed and opened *The Gifts of Glistening Glen*. Judging from its tone, it was the last book in the series.

"*The old magic was passing,*" Rufus read. "*A new kind of magic had come into the world—the magic of cars and telephones and airplanes and clever inventions of every kind.*"

He flipped to the back to see how many pages were in the book. One hundred and fifty-four. He soldiered on.

"Lacy, the fairy queen, called a meeting of the fairies. 'Our time on Earth is coming to an end,' she told her pretty subjects. 'But each of us has a gift to give the world. You must now bestow your gifts before your bright spark fades away forever.'"

"She writes about them *dying*," Rufus said indignantly. "She must have been planning to hide the train—or she'd hidden it already."

"Why do you think she left Feylawn and moved to Seattle?" Abigail asked. "Do you think once she took their train, the feylings made it impossible for her to stay?"

"I don't know," Rufus said. He flipped through the pages. "It doesn't make any sense," he said. "She writes all these books about feylings. And then she cuts down their Roving Tree, steals their train, and moves to Seattle. Why? Why did she turn on them like that?"

"This seems like the perfect moment to tell me how brilliant I am for suggesting that we research Carson Collins," Abigail said. "But if you're not ready, you could also tell me tomorrow, when we go to Feylawn to interview Grandpa Jack."

Rufus rolled his eyes. "I'll tell you you're brilliant when you figure out what BDNC means," he retorted. "Not before."

"Fine," Abigail said. "I can wait."

WHISTLING
IN THE DARK

Rufus was dreaming about rats. Rats that scrambled up the walls, trying to get inside.

"Shoo," he murmured. "G'way." The rats nibbled the walls with busy teeth. He flailed and slapped the wall to frighten them, and found himself awake.

The scratching and nibbling continued. It came from somewhere outside. Rufus tiptoed to the window. A lumpish shadow sidled across the roof of the porch, hands pressed against the wood shingles of the house. It had thin, birdlike legs. Large ears. A head that seemed too large for its body. Rufus recognized the shape immediately: Mr. Diggs, the goblin from the model train store.

Heart hammering, he dropped to a crouch and peered over the windowsill. The goblin moved in slow, methodical steps, tapping at the shingles as he went.

"Here it is," he said as he reached Rufus's window. "Come to Papa, my pretty toy."

A low hum buzzed from under the bed. Rufus sank onto his belly so he could see the place where he'd hidden the train. A glow came from behind the wall of boxes, like the moon behind the clouds.

When Rufus looked back at the window, Diggs was gripping the edge of the outer sill with the talons of one foot. With the other, he etched a large square in the glass, one squeaky line at a time. Rufus flattened himself against the floor, certain that Diggs would see him among the shadows. But Diggs didn't seem to be looking. The square complete, he tapped its center with one talon. A whisper of cool night air sighed into the room as the glass inside the square faded away. The goblin hopped off the sill, landing once again on the roof of the porch.

Rufus army-crawled toward the space under his bed. Mr. Diggs leaned forward, put his lips to the hole in the glass, and whistled.

The sound plunged into every corner of the room, questioning, calling, demanding a reply. Rufus heard the swish of shoeboxes being nudged aside, then a click as the tender fastened itself to the back of the locomotive. The train was moving.

He grabbed the train just as it emerged from under the bed. It strained against his grip, beckoned by the goblin's unceasing whistle.

"Stop it!" he hissed at Diggs's whistling lips. "It's not yours!"

The whistling stopped. "Go back to sleep," Diggs rasped. "It's only the whistling wind."

"No, it's not," Rufus said. "It's *you* whistling. You're Mr. Diggs from the train shop, and you're a goblin!"

The goblin frowned and withdrew his face from the hole in the window to look down at his body. After a moment the face returned. "I am currently wearing a glamour which makes me appear human. You cannot see my true form."

Rufus felt keenly aware of the absurdity of this statement, but since the goblin seemed bewildered he decided to press his advantage. "I see you perfectly. Just like I saw you in the store, messing around with my engine."

"*My* engine, you mean," Mr. Diggs said. "I made it, after all. It even comes when I call."

He pursed his lips again. The whistle thrummed through the room, rising in pitch. The train snaked toward the window, dragging Rufus along with it. He braced his feet against the floor and tried to yank it backward, but it lurched forward, its front wheels rising into the air as if climbing an invisible hill.

"Stop it!" Rufus shouted, trying to drown out the ear-piercing sound. A door opened down the hall. As Mr. Diggs glanced in the direction of the sound, Rufus charged forward, adding his own momentum to the pull of the goblin's whistle. The door to his room opened just as the engine smacked into Mr. Diggs's puckered lips and sent him flying backward. Talons scrabbled against the shingles for a moment, then the goblin disappeared over the edge of the porch roof.

"Rufus? Is something wrong?"

Rufus turned away from the window, still holding the engine and tender. His dad stood in the doorway in his bathrobe. "I heard you shouting," he said. "Did you have a nightmare?"

Rufus exhaled a shaky breath. "A goblin was at the window," he said. "Mr. Diggs from the train store—he was trying to take the train!" He looked over his shoulder. The hole in the glass was rapidly filling in, like steam clouding over a mirror.

"No one's trying to take your train," his dad said gently, drawing the curtains closed. "There's no such thing as goblins, Ru. It was just a dream." He waited for Rufus to return the engine and tender to the floor and climb under the covers. Then he sat down on the edge of the bed.

"I know that train means a lot to you," he said. "I shouldn't have put so much pressure on you at the store today." He brushed a hand over Rufus's hair, then kissed his forehead. "Sleep tight."

Rufus nodded and shut his eyes. But as soon as his father had left the room, he opened them and went to the window. The glass was smooth and whole again, the night breeze snuffed out. There was no sign of Diggs.

EASY AS 1-2-3

The next morning, Rufus roamed the house looking for a place to hide the train. It had to be far away from any windows, and enclosed enough to keep the train from rolling away if the goblin whistled for it. He ended up wrapping the two pieces in a sheet, stuffing the sheet into a pillowcase, and then wedging the bundle into the drawer of a filing cabinet in the garage. He stuck the papers that had previously filled the drawer into a cardboard box. Hopefully they weren't important.

He had arranged to meet Abigail at the Galosh Public Library to see if they could find out what BDNC stood for. He found her on the front steps, hunched over a spiral-bound notebook.

"I'm writing my pen pal in Shanghai," she explained when Rufus looked over her shoulder. She tucked the notebook into a khaki backpack at her feet. "By the way, my mom was at Feylawn this morning, visiting Grandpa Jack. Guess who hitched a ride back in her purse?"

She opened the backpack's pencil compartment, where Iris lay sleeping.

"Good," Rufus said. "I have questions for her. About this guy." He handed Abigail Mr. Diggs's business card. "The goblin you didn't believe was really a goblin. He tried to break into my room last night."

Abigail stared at him. "Are you sure?"

Rufus rolled his eyes. "Yes, I'm sure. He wants the train. I'm just not sure why."

Abigail read the business card aloud:

Rance Diggs
Repairs and Special Projects

$\rightarrow$ ———————————————— $\leftarrow$

GRUEN'S TRAINS AND HOBBIES
Serving the public since 1925
at the intersection of Beady and See Streets
in historic downtown Galosh

"Wait," Rufus said. "Read the address again."

"At the intersection of—"

"Beady and See!" Rufus said. "It wasn't BDNC at all!"

"Leave it to Iris to get it wrong." Abigail flashed Rufus her brightest smile. "I think now's the moment you tell me I'm brilliant."

"*You're* brilliant? We figured it out together."

Abigail shrugged. "You'll say it eventually." She bounded down the steps as if she knew exactly where she was headed.

"See Street's this way," Rufus called after her. He led her across the library lawn and toward the old part of downtown, his stomach fluttering. He was not looking forward to another meeting with Mr. Diggs.

❧

They had been walking for about fifteen minutes when Iris's head peeked from the pencil compartment. "Where are we?" she asked, yawning.

"On our way to the train store," Abigail said.

"Where the coach car is hidden," added Rufus. "We figured out what BDNC meant—"

"Spare me the details. I already have a headache." Iris stretched and flew to Rufus's shoulder, coughing. "Why are there no other glompers around here? Not that I'm complaining."

With each block they'd walked, the traffic had grown sparser, the sidewalk emptier. "People stopped coming to this part of town when Key Station closed." Rufus gestured at the boarded-up building that loomed ahead of them— the decaying remnants of Galosh's old stone train station. "It's not earthquake safe, so they built a new station closer to city hall."

He stopped in the middle of the sidewalk and stared up

at the old station's tall, key-shaped clock tower, its hands stopped at ten minutes before five o' clock.

"*Key Station!*" he exclaimed. "There's a miniature one at the train store—it's part of Mr. Diggs's train layout. That's got to be where the train car is hidden!"

Abigail looked at him with grudging admiration. "*Find the key at Beady and See,*" she repeated. "That's pretty smart."

"It won't be easy to get it out of the store," Rufus said. "Mr. Gruen watches everything like a hawk."

"One of us will distract him; the other will find the train," Abigail said. "Then we stick it in the backpack and go home."

"Easy as peas," Iris said.

"You mean, easy as *pie*," Rufus corrected.

"Why would I mean that?" Iris asked. "You have to *bake* a pie. Peas you can eat right out of the pod."

⁂

"Rufus!" Ray called out when they walked into the store. "I see you brought a friend."

"My cousin," Rufus said. "Abigail, this is Ray." He looked around for Mr. Gruen and Mr. Diggs, but the rest of the store appeared to be empty. He felt a surge of relief. Ray had stood up for him the day before. Whatever Gruen and Diggs were up to, he didn't seem to be part of it.

Iris flew from Rufus's shoulder and circled the room, her tiny coughs echoing through the empty store.

"It's hot as a cauldron in here," she noted. "And it stinks something awful."

"The boss isn't here at the moment," Ray said. He was using a paintbrush to daub glue onto the branches of a miniature tree trunk. "If you're thinking of trading in your train, you'll have to wait till he gets back. Not that I think you should."

"We just want to look around," Abigail announced, flashing her best impress-the-grown-ups smile. "I'm *really* interested in learning about model trains." She unzipped her hoodie and tied it around her waist.

"You came to the right place." Ray grinned. "I'm betting you've never seen a man make a forest before." Holding the tree trunk between two thick fingers, he used a pair of tweezers to attach small clumps of green fluff to its branches. "*Voilà*," he said, holding it up. "A tree."

"That's so *cool*!" Abigail said, widening her eyes. She gave Rufus a nudge with her elbow. "How did you make the trunk?"

As Ray explained the intricacies of crafting tiny trees, Rufus strolled over to Mr. Diggs's model railroad at the back of the room. He cast an anxious glance through the door marked REPAIRS, but Mr. Diggs wasn't inside. A terrible thought occurred to him. What if Mr. Diggs was at his house, sneaking from room to room, hunting for the train? He wiped the sweat from his forehead with the hem of his T-shirt. *Calm down*, he told himself. *Stay focused.*

The miniature Key Station in front of him was exactly like the real one, except shrunk to the size of a toaster oven: long stone walls lined with keyhole-shaped windows and sets of double doors; a tall clock tower topped with the shape of a key; a pair of platforms where the trains loaded and unloaded passengers. Most of it looked too small to fit one of the Roving Trees Railway cars, which were likely to be around a foot and a half long.

Iris alighted on the platform. She was four or five times taller than the tiny people in the layout—a winged giantess.

"Can you see if there's anything inside the station?" Rufus whispered.

Iris bent down to peer through a keyhole-shaped window. "Nothing."

"Hey, Rufus!"

Startled, Rufus swiveled. Ray stood at the bottom of a roped-off staircase near the front of the store. "Abigail's asking to see the layout I'm making. Want to come?"

Rufus hesitated, unsure how to decline without sounding rude.

"Go ahead," Iris said. "I'll stay here and look."

Reluctantly, Rufus followed Ray and Abigail up the staircase to a small office, bare except for a desk and a computer in one corner. Ray had built his layout on a sheet of plywood that rested on two sawhorses. Tracks ran through a forest, along a river, past a logging camp.

"Awesome!" Rufus said. The room was even hotter and

stuffier than the main part of the shop. He blinked, trying to clear his head. He needed to get back downstairs.

"The trees look so real!" Abigail enthused.

"I'm pretty proud of this river," Ray said, pointing to a ribbon of glass bordered by gravelly banks. "The trick is getting it to look like it's moving. What I did was . . ."

Abigail's face was frozen in a smile that was on the verge of hardening into a grimace. Her eyes met Rufus's and she tilted her head almost imperceptibly toward the stairway.

"Um, Ray?" interrupted Rufus. "Is there a bathroom?"

"Sure, downstairs. Right through the repair room. The light switch is on your left."

Rufus dashed down the stairs. The coach car *had* to be hidden somewhere near the miniature Key Station. He just needed to find it before Ray came back downstairs. A trickle of sweat slid down his ribs.

Iris sat in front of the station, head on her knees. "Something about this place makes me queasy."

"Did you try opening the clock tower?" He looked around to make sure they were alone, then reached into the layout and pushed against the clock tower.

It didn't move. He tried wiggling the roof. Nothing.

A loud electronic bleat filled the room. Rufus jerked his hand back. The sound died out, then started again. Rufus almost laughed with relief. It was just a phone ringing. He could hear Ray's cheerful voice drifting down from upstairs: "Hey, boss! How's it going?"

Was Mr. Gruen on his way? *Don't panic, think,* he told himself. There had to be a way to open the tower and look inside. He recited the clue in his mind: *Find the key at Beady and See. It's as easy as . . .*

What if there was a keypad where he could punch in the numbers *1-2-3*? Or a dial like on a safe? He looked behind the clock tower, then crawled under the table that held it. Why else would there be numbers in the clue?

But there was no lock, no keypad, nothing. He got to his feet, staring at the clock on the tower as if it would tell him exactly how many seconds he had left to search. It was stuck at ten minutes to five, just like the real Key Station clock.

"No," he said, as the answer came to him. "Not ten to five. It should be"—he adjusted the clock hands with his fingers so that the small hand was on the three and the large hand was just slightly to the left of the twelve—"one to three."

As the hands of the clock fell into place, there was a sudden whirr. In the train yard, a train blew billows of steam and began chuffing toward town.

"Ssssh!" Rufus hissed at the layout. "Iris! Do that muffling thing—quick!"

The entire layout had come alive. On the platform of the station, tiny porters wheeled carts of luggage. Passengers opened newspapers or checked their watches. At the carnival, the Ferris wheel began to spin. A couple who had been fixed in the act of buying tickets at the cinema walked in jerky clockwork steps toward the door of the theater. The bears by the river ambled along the banks, and a little dog ran after them, barking.

"How do I make it stop?" Rufus whispered. He spun the clock hands back to their original positions but nothing happened. "Iris—what do I do?"

The two pitched sides of the Key Station roof were separating, folding away from each other like the halves of a drawbridge. As they split apart, the floor of the station slowly rose toward the open roof, exposing a miniature interior of benches and ticket counters. Tiny telephones rang inside the ticket office. A woman's voice announced the arrival of a train at platform 3. Rufus couldn't believe how much noise everything made. He glanced anxiously at the steps leading to the upstairs office.

"Calm down. It's muffled," Iris said, patting the pouch she wore at her waist. "And look."

As the train station interior rose above the roofline, it revealed a hidden compartment beneath its floor. Inside the compartment was a bright green coach car, its sides emblazoned with gold letters: ROVING TREES RAILWAY, LTD.

"We got it!" Rufus breathed. He lifted the car from the compartment with trembling hands and held it out for Iris to see.

Talons scrabbled on the floor behind him.

"Good little boys," rasped a voice, "don't steal other people's toys."

KEYS AND CLOCKWORK

Mr. Diggs had a purple bruise on the left side of his face and a swollen lower lip. He was in a different suit today, kidney-colored with wide lapels.

"Hand me the coach car," he said. "Don't test my patience."

"I—I didn't mean to hurt you last night," Rufus stammered. "But you were trying to steal my train."

"And now you're trying to steal *mine*." Mr. Diggs stepped closer to the layout, talons clicking on the linoleum. "Does that mean I have to hurt *you*?"

"But it's *not* your train," Rufus said. He glanced at Iris. She stood trembling next to the dismantled train station, her wings pressed tightly together like a pair of praying hands. He took a step backward, the edge of the layout pressing into his hip, and tried to stall for time. "Why were you hiding it in the first place?"

"A human named Carson Sweete Collins gave it to me

for safekeeping. A relative of yours, perhaps?" The goblin moved closer to Rufus in a series of birdlike hops.

Rufus drew the coach car to his chest. "My great-grandmother."

The goblin looked up at Rufus's face. "And you inherited her clearsight. Allowing you to see me as I am."

"So Carson Collins knew you were a goblin?"

"Mrs. Collins admired my work." Mr. Diggs indicated the train layout, which still hummed with activity. He hopped onto the table that held it and scooted along the edge like a parrot on a perch until he hovered directly over Rufus. "She asked me to hold one of the train cars for her. It was my idea to keep it inside the Key Station. Clever, no?"

Rufus eyed the staircase that led to Ray's layout. Why didn't he and Abigail come down?

"Missing your friends?" Diggs asked, following his gaze. "They may be a while. Ray's boss is on the phone. As long as Mr. Gruen wants to talk, Ray has to listen. Your cousin's probably thinking you're in luck. So much time to poke around down here by yourself."

He rotated the hands of the Key Station clock in a pattern Rufus couldn't quite follow. The clockwork figures lapsed into stillness. "The feyling muffled the room," he continued. "Which is a problem if you planned to shout for help." He bent down and peered at Iris, who had begun to cough violently. "I wonder if she has the energy to lift the muffle. She doesn't look so good."

Iris bristled, her wings spreading in a green fan behind her head, but she was too racked by coughs to speak.

"I'm curious how you knew where to look," Mr. Diggs said to Rufus. His tone was casual. "Did Mrs. Collins leave instructions?"

"When you tried to take the engine, I knew you must have the other cars," Rufus said. "I just happened to look in the right place."

A shadow of disappointment flickered over Mr. Diggs's face. "I don't like looky-loos," he said, and leaped from the edge of the layout, knocking Rufus to the floor. The coach car flew from Rufus's hands and rolled out of reach.

"Let me go!" Rufus struggled and kicked, but the goblin had him pinned. Sharp talons bit into his legs. One hand held him by the shoulder, the other raked his eyelids. Rufus squinched them tight.

"Clearsight is easily removed," Mr. Diggs hissed. "I just need to get my finger in your eye."

"Iris!" Rufus shouted. He tried to push away the goblin's clawing hand, but Mr. Diggs was too strong. Long-nailed fingers scraped at his clenched eyelids. Rufus thrashed, screaming. "Abigail! Ray! Help!"

Wings fluttered against his cheek. Tiny fingers pushed something small and firm between his teeth. "Bite!" Iris whispered in his ear. He did.

The taste of pond water flooded his mouth. His body writhed and squirmed. He was being twisted into an unfamiliar shape, yanked into a knot. He slid out of the goblin's grip, landing on his side. Mr. Diggs swore under his breath and reached for him, his hand suddenly enormous.

Rufus tried to stand but his legs seemed sewn together. His lungs felt as flat as cardboard. He flopped across the floor, bouncing on his side, gasping for breath. *What was happening to him?*

"Here, fishy, fishy, fishy," Mr. Diggs called as he chased Rufus across the floor.

Fishy? Then Iris was next to him again, pushing something round between his gasping lips. He shook his head—whatever she gave him before had made him helpless. Breathless.

"Swallow it!" Iris hissed in his ear. "It'll make you human again."

"I *am* human," he tried to say, and the round thing rolled down his throat.

Almost at once, air filled his lungs. His limbs unstuck themselves in a ripple of strength and coordination. He looked down at his arms in time to see a shimmering rainbow of scales fade into his familiar light brown skin.

Footsteps thudded down the stairs. He rolled to a sitting position. Abigail and Ray stood over him, looking panicked.

"Rufus?" Abigail said. "What happened?"

Mr. Diggs stood next to the layout, brushing dust from his kidney-colored suit. "The boy took ill."

Rufus rubbed his stinging eyes, relief rushing over him. He could still see the goblin's birdlike feet and piglike ears. He was still clear-eyed.

"I'm fine," he said. He stood, trembling with fear and fury. The Key Station roof was closed tight. He spun around, scanning for signs of the coach car. The floor rolled woozily under his feet. He bent over, resting his hands on his knees, and tried to steady himself.

"You don't look fine," Ray said. "What happened to you?"

Iris fluttered to Rufus's shoulder. "Sorry about that," she whispered. "I needed to make you slippery. A trout was the best I could do on short notice."

Rufus frowned. *Trout?* His legs were noodly, as if he'd just gotten off a boat. Had he just been a *trout*?

"He has fainting spells," Abigail announced. "It's better if we don't make a big deal about it. We're just going to go home now so he can rest." Her hoodie lay in a pile on the floor. She picked it up with both hands and stuffed it in her backpack.

Mr. Diggs's eyes narrowed. "Stay."

"I agree," Ray said. "Maybe your parents should come get you."

"No need," Abigail said, zipping up the backpack. "My mom's just around the corner, waiting for us in the car.

Thanks for showing me your train layout, Ray. It was very interesting."

As she spoke, she took Rufus by the arm and moved him toward the door. He pulled away, annoyed. After all that, they were just going to leave? He'd been holding the coach car in his hands seconds earlier. It couldn't have gone far.

"*Wait*," he growled.

"Don't be an idiot," Iris hissed in his ear. "Keep moving." She gave him a small, forceful pinch on the earlobe. "*Walk*."

Reluctantly, Rufus allowed Abigail to lead him out the door.

"Could you run?" she asked as she propelled him down the sidewalk. "If you had to?"

"I guess so. If I had to."

"You have to," Abigail said. "*Now*."

FOUR LITTLE DOGS

Rufus's legs felt slushy, as if he were running on a trout's floppy fins. He gasped for breath.

"Can't you run any faster?" Iris shrieked from his shoulder. She gripped his ears with both hands to keep from falling off.

"Why—are we—running?" Rufus panted. He collapsed on a bus stop bench.

"Because I have the coach car!" Abigail pulled him to his feet, looking around frantically. A bus was lumbering toward them. "Get on—*quickly*!"

As soon as they were sitting at the back of the bus, Iris kicked Rufus in the shoulder, hard. "*That's* for taking me into a goblin nest with nothing in my pouch but mufflewort and trout lily bulb. He could have killed us all!"

"I'm the one who almost died!" Rufus rubbed his smarting arm. "Next time you turn me into a fish, try doing it near water."

"Keep your head down—we don't want anyone to see us," Abigail hissed. She had abandoned her usual erect posture and was so slumped in her seat she was practically lying on it. She shoved Rufus down by the shoulder, then wrinkled her nose. "You smell awful. Did you just say you were a fish?"

"A trout to be exact," Iris said, settling on Abigail's shoulder. "In the train store. Just before you came in. I needed him to be slippery."

"You can do that—turn people into trout?"

"With the right seeds, you can do almost anything," Iris said. She hacked for a long minute, then wiped her nose with her hand. "That was quick thinking," she said to Abigail. "Dropping your sweatshirt over the coach car and then putting the whole bundle in your backpack. But that goblin's going to want it back."

"Believe me, I know," Rufus said. He told Iris about Diggs's visit the night before. As he did, Iris seemed to crumple.

"I don't like this at all," she said. "I don't understand what he wants."

"There's a lot I don't understand," Rufus said. He shuddered, remembering the goblin's fingers prying open his eyelids. "Like why he tried to claw my eyes out."

"No mystery there," Iris said. "Goblins don't like to be seen for what they are. When they do business with glompers, they wear a glamour."

"A *glamour*?" Rufus remembered the goblin using the same word.

"A disguising spell. It makes them look human to any-one who doesn't have clearsight."

"What do you mean *do business?*'" Abigail asked. "I didn't think there *were* goblins outside of Feylawn."

Iris sighed. "*Most* goblins are outside of Feylawn. When we're healthy, we keep them off the property. But you humans work with them all the time, particularly when you're mining, drilling, or tunneling."

"But the train doesn't have anything to do with mining or tunnels," Rufus said. "So why is Mr. Diggs so obsessed with it?"

"I don't know." Iris's wings twitched anxiously. "Tell me what you've done to keep him from breaking into your room a second time."

"Nothing, really," Rufus admitted. "I hid the engine and tender in a filing cabinet."

"Hid it?" Iris slapped her forehead with her palm. "You don't seem to understand what we're up against. We need goblinsbane at all four corners! Fill-mallow seeds to protect against tunneling!" She coughed into her fist. "We have to get to Feylawn. If we're going to keep that goblin from get-ting his hands on our train, we're going to need help."

꧁ꂌꀤꈡ

By the time they'd walked from the bus stop to Feylawn, Iris was asleep in the backpack. Rufus wished he could join her. His legs still felt weak and rubbery, and he had an almost overpowering urge to take a bath. He wasn't sure if this was because he was still thinking like a trout or because he still smelled like one.

Feylawn was strangely quiet as they trudged across the meadow. No feyling swooped down to pinch or throw things at them, not even when they pushed open the door of the farmhouse. All was silent.

They found Grandpa Jack in the kitchen. He was wearing a pair of bright red eyeglasses and ironing a sandwich. "Stove's on the fritz again, but the clothes iron works dandy for grilled cheese," he explained. "Want one?"

"Please!" Abigail said. "We're famished!"

Rufus glanced at the kitchen windows, half expecting to see Mr. Diggs leering back at him. How long would it be before the goblin came looking for the coach car?

"Everything all right?" Grandpa Jack said as he ironed sandwiches. "You look a little jumpy. You're not hiding from your parents, are you?"

"They said it's okay for us to be here," Abigail said. "My mom's going to pick us up at four, drop off Rufus, and take me to swim practice."

Grandpa Jack raised an eyebrow. "We're talking about my daughter, Chrissy, right? Last time you were here she wouldn't let you out of the car."

"It's because we're doing a research project," Abigail explained. "About your mother, actually. Carson Sweete Collins. We're going to make a website."

Grandpa Jack switched off the iron. "A website about my mother," he said, carrying a plate of toasted sandwiches to the table with his good hand. "That's a nice tribute." He stared at them through the enormous lenses of his red glasses, his expression unexpectedly sad. "She was a true child of Feylawn. Born here. Buried here."

"Buried here?" Rufus said. "I thought she left and didn't come back." He knew he sounded accusing, but he couldn't help it. How could someone who loved Feylawn have abandoned it for a big city like Seattle?

"Her father, Pop Avery, is buried on the ridge above the woods. My mother wanted to be buried next to him. So that's what I did."

"We should be writing this down," Abigail said. She devoured half a sandwich in three enormous bites and bent down to retrieve her notebook and a pen from her backpack.

"So she was born at Feylawn?" she asked, tapping the pen against her chin.

"Upstairs, in the master bedroom," Grandpa Jack said. "A year later, her mother died in the flu epidemic."

"And Carson's father raised her by himself?" Abigail scribbled furiously with one hand, while shoving the second half of her sandwich in her mouth with the other.

"Avery Sweete—we called him Pop Avery," Grandpa Jack said. "He raised her his own way, the way he did everything. My mother didn't go to school until she was fourteen years old. Just ran wild here at Feylawn, drawing pictures and writing stories and helping Pop Avery with the apricot orchard."

Rufus sighed. Some people had all the luck.

"But she went to school eventually, right?" Abigail asked. "And got married, too."

Grandpa Jack nodded. "My father was Lloyd Collins, the station agent for Key Station. After they married, they lived in town, but my mother never liked it there. Then he went overseas to fight in the war, and she went back to spending her days at Feylawn, with me and Biggy by her side."

"Great-Aunt Biggy said your mother was in a mental hospital." Rufus felt awkward mentioning it.

Grandpa Jack looked grave. "Mental hospitals were terrible places in those days," he said. "And in a small town like Galosh, it was pretty easy for a man to get his wife committed to one. My father came back from the war and didn't like what he saw—his wife and kids running wild in the woods, talking about fairies. Maybe he was doing what he thought was best. I was only three at the time, but I still remember the men taking my mother away. I don't know which of us screamed louder—her or me."

Abigail scowled, still writing. "How long was she in there?"

Grandpa Jack shook his head. "Not long," he said. "A few weeks? Pop Avery got her out of there pretty fast. He must have given my father some kind of ultimatum because he left town and didn't come back."

"*Ever?*" Abigail said.

Grandpa Jack gave her a small, sad smile. "He'd come through Galosh every now and then and take Biggy and me out for hamburgers," he said. "But we barely knew him. It was Pop Avery who helped raise us, just like he raised my mother. We all lived here at Feylawn."

Rufus remembered what Great-Aunt Biggy had said when they visited her at Orchard Meadows. *Those were nice times. Just Mama and Pop Avery and Jack and me.*

"And that's when your mother got famous for her books," he said.

Grandpa Jack nodded. "No one worried about her sanity after that," he said. "Those fairies she saw had dollar bills for wings."

Abigail twisted one of her braids in her fingers as she wrote. "Could anybody else see them?" she asked, keeping her eyes fixed on her notebook. "Could you?"

Grandpa Jack threw back his head and laughed. "They were just stories, kids. Even my mother stopped claiming they were real once she saw she could be misunderstood."

"But what if that was just because she was scared to tell the truth?" Rufus said. "What if she really *could* see things other people couldn't?"

"Like little creatures flying around the house?" Grandpa Jack flapped his hands like they were tiny wings. "Come on now, Rufus. Some things are, and some things aren't." His voice was louder than usual. "My mother had a marvelous imagination, but that doesn't mean she was delusional."

"I don't mean that she was delusional," Rufus said. He was sure Grandpa Jack would believe him if he just explained. "Abigail and I can see the exact same—"

Abigail broke in to finish the sentence: "—landscapes at Feylawn that she painted for the books." She glared at Rufus before adding, "It *almost* makes it seem true."

"Feylawn was her inspiration," Grandpa Jack said, and his voice was quieter now. "When she was here, all she saw was magic."

"But then why did she leave?" Rufus asked.

Grandpa Jack got up and went into the living room. He returned with a framed photograph.

"That's Pop Avery." Grandpa Jack tapped the photo. It showed a tall blond man who gazed at the camera with a mischievous expression, as if he had just said something funny. His lips were clamped around a lit cigarette in an upside-down grin.

"That cigarette's what killed him," Grandpa Jack added. "He died of lung cancer when I was twelve. My mother took it pretty hard. I think it was just too sad for her to be here after that. So we went to Seattle."

"Did you remember her having a friend from town?" Rufus asked. "A short guy named Mr. Diggs who worked with model trains?"

To his surprise, Grandpa Jack nodded. "Time was, every-body in Galosh knew Mr. Diggs and his boss, Mr. Gruen," he said. "They both must be long dead by now. I remem-ber going to their store to see their model railroads. Those railroad displays were like Disneyland to us." He frowned, as if remembering something. "You know, I think we had a model train set of our own—that must have been where that steam engine I found in the icebox came from. I just remembered a miniature train going through the backyard—right by the porch. Maybe Pop Avery set it up."

Rufus gave Abigail a meaningful look. The Roving Trees Railway. Grandpa Jack had seen it running.

"Do you remember anything else about Mr. Diggs?" Rufus asked. "Did he ever visit Feylawn?"

Grandpa Jack shook his head. "My mother pretty much kept to herself," he said. "Especially after what happened with my father."

He got up and retrieved a plate of oatmeal cookies from the stove. As he carried it to the table, Rufus saw that he was walking with a slight limp.

"What happened to your leg?"

"Nothing much." Grandpa Jack set the plate on the table. "Tree fell on me last night, out past the barn."

"A *tree*?" Rufus repeated.

Grandpa Jack handed him a cookie. "Don't get excited. Could have been worse—if those dogs hadn't come by, I'd still be there."

"What dogs?" Abigail asked.

"Weirdest thing, actually," Grandpa Jack admitted. He sat down in his chair again, a little stiffly, Rufus saw now. "It wasn't much more than a sapling, but with my arm busted, it had me pretty well pinned. I figured I was spending the night there."

Rufus swallowed. Two days ago, All-Outers had been pelting them with marbles and sharpened pencils. If they'd started dropping trees on people, things at Feylawn were worse than he'd imagined. "How'd you get free?" he asked.

"Along came these four little dogs, Chihuahuas or some such. They started digging underneath my leg, just digging away. Next thing I know, there's enough room for me to pull my leg out."

"But where did they come from?" Abigail said.

"Chihuahuas are a Mexican dog, aren't they? Probably came from Mexico. All I know is, they set me free and then took off running."

"But you hurt your leg," Rufus said.

"Nah, it's almost healed," Grandpa Jack said. "I've got a nasty bruise though—six shades of purple, like one of those modern art paintings." He laughed.

"It's not funny," Rufus said. "That's two accidents in a week."

"It's not as bad as you make it sound. This place has funny moods; always has. Wild places are unpredictable, same as wild animals." He winked at Abigail. "I hope you like wild animals."

"I do," Abigail said. She sounded surprisingly fierce. "I mean, it's . . . dangerous and aggravating here, and I wish you'd be more careful, Grandpa Jack. But even so—I *like* how wild it is. I feel different when I'm here. More . . . *me*."

"Uh-oh," Grandpa Jack said. "Sounds like you've got the Feylawn bug, just like Pop Avery and my mother and Rufus and yours truly." He shook his head. "Trouble is, my children don't have it. Never have."

REFLECTIONS

It was hard to wake Iris from her nap. She staggered out of the backpack and collapsed on the living room floor with her head in her hands. "Everything hurts," she groaned. "How do you glompers stand being mortal?"

The sound of clattering dishes and running water drifted from the kitchen, punctuated by Grandpa Jack's spirited humming.

"I guess we're used to it," Rufus said. "Listen—we need a plan of action."

"Grandpa Jack got attacked again," Abigail said. "Somebody's got to persuade the All-Outers to calm down before he gets really hurt."

"We found out something else," Rufus added. "Grandpa Jack said he remembers Mr. Diggs from when he was a kid. So he definitely did meet Carson Collins. Except he doesn't look old enough for that."

"Goblins live about 150 years," Iris said slowly. "So it's

perfectly possible. But I still don't understand why they want—" She broke off and clapped a hand over her mouth. "Oh no. No, no, no, no, no."

"What?" Abigail said. "What's wrong?"

"Why didn't I see it before?" Iris wailed. "How could I have been so stupid?" She buried her face in her hands and began to sob.

"Hey now," Abigail said. "Don't cry. It can't be that bad."

"Not that bad?" Iris said between sobs. "The goblins— they're planning—to invade the Green World."

"Invade the Green World?" Rufus asked, not sure he'd heard correctly. "Why?"

"And how?" Abigail added. "Even *you* can't get there—"

"Without the complete train," Iris said. "But *with* the train, anyone can." She rocked back and forth, moaning. "They'll kill every last one of us, even the ones we thought were safe at home."

A puddle of fear settled deep in Rufus's chest. Iris was always dramatic, but he'd never seen her look so defeated. "Why?" he asked.

"They're greedy, that's why." Iris's voice was barely a whisper. "Greedier than I ever imagined."

Abigail looked at Rufus as if expecting him to say some-thing. The clatter of dishes had ended, but they could still hear Grandpa Jack humming to himself in the next room.

"They haven't won *yet*," Rufus said. He tried to think of

a plan of action. "You said there are seeds we can use to guard the train from Mr. Diggs."

Iris slumped on the floor, weeping into her fists. "There's no point."

"Iris. Look at me." Rufus lifted the feyling by the back of her dress and held her at eye level. Iris remained limp, drooping from his fingers like a wet sock. "I've traipsed all over town, made an enemy of a goblin, and been turned into a fish. It's a little late to announce you're giving up."

Iris raised her head and met his gaze. "Well, I *am* giving up," she said. "I'm too sick and too scatterbrained and whenever I try to fix anything it just makes everything worse. Leave me to die in peace."

Abigail snorted. "Fine," she said. "I guess we have the afternoon to ourselves. What do you want to do, Rufus?"

Rufus carried the coach car to Grandpa Jack's coat closet, stuffing it into an enormous wicker picnic basket.

"Let's find Quercus and Trillium," he said once he had wedged the picnic basket beneath a pile of coats, a pair of umbrellas, and a croquet set. "Maybe they'll be willing to guard the train."

෧ᅇᅇ෨

It took some searching, but they finally found the young feylings at the base of the cluster of tall granite stones that Rufus called the Boulder Dude. Trillium was quietly stroking Smacker, her green caterpillar. Quercus's eyes, Rufus saw, were red and puffy.

"Where is everyone?" Rufus squatted down beside them. "The house is deserted."

"They're at the funeral." Trillium's wings drooped.

"What funeral?" Abigail asked.

Quercus tugged at a tendril of a plant that had been curling around the rock. The motion shook loose a confetti of flat green seeds.

"Rosemary and Buckeye—the ones who died saving your grandfather from the fallen tree," he said, kneeling to collect the seeds and put them in the pouch he wore at his waist. He wiped his nose with the back of his hand.

"You mean the little dogs *died*?" Abigail said. "That's terrible!"

Quercus gave the tendril another vigorous yank and tumbled backward as it gave way. "They weren't real dogs—they were just dogwood seeds. But the two feylings who called the seeds into dog shape and sent them to rescue Jack, they died after doing it."

"That's how it is these days." Trillium rested her cheek against Smacker. "Anytime somebody has to do a complicated bit of seedcraft, there ends up being a funeral. Everybody's too weak."

"But that's awful!" Rufus wished he could think of something more comforting to say.

"Listen—we need your help with something," he said

instead. "We've found two pieces of the train, but there's a goblin after them. Iris thinks he wants to use the train to get to the Green World. We need someone to guard it."

Quercus frowned. "Why would a goblin go to the Green World?"

Trillium wrapped Smacker around her neck. "It doesn't matter. If Iris thinks the train needs guarding, you've come to the right place. Querc and I know a lot of goblin-fighting seedcraft."

"There's something else," Abigail said. "Can you get the All-Outers to stop attacking Grandpa Jack?"

Quercus snorted. "I doubt they'll listen to us," he said. "But I suppose we can try. They'll be at the funeral, pretending to be sad about Rosemary and Buckeye. We were on our way over there anyway."

"We just have to feed the umbrals first," Trillium said, flying to a low cavern formed by a cluster of leaning boulders. "Come watch!" she called over her shoulder. "It's not something you see every day!"

They followed her, kneeling down to peer into the opening. A dank, moldering smell hit their nostrils. They heard a series of shrill, piping cries, like a cascade of icicles interspersed with the whistle of a teakettle. Alarmed, Rufus backed away, but not before glimpsing a writhing mass of shadows inside the cave. The sight gave him a jolted, sick feeling, like missing a step on a staircase. They reminded him of something, but he couldn't think what.

"Glompers don't usually get to see them," Quercus said, landing on his shoulder. "Umbrals are super shy. If their mother was here, you'd be dimpsied by now."

Rufus had no idea what *dimpsied* meant, but he didn't care to find out. The umbrals gave him the creeps.

Abigail was still crouched at the front of the cave, watching the creatures undulate like an inky ocean. "Why are they crying like that?"

"They're hungry," Trillium said, flying over to Abigail. "Their mom's gone missing." She dug a few wooden kitchen matches out of her pouch and offered them to Abigail. "You can feed them if you want. Strike a match on the rock and then hold it inside the cave. Just don't get too close."

"They eat fire?" Despite his revulsion, Rufus leaned in to look. The baby umbrals looked like wriggling black napkins. One of them glanced at him, its eyes pure white. He flinched.

"They eat reflections," Trillium said. She nudged Abigail. "Go on."

The umbral babies' cries thickened into a knot of shrieks as the flame cast an orange glow on the granite walls of the cavern. Long violet tongues emerged from their tiny mouths and licked at the reflected light. In a moment the cave was dark, except for the flame itself.

"Normally the mother feeds at the creek: sun-dapples in the afternoon, moonlight at night," Quercus said from Rufus's shoulder. "Then she carries the reflections to them inside her stomach, like a bird. This is the best substitute we could think of."

The umbral babies piped and whistled. Abigail piped back at them as she struck a second match, mimicking their calls with uncanny accuracy.

"What happened to their mommy?"

"Don't know," Quercus said. "Although I have my suspicions."

"He means Nettle and his mob," Trillium said. "They're always harassing umbrals."

"Why?" Abigail asked. She leaned farther into the cave. "Why would anyone want to hurt them?"

Trillium shrugged. "Umbrals make stuff malfunction. They don't do it on purpose—it just happens."

"Malfunction how?" Rufus asked. The words had snagged the edge of a memory, but the more he tried to bring it into focus, the more the memory eluded his grasp.

"Pretty much any way you can think of," Trillium said. "When umbrals come around, everything starts going on the fritz—phones, computers, appliances. Clocks stop. Zippers jam. The roof leaks."

"So the All-Outers wait until an umbral comes out to feed, and then they chase it over to Jack's house to get something to break," Quercus said. "They think it's abundantly funny." He sighed. "I don't know how we're going to persuade that group to do anything besides fight and make trouble."

"We have to try though," Trillium said. "Let's go."

"Bye-bye, babies!" Abigail sang. She stuck her head deeper into the cave and kissed the air above the umbral nest. The baby umbrals flapped in alarm, their ropy tails lashing. One squirted out a puff of violet smoke. Abigail yanked her head out of the cave. "Blecch!"

"You okay?" Rufus asked.

Abigail stared past him, unseeing. Her cheeks flamed pink. She looked uncertain and—was it possible?—*ashamed*.

"Abigail?"

Instead of answering, Abigail took off running across the meadow.

UNUSUAL APRICOTS

"Abigail!" Rufus yelled. "Where you are going? Wait!"

Abigail kept running.

"Blight and mildew!" Trillium yelped. "I thought they were too little to dimpsy anyone."

"What are you talking about?" Rufus's heart was pattering in his chest. "What's *dimpsy*?"

"It's how umbrals defend themselves," Quercus said. "That violet smoke. It makes you remember every mistake you ever made and every doubt you ever had."

"It's abundantly effective," added Trillium. "Most humans want to get away from it as quickly as possible."

"And then when the smoke fades, the memory of seeing the umbral fades as well," Quercus said. "People forget they ever saw it."

Rufus shook his head. That couldn't be why Abigail was running. He was pretty sure she'd never made a mistake in her life.

"Stop!" he called after her. "Abigail! We need to go to the funeral!"

But if his cousin heard him, she gave no indication of it. When she reached the end of the meadow, she made a hard right turn and pelted toward the apricot orchard.

Rufus bolted across the meadow to catch her, Quercus and Trillium at his heels.

The orchard was half-wild now. Decades had passed since the Collinses had last brought Feylawn apricots to market; knee-high grass now carpeted the lanes between the trees. The trees themselves fairly glowed with immense orange globes the size of a man's fist.

"Abigail?" Rufus called. "Where are you?"

Then he noticed that one of the trees was being hit by a very localized storm. Branches thrashed from side to side, sending a light rain of leaves wafting to the ground.

Abigail perched on a spindly upper branch some fifteen feet off the ground.

"I'm sorry," she said. "I shouldn't have."

"What are you talking about? Sorry for what?"

Abigail climbed up to another branch. "Go away! Don't look at me!"

Trillium landed on her shoulder. "What did you do for your eighth birthday?" she asked. "What's the most delicious thing you've ever tasted? Who's the nicest person you've ever met?"

Abigail slowed in the midst of ascending to a higher

branch. "I went horseback riding on a pony named Ambrose and . . . chocolate éclairs? . . . and . . . why are you asking me so many questions?"

"You've been dimpsied," Trillium said. "It helps to remember happy things. Burns through the dimpsy smoke."

"Whoa. It's super high up here." Abigail gripped the tree more tightly and looked around as if waking from a dream. "But what an amazing view! And did you know there are apricots?"

"That's because it's an apricot tree," Trillium said. "Do you remember the umbrals?" Abigail's forehead wrinkled. "Umbrals? No. Wait. *Yes!* Babies with high voices and bad breath." She began to climb down, one branch at a time. "Why have I never climbed a tree before? It's fun! And look!" She held out two slightly bruised apricots. "Want one? They look delicious!"

"Wait!" Trillium shouted as Rufus took one. "Before you bite, you have to check for—"

A streak of orange shot from the fruit in Abigail's hand and landed with a muffled splat on her nose.

"What was *that?*" Abigail yelled, dropping her apricot.

The streak of orange planted a noisy kiss on her right nostril. "Ooooh!" it squeaked. "I *love* you!"

"Apricot imp," Quercus said, landing on Rufus's shoulder. "We call 'em cotters. The males wait inside the apricots to be discovered by a potential mate. You might as well eat yours," he added, indicating the fruit in Rufus's hand. "There's not much chance of finding two in the same tree. And if you do, maybe they'll fall in love with each other."

"No, no, no!" squeaked the cotter. "I won't love anyone but—what's your name?"

It drew back and examined Abigail tenderly, still clinging to her face with what appeared to be suction-cup paws. It was about the size of a hamster and bright orange, with a pointed head, a potbelly, and wide-set green eyes, a combination that made it look like a cross between a carrot and a lemur with a glandular problem.

Abigail put her hand to her face and the cotter obligingly clung to her finger and let itself be lifted off.

"He's adorable!" she cooed when she got a good look.

"You are adorable, too!" the cotter said.

"*We need to get to the funeral!*" Rufus said. He tossed away his apricot, bouncing on his toes. "Remember? We have to talk to the All-Outers!"

"Okay, okay," Abigail said, tearing her eyes from the creature in her hand. She tried to set the cotter on the ground, but it clung to her finger.

"I'm yours *forever*," it insisted. "But tell me, what is your name?"

"Don't tell him!" interjected Quercus.

"Abigail," said Abigail.

"Here we go," sighed Trillium.

"Abby-gell!" cooed the cotter. "Oh, Abby-gell! You suit me well, Abby-gell. Of your charms, I'll tell, Abby-gell. You cast a spell, Abby-gell!"

"And what's *your* name?" Abigail asked, batting her eyes a little.

"Don't *ask* him that!" Quercus said, clutching his head in his hands.

"You ask because you love me!" declared the cotter. "And now we are bonded—me to Abby-gell, and you to Bobalo Fling!"

Abigail looked up. "What does *bonded* mean, exactly?" she asked Quercus.

"It means you've got yourself a devoted husband." Quercus sighed. "I hope you like love poems and presents."

Abigail shrugged. "That doesn't sound so bad."

"It *isn't* bad, Abby-gell!" squeaked Bobalo Fling. "Bobalo will get presents for presenting to his Abby-gell! Back soon!"

The cotter leaped from Abigail's hand and hit the ground rolled up tightly in a ball. He bounced a few times on impact, then unfurled and scampered off.

"Okay, he's gone," Rufus said. "Let's go to the funeral."

"You can divorce him," Quercus said in an urgent whisper. "All you have to do is say *I cut the bond with Boppy Flop* three times."

"It's Bobalo Fling not Boppy Flop," Abigail said. "And I don't want to divorce him. He's cute."

"In love I fell, with Abby-gell! I ring a bell, for Abby-gell!" Bobalo squeaked as he returned, climbing up Abigail's T-shirt while awkwardly clutching a bundle of tiny parcels. Each one was wrapped in a leaf and tied with a blade of grass.

Abigail beamed. "Wow, thanks!"

"Open them! Open them!" the tiny cotter commanded, dropping the gifts onto the flat of her hand. "Presents for Abby-gell!"

Using her free hand, Abigail untied the first parcel. Then she shrieked and dropped the leaf bundles on the ground.

"Abby-gell doesn't like spiders?" Bobalo asked sadly. "Not a nice surprise?"

"Thanks for the thought," Abigail said. "It was very large and hairy. But I don't like spiders very much."

"I will eat then," said Bobalo. He rolled off Abigail's palm, snatched up the spider, and stuffed it in his mouth. "Open the others!"

"Maybe you could open them for me?"

"With pleasure, Abby-gell!" The cotter darted to collect the packages on the ground as Abigail squatted next to him. "Ants! Many, many ants!" he announced. And then, seeing Abigail's expression: "You don't like? Okay, I eat."

The following parcels contained a fragment of blue eggshell, an unremarkable gray pebble, and a shoelace. "A ribbon for Abby-gell's lustrous black hair!" Bobalo said, climbing up Abigail's leg again, this time with the intention of wrapping the shoelace around one of her braids.

"Wait a minute—that's mine!" said Rufus. He had just noticed that his right sneaker was loose.

"No longer!" said Bobalo. "It's for the lustrous hair of beautiful Abby-gell!"

"Actually, I need it." Rufus reached to take the shoelace. "My shoe's going to fall off—hey!" A gooey wad of masticated spider hit him in the face.

"Don't steal presents from Abby-gell!" Bobalo admonished, his orange fur bristling.

"I warned you," said Trillium. "Now, let's head over to the funeral. It's probably winding down by now."

"Yes, let's," Rufus said, wiping his face. "Trillium, you'll do the talking, right?"

"I'll talk to them," Abigail said, stroking Bobalo's head. "I was in the speech and debate club in Houston."

"Abby-gell is eloquent!" Bobalo sighed. He flung himself at Abigail's face and planted several loud, wet kisses on her cheek. "And also very elegant! And smaller than an elephant!"

"*Okay*," Rufus interrupted. "We get the picture."

22

DEADLY CENTIBERRY

Abigail and Rufus crouched behind a flowering bush with the two feylings on their shoulders. They were at the edge of a clearing dominated by an immense madrone tree. Feylings perched along the tree's red-gold branches, looking down at a flat spot in the center of the trunk where two bundles lay wrapped in lichen and flowers like intricate birds' nests. Those, Rufus realized, must be the dead feylings. They were so small and still, like a gerbil he'd had once that had died in its sleep.

A wrinkled feyling with heart-shaped wings stood between the two shrouded bodies. "Most of us figure the tree that nearly killed Jack Collins didn't fall on its own," he was saying. "But Rosemary and Buckeye thought quick and they worked seedcraft like we haven't seen in years."

"That's Penstemon Cottonwood," Trillium whispered. "He used to run the train, back when we had one."

Rufus glanced over at Abigail. She was stroking Bobalo's armpits with her thumb and forefinger, which seemed to lull him into a kind of stupor. It was the only way she'd found to stop him from singing or reciting poetry.

"But it was too much for them, as sick as they were," the old feyling continued. "They stopped a murder, but they was killed in the process." He glared at Nettle Pampaspatch, the leader of the All-Outers, who sat in the front row in his lizard-skin suit.

"Murder?" Nettle shouted, tossing his spiky topknot. "What do you call what's happening to all of *us*?"

There was scattered applause and someone shouted, "*We're* dying, why not Jack Collins?"

Abigail lifted her hand from Bobalo's armpits and touched Rufus's arm. "Uh-oh. This might not be the best time to explain—"

Released from the lulling effects of Abigail's armpit rub, Bobalo sat up on his haunches like a prairie dog. "*I am going to explain*," he squeaked. "That I love Abby-gell, again!" Abigail pushed her fingers back into his armpits, but it was too late. "I love her during the months of rain. And now I'll shout my loud refrain—"

"Please don't," Abigail said, trying to cover Bobalo's mouth with her hand.

"—I HAVE ABBY-GELL ON THE BRAIN!"

Every feyling head swiveled to look at them.

"Glompers!" several shouted. "There, behind the bush!"

Nettle Pampaspatch leaped to his feet. "You were spying on us! You're spies!"

A tremor passed through the crowd. There was an eruption of outraged coughing. Wings vibrated furiously, filling the air with an angry whir.

"That's not true!" Rufus cried. "We're here because we want to help you." His voice sounded thin and tentative even to his own ears.

"Help us? Since when have glompers cared about feylings?" Nettle retorted. "We know why you're here. You're plotting to kill the rest of us!"

The voices in the crowd grew louder. "Spies! Murderers!"

"If I were you, I'd start running," Quercus said in Rufus's ear. "Get yourself a good head start."

"But we have information for you!" Rufus blurted. He gestured for Abigail to step forward, but she was still wrestling with Bobalo. He made himself walk to the front of the feyling gathering. About two hundred feylings watched him from the limbs of the tree, some yelling accusations, some coughing, some whispering to their neighbors. Scattered throughout the crowd were the feylings who called themselves All-Outers, dressed in shiny lizard-skin outfits.

"We want to help you," Rufus said, trying to be heard above the din, "but we can't if you keep attacking." He tried to think of something convincing to say, something that would make up for all the funerals that the feylings had been to since their train disappeared. His eyes fell on a familiar form. Iris sat on a branch in the back, her shoulders slumped. She met his eyes and gave a small nod.

"I'm sorry my great-grandmother stole your train," he said. His mouth was dry, his tongue thick. "I know what it's cost you. But we've been looking for it, Iris and Abigail and I"—Rufus gestured at his cousin, who had finally lulled Bobalo into silence—"and we've found half of it already."

There was a collective gasp. The noise around them grew even louder as the feylings murmured among themselves.

"But the goblins want it, too," Rufus continued, pitching his voice to be heard over the crowd. "If they have it, they can invade—"

A marble hit him square in the forehead. He ducked, covering his head, as Nettle Pampaspatch circled him. "*He lies!*" the feyling shouted, pointing at Rufus. "Where is this train, anyway? Who here has seen it?"

"I have," Iris said. She stood, wings trembling.

"Iris Birchbattle," Nettle said in a mocking tone. He settled on a branch beside her. "What a surprise. You've always been a glomper-lover, haven't you? You and Carson were thick as thieves."

Rufus stared at Iris. They were?

"That was before," Iris said. She looked rattled. "Before she did what she did."

"All righty then, let's see this train," Nettle said. He

turned back to Rufus and folded his arms. "Go ahead. Show us."

"It's not here at Feylawn," Rufus stammered. "Well, one of the cars is, but it's hidden." He tried to remember what he'd been trying to say before Nettle interrupted. "The goblins want the train so they can invade the Green World—"

"And how do *you* know so much about what the goblins want?" Nettle interrupted. "Have you been talking with them?"

"*No!*" Rufus said. "I mean, yes, but only because one of them had the coach car and—"

"And he just *gave* it to you?" Nettle said. "And told you all about his plans while he was at it? Is that what you expect us to believe?" He laughed, a high, derisive cackle. Then he stopped abruptly. "Or did he tell you his plans because you're working with him—as a goblin spy?"

"What?" cried Rufus. "Don't be ridiculous!"

A loud cry came from the All-Outers in the crowd. One by one they lifted off from the tree and circled Rufus and Abigail in tight formation. "Spy! Spy! Spy!" they chanted.

"This isn't good," Quercus said. Rufus was thinking the same thing. Apparently he'd made another Fatal Error.

All at once, a dozen All-Outers swooped down and grabbed Abigail's braids, tugging them in opposite directions. She dropped Bobalo and tried to break free, but she was fastened in place as if roped there. "You creeps!" she shouted, thrashing. "Ow! Stop *pulling*!"

"Leave her alone!" Rufus tried to wrench Abigail's braids from the All-Outers. A marble caromed off the bridge of his nose, sending a jolt of pain into his sinuses. When his vision cleared, he saw that Abigail had suddenly gone very still.

Nettle Pampaspatch stood on her shoulder, his legs wide, his stance triumphant. In his hands he held a cord that was looped around the body of a writhing foot-long centipede. It dangled in midair, inches from Abigail's throat. "Nobody move!" he warned. "Or I'll let it sink its fangs into her."

The feylings gasped. "Deadly centiberry!" someone whispered. "Where'd he find it?"

The centipede was twice the size of Nettle himself, its body armored in overlapping crimson plates. Its scarlet legs were tipped with sharp black claws. Two wriggling antennae strained toward Abigail's neck.

"Let go of my beloved Abby-gell," Bobalo squeaked. He clambered up Abigail's leg, shaking violently. "She is not liking bitey centy-pede."

"Then maybe she'll tell us the truth about this train they claim to have," Nettle said. "Where is it? Where did you get it?" He dangled the centipede a hair closer to Abigail's throat. It arched toward her, its legs wriggling.

Abigail lifted her chin. "It's somewhere safe," she said.

"Where?" Nettle demanded. "No more of your glomper lies!"

"Come on now, Nettle," Penstemon called from the tree. "She's a child."

"She's a glomper," said Nettle. "Two of us are dead today, why not one of them? An eye for an eye, I say."

Iris gave a shriek of frustration. "You've got it all wrong!" she exclaimed, circling Nettle and Abigail. "The expression is actually, *I foreign I*. It doesn't have anything to do with hurting anyone. It means that people are the same, even if we seem foreign to each other. I am just a foreign you, and vice versa."

"Quiet!" Nettle twitched the cord that held the centipede. It swung like a pendulum—closer to Abigail, then farther, then closer again. "Now for the last time," he hissed, "tell us how to find our train!"

"Do not scare my Abby-gell!" squeaked Bobalo. His fur had puffed into orange spikes so that he looked like a child's drawing of the sun. He scampered up Abigail's body with his suction-cup paws until he was clinging to the collar of her T-shirt. Then he gave a bloodcurdling screech and flung himself onto the centipede.

The insect tumbled to the ground, pulling Nettle with it. Bobalo grabbed it by the neck and expertly bit off its head. Then he straddled Nettle and spat a large clump of partially chewed centipede into his face.

"No, no, no threatening my Abby, my Abby, my Abby-gell!" he squealed, pinning Nettle to the ground with his tiny furry paws. "No, no, no pulling her lustrous hair!"

Abigail yanked her braids free of the All-Outers' hold. "Maybe we'll bite *your* heads off next!" she yelled.

The feyling crowd had been watching the fracas from the limbs and branches of the old madrone, their expressions ranging from outraged to frightened to amused. Now Rufus turned to face them.

"We're trying to find the rest of the train," he said. "But we can't do it when you're attacking us and Grandpa Jack."

"Just give us a little time," Abigail said. "All we want is a ceasefire."

The feylings whispered and murmured among themselves, their voices growing louder and louder. Then Penstemon spoke. "Show of wings," he said. "Fan your wings if you want to help them. Fold your wings to refuse."

The All-Outers, clustered together in their matching lizard-skin suits, pressed their leaf-shaped wings tightly together. Iris, Penstemon, Trillium, and Quercus opened theirs. In the silence that followed, all that could be heard was a faint rustling as feylings opened or closed their wings.

"The fans carry it," Penstemon said at last.

"Fools!" shouted Nettle, still struggling to extract himself from Bobalo's grip. "Dupes!"

Penstemon landed beside him. "We've made our choice, Nettle. We're making peace with the glompers." He looked up at Abigail. "Tell your cotter to let him go."

"Go ahead, Bobalo," Abigail said.

Reluctantly, the cotter rolled to his feet and scampered up Abigail's leg.

Nettle wiped crimson saliva from his face.

"You'll get no peace from me, glompers!" he hissed as he took wing. "I'll be trailing you like a shadow, watching your every move." He uttered a hoarse, ugly cry, something between a screech and shout, and the other All-Outers fell in behind him, circling Rufus and Abigail a final time before they swooped into the trees.

Rufus let out a breath he hadn't realized he'd been holding. "Are you all right?" he whispered to Abigail.

She nodded, cradling Bobalo under her chin.

A feyling in a long dress that looked to have been made from a single black glove began to sing a slow, wistful melody. One by one, other voices joined in. A half dozen feylings lifted the bodies of Rosemary and Buckeye from the tree and hovered in the air. The others lined up behind them in an airborne procession, their wings rousing a swirl of skittering leaves. Slowly, they drifted away through the trees until only Iris, Penstemon, Quercus, and Trillium remained perched on the old madrone.

"Well done," Trillium said excitedly. "Abundantly well done!"

"Let's not count our chickens before they're hatcheted," Iris warned. "I don't trust Nettle Pampaspatch or the rest of his mob. They're not done making trouble."

"Trouble's one thing we haven't run short on," agreed Penstemon. He turned to Rufus. "Iris tells me you need a few good seed-speakers to guard the train. I'm ready, if you'll have me."

"Of course we'll have you," Rufus said. "And you'll come, too, right, Iris?"

Iris nodded. "I suppose I'd better."

"Trill and I need some supplies for our pouches," Quercus said. "Meet us back at the house in half an hour. And if I were you," he said to Abigail, "I'd use the time to divorce that cotter."

23

SEED SPEECH

Rufus was in the garage, kneeling in front of the filing cabinet where he'd hidden the train, when his father came in from the kitchen.

"How was your day?" His dad stood in the doorway, hands in the pockets of his shorts.

For a moment Rufus thought about telling him. *My day? Funny you should ask.* But then he remembered what he was supposed to say. "Great. We did some library research. Interviewed Grandpa Jack. Everything's on track."

"Glad to hear it." Rufus's father nodded, although he didn't seem to have been listening. "I'm glad you two are documenting our family history. It's important. But I don't want you to get too attached to the past." He cleared his throat. "Feylawn has been in our family a long time. But sometimes things have to change."

Rufus looked up. "Like what?"

His father ran a hand over the lumpy waves of his hair.

"Grandpa Jack is getting older. He's not going to be able to live at Feylawn forever—"

The rest of the sentence was lost in the buzzing of Rufus's ears. "You want to *sell* it," he said. "You want to move Grandpa Jack into Orchard Meadows so you can sell Feylawn! That's why you and Aunt Chrissy have been going there so much!"

"Nothing's been decided. We're just exploring options."

"Is that why you didn't want me spending my summer at Feylawn?" Rufus demanded. "So you could sell it while I was at summer camp?" Tears stung his eyes and he blinked them back, his mouth contorting with the effort it took not to cry.

"Rufus." His father's voice was pained but still calm. "I know how you feel about Feylawn—"

"You *don't* know," Rufus interrupted. "You don't know how I feel at *all*."

"I *do* know," his father said, and now his voice had an edge to it that Rufus hadn't heard before. "You love Feylawn and that's wonderful. I'd love to keep it in the family just for you. But it's a very big and very valuable piece of real estate. If a developer makes us the offer we're expecting, there's no way we can say no."

"Sure you can," Rufus said. "It's easy: No. No. *No*." He kicked the wastebasket next to the filing cabinet and it tipped over, discharging a stained paper coffee cup and a wad of dryer lint.

His father bent down, righted the wastebasket, and replaced its spilled contents. When he stood up again, his face was flushed and angry. "This might be hard for you to hear, but I do know a few things that you don't. I know that children grow up and develop new interests. I know that college is expensive and houses are expensive and money doesn't grow on trees—not even the trees at Feylawn. I know that I've been looking for work for months and your mother had to take a job out of state. Sometimes adults have to think about more than what a twelve-year-old wants."

"*Two* twelve-year-olds," Rufus said. "Two twelve-year-olds and an old man—an old man whose property it is."

His father said nothing for a moment. Then he shoved his hands in his pockets, as if trying to resume the jovial stance he'd taken when he first appeared in the doorway. "Grandpa Jack cares about his family," he said. "He's going to do what's best for all of us. Just as I am. Just as Aunt Chrissy is."

"It's not best for *me*," Rufus shouted. "Don't you get it? I love Feylawn more than anything. I love Feylawn more than I love *you*."

He turned and yanked open the filing cabinet drawer. The pillowcase-wrapped bundle containing the train and tender was just as he'd left it. Rufus grabbed it in both hands and turned to face his father. "I'm going to my room."

His father reached out and stroked Rufus's forehead,

brushing the bangs out of his eyes. "I know you can't understand this now, but I'm doing this for you."

"For who you *want* me to be," Rufus said. He shook off his father's touch and pushed past him, clutching the pillow-case to his chest.

⚬⚬⚬

He'd left Iris, Penstemon, Quercus, and Trillium in his room. They were so excited to see the train that they didn't seem to notice the force with which Rufus placed it on the floor, or the way his jaw clenched as he attached the engine and tender to the coach car he'd brought home in the picnic basket.

"Shouldn't we get to work?" Trillium said after they'd spent several minutes admiring it. "While we're standing around gloating, that goblin may show up to snatch it out of our hands."

"All right then, what do we have?" asked Penstemon, peering into his pouch. "I didn't have much time to gather supplies, but I have fern seed."

"Trillium has three kangerlen pods," said Quercus, pulling open his own pouch. "And I've got chokecherry."

Within moments, the feylings were dropping piles of seed on the bedroom floor, engaged in a conversation that Rufus found completely incomprehensible.

"We should start with nodding needlegrass."

"There's a kitchen here. Maybe they have caraway."

"Mustard—to confuse him!"

Rufus listened with interest, trying to figure out how seed speech actually worked. Did the feylings actually talk to the seeds? And how could *talking* turn something as ordinary as mustard or caraway into the kind of magic you could use to fight a goblin?

Curious, he dug out the toolbox that held his own seed collection and opened the lid, surveying the assortment of seeds and seedpods, dried flower heads, and withered berries. He picked up a pod that held a thimbleful of poppy-size seeds inside six paper-thin chambers.

"Hello," he breathed, barely making a sound in case the feylings noticed what he was doing.

There was an answering sigh from the seedpod in his hand. *Cross paths*, a chorus of little voices seemed to whisper. *Cross tracks. Turn. Twist. Go back.*

With a jolt, Rufus dropped the seedpod. The sound had probably been the murmur of his own tired imagination. But if it hadn't been? He lifted a cluster of shriveled red berries and again breathed an almost inaudible greeting.

"*Prickles,*" whispered the berries.

Rufus blinked and held them to his ear. But the sound didn't come to him that way. It seemed to have sighed directly into his thoughts. *Prickles have I, for those who pry.* He cast an eye over at the circle of feylings on the floor, wondering if they could hear it, too.

Trillium was balancing on her forearms with Smacker dangling from her feet. When she saw Rufus looking at her, she flapped her wings, flipped over in midair, and landed on the edge of the toolbox with Smacker in her arms. "What's all this?"

Then her jaw dropped. "Sticks and weeds! Guys, get over here! You're not going to believe what Rufus has."

A moment later the feylings were digging through the compartments of the toolbox, tossing seeds and seedpods into piles with no regard for the order that Rufus had painstakingly created.

"Look at this—tanglevine," Iris hooted, holding out a flat, furry seedpod. "Not a lot, but enough!"

"And nackleburr!" Penstemon said as he clawed through the seeds at the bottom of the box. "Crowcock. Zaniums. Slickspit! This goblin won't know what hit him."

"What about this one?" Rufus said, holding up the cluster of berries that was still in his hand. "It says it pricks those who pry."

"Sure," Quercus said. "Wall of Thorns, we call it." He flew over to take the berries from Rufus, then gave him a puzzled look. "But you couldn't have heard—"

Penstemon tapped Quercus on the shoulder. "Sun's sinking," the old feyling said. "We'd best get started before our visitor comes knocking. You and I will do the boundary line."

Quercus hitched up his silver pants and threw back his

shoulders. "Let's go," he said, and flew off with Penstemon, his question forgotten.

❧ ❧ ❧

Rufus woke in the middle of the night to the sound of something scuttling methodically around the outside of the house. *Click. Scrape. Tap.* The feylings were nowhere to be seen. He crept to the window and drew aside the curtain, muscles tensed. He heard a familiar cough.

Iris sat on the windowsill with her legs drawn up, looking out at the street and coughing as quietly as she could.

"He's persistent, I'll give him that," she said, wiping her nose on her knees. "He's been circling for the past three hours."

Rufus remembered the sting of Diggs's fingernails on his eyes, the stench of his breath in his face. His father was sleeping down the hall. He'd come running if Rufus shouted for him. But what could his father do against a goblin? What could any of them do?

"What happens if he finds a way in?" he asked.

"He won't." Iris turned her head at last and gave him a weak smile. "Between the four of us, we'll keep him out."

"Good." Rufus cloaked himself in the folds of the curtain. "Before, he just wanted the train. Now I think he'd like to kill me."

Iris turned her gaze back to the street. "He brought someone with him," she said. "There, in the shadows."

Rufus moved closer to the window. A figure stood under the boughs of a tree in the front yard, draped in a long gray overcoat. He looked up, met Rufus's eyes, and gave a slight nod. Rufus stepped backward, an icy chill traveling down his spine.

"That's Alastair Gruen," he said. "He owns the train store where Diggs works."

"Is he the boss, then?"

"Of the store, yes," Rufus said. "But I don't think he's the boss of Diggs. I'm not sure what he is."

"Me neither," Iris said. "Not a red-blood. Not a gray-blood either. Definitely not a green-blood. Something else." She coughed again, her lungs making a sharp squeak.

"What else could he be?" Rufus asked. "What is there besides humans and goblins and feylings?"

Iris rolled her eyes and Rufus saw a spark of her old feistiness. "More than your little glomper imagination could ever conceive," she said. "And most of it, I wouldn't want on my front lawn." She turned and looked at him, her pupils very large in the dark room. "Go to sleep," she said. "You did a lot today. More than I could ever have expected."

Rufus nodded and turned back to his bed, his eyelids drooping. As he pulled up the covers, he remembered something.

"Iris?"

"Still here."

"Nettle said you were friends with Carson Collins."

"That was long ago."

"But what happened? If you were friends, how could she have destroyed your only way home? Didn't she know it would kill you?"

There was a long silence.

"We saw things differently," Iris said at last. "Humans and feylings always do in the end."

24

ALL THE FINISHED STORIES

Tucked on the third floor of the public library, the Galosh History Room was crammed with filing cabinets and rows of mismatched bookshelves. Rufus and Abigail had arranged to meet there at ten o'clock that morning, to look for information about Carson Collins that might help them solve the next clue. But Abigail hadn't arrived yet. Rufus hovered at the door, wondering whether to go in. The jump rope rhyme riddled around in his mind: *You found the coach car good for you. But every good train must have two. Waltz and fox-trot, twirl and prance! Wake the dancer! Make him dance!*

A tall woman sat at the back of the room typing on an electric typewriter next to an electric fan. She wore a fluorescent green skirt and an oversize button-down shirt and had piled her bushy red hair into a loose knot on top of her head.

"The Children's Room is two floors down," she said as Rufus approached her desk. "Look for the bright yellow rug."

"No," Rufus said. Why hadn't he waited for Abigail? "I mean—I'm not looking for the children's section. I'm looking for information about a person. A writer."

"Biographies are on the first floor. The reference librarian can help you." The librarian was still typing. Her name tag said ANNE THORPE.

"But the writer lived in Galosh," Rufus said. "I thought this room had information about the town's history."

Ms. Thorpe continued to flutter at the keys of the typewriter for a long minute, the silver bangles on her wrist jangling. At last she looked up. "I'm sorry," she said. "This room contains historical reference materials. For researchers."

"But I'm *doing* research." Rufus tried to smile the way Abigail did, with all his teeth showing. "My great-grandmother—Carson Sweete Collins—was a famous children's book writer a long time ago and—"

Ms. Thorpe emitted a high-pitched noise that was something like the sound a cat makes when you step on its tail. "*The Fair Folk of Glistening Glen!*" she squealed. "I absolutely *love* those books!" She rolled up one sleeve of her shirt. "*Look!*"

Tattooed on her pale forearm was Iris, if Iris had been given a Hollywood makeover. Her knobby legs were smooth and shapely, her leathery green wings thinned into pale green silk, and her bedraggled black hair was arranged in elegant swirls.

"Cool," Rufus said, hoping that was what you were supposed to say when a librarian showed you her tattoo.

"It's from the final book," Ms. Thorpe said. "*The Gifts of Glistening Glen.*"

"Right." Rufus still hadn't gotten around to reading past the first twenty pages.

"Did you see the quote?" Ms. Thorpe flexed her wrist so the feyling on her forearm seemed to shimmy. A phrase was inked in a banner above Iris's wings: *All the finished stories will begin again.* "The last line of the book," she prompted.

Before Rufus could manage to stutter out a response, Ms. Thorpe had extracted a familiar green volume from a drawer in her desk and begun to read the final page aloud, her voice taking on just the hint of an English accent.

"*Stories might seem to end, but they never do, no more than rivers stop flowing or trees stop reaching for the sky. The fair folk of Glistening Glen have faded into the shadows, but perhaps we shall find them again before long. A time will come when all the lost things are found, and all the finished stories will begin again.*"

She closed the book, her face wistful. "You probably know those books by heart," she said. "What's your name?"

"Rufus Collins."

"An actual Collins!" The librarian sighed. "I feel like I'm meeting a movie star."

Rufus shrugged modestly. "What do you think she meant?" he asked. "About the lost things being found, I mean."

Ms. Thorpe rolled down her sleeve. "As you know, Mrs. Collins lost her father just before the book was published. She was probably wishing she could see him again one day."

She opened the book to the dedication page and tilted it so that Rufus could see.

In memory of my father, Avery Sweete,
who knew the way to Glistening Glen

Rufus ran a finger over the inscription. "So, can you help me with my research?" he asked. "I'm trying to find information about dancers that my great-grandmother might have known when she was alive."

Ms. Thorpe frowned and led him over to an island of filing cabinets in the center of the room. "Unfortunately, we don't have much information about Mrs. Collins. She was a bit of a recluse." She handed him a thin folder, then topped it with two thick, musty-smelling books. "You might find something in these—they're scrapbooks one of our early curators made about notable Galoshites."

When Ms. Thorpe had returned to her desk and begun typing again, Rufus settled at a table near the filing cabinets. Where was Abigail? He checked his watch, but it had stopped working the day he went to the barn to find toys for Mump.

He had finished reading the file on Carson Collins and was starting on the first scrapbook when he heard running footsteps in the hallway outside. Abigail burst in, looked wildly about, and then made an effort to compose herself. Bobalo was perched on her shoulder, crooning a tuneless song about Abigail's hair, eyelids, and knees.

Ms. Thorpe didn't seem to be able to see or hear him. She gave Abigail the once-over. "The Children's Room is two floors down."

"It's okay; she's with me," Rufus said. "She's my cousin."

Abigail flashed Ms. Thorpe an abbreviated version of her politician's smile and flopped into a chair. "Our parents want to sell Feylawn," she announced. "I heard my mother talking on the phone this morning."

"My dad told me last night." Rufus swallowed, his throat suddenly dry and tight. He was, he realized, extremely glad to see her.

"But they can't, right? Not without Grandpa Jack saying yes?"

"I don't know. They sure want to." Rufus shook his head, fury turning his stomach into a popcorn machine. "Did you say anything to your mom?"

Abigail shook her head. "I wasn't supposed to be eavesdropping. I was supposed to be writing pen pal letters in Mandarin *and* Spanish. Then my mom wanted to check that we'd made progress on our Carson Collins website."

"But we haven't!" Ms. Thorpe looked over at them and frowned. Rufus lowered his voice. "We haven't done anything!"

"*You* haven't done anything. *I* threw something together last night after we got home." Abigail raised her eyebrows expectantly. "Three little words."

"Fine." Rufus sighed. "You. Are. Brilliant. Although"—he took in her disheveled appearance—"you're not usually so dirty."

Abigail flushed. "I fell," she said. "I rode over here on my bike and a bird—you know, like the blue one you pointed out on the way to Orchard Meadows? It was following right behind me, weirdly close for a bird. I was so freaked out, I hit a pothole and crashed."

"A Steller's jay was *following* you?" Rufus felt a shiver of anxiety. "Why?"

"I don't know." She rubbed her scraped knee with her palm. Bobalo stroked her cheek.

"Abby-gell was in terrible pain, but Bobalo was there to comfort her," he announced. "With comforting poetry! And comforting songs! And comforting presents!"

"Yes, I'm very comforted now, thanks," Abigail said. She picked up one of the scrapbooks. "Have you found anything?"

Rufus shook his head. "Not yet."

They worked in silence—or at least, *they* were silent. Bobalo continued singing the song about the beauty of Abigail's hair, eyelids, and knees at steadily increasing volume.

"How can you stand it?" Rufus asked after the eighteenth

or nineteenth verse. "It's like being waterboarded in a vat of artificial sweetener."

"It's not *artificial*," Abigail protested. "He means every word of it. Anyway, he'll calm down eventually. This is just the honeymoon stage."

"Honeymoon!" squealed Bobalo, assuming his poetry-reciting pose. "I met my Abby-gell in June! And we went on our honeymoon!"

"And I will murder you by noon," Rufus muttered.

Bobalo's fur bristled. "*Please* be quiet, Bobalo," Abigail said in a low voice. "We need to find the dancer and it's impossible to concentrate with you screaming in my ear."

"I understand you, my beloved," Bobalo said, his eyes taking on a tragic gloom. "I will go." With that he threw himself from Abigail's shoulder and rolled away.

"Wait!" Abigail cried.

Miss Thorpe looked up from her desk. "Do you need assistance?"

Abigail shook her head, watching the cotter roll out the door. "Do you think I should go after him?" she whispered to Rufus.

"Go after him?" Rufus said. "How about bolting the door so he can't come back?"

"Don't be mean." Abigail chewed her lip. "I think I hurt his feelings."

They continued paging through the scrapbooks: programs from long-ago performances, menus from gala luncheons, men in fedoras shaking hands. There was nothing about Carson Collins or any dancers. Rufus's eyes watered from yawning.

But then he saw a familiar face. He bent forward to look more closely. "That's weird."

"What?" Abigail leaned over to look at the page.

"This picture—it's of Alastair Gruen, the guy who owns the train store. But it's from, like, seventy years ago." Rufus indicated the caption under the photo, which read, *Alastair Gruen, industrialist and miniature railroad hobbyist.*

Abigail got up and went over to Ms. Thorpe's desk. She returned a few minutes later with a folder labeled *Alastair Gruen/Clockwork Displays.*

The folder held a series of newspaper clippings arranged in chronological order. Rufus peered over her shoulder as Abigail riffled through them. The first ones were all about the hobby shop's railroad layouts, the display of which seemed to have been an annual event in Galosh. But then a different sort of headline leaped out at them.

MINIATURE RAILROAD BARON
KILLED IN KEY STATION PLUNGE

Rufus took the clipping from the file, the hairs on the back of his neck tingling. "It says he died in 1949 after falling from the Key Station tower when he and Mr. Diggs were trying to repair the clock."

"But look—he didn't die after all." Abigail handed him the last clipping in the folder.

March 18, 1949

HOBBYIST MAKES
MIRACULOUS RECOVERY

GALOSH, CALIF.—In a twist worthy of Edgar Allan Poe, industrialist and hobby shop owner Alastair Gruen astonished both his doctors and the workers at Ibbotson's Mortuary Services by waking from what everyone had believed was his final sleep. Gruen, 50, was killed—or so it was thought—in a fall from the Key Station clock tower on Thursday morning. At around 5 a.m. on Friday, Sven Ibbotson, the mortuary owner's son, heard a loud crash in the room where the dearly departed are kept before embalming.

"The day you see the dead walk is the day you start thinking about getting out of the mortuary business," said Ibbotson, 22, when the Daily Drenching located him at Dry Socks Tavern.

Doctors say Gruen's return from the great beyond, while extremely rare, is not unheard of. According to Dr. Steven Ransome, chief of surgery at Good Samaritan Hospital, the human body

is capable of husbanding its resources in times of
acute stress, as after a dramatic fall.

"But then why hasn't he aged?" Rufus asked. "If he was fifty then, he'd be over a hundred and twenty years old by now."

"Maybe that was his grandfather."

"He said his grandfather founded the store," Rufus said doubtfully. "But I don't buy it. I think it's the same guy."

As Abigail opened her mouth to reply, an orange blur streaked across the table and collided with her left cheek.

"Bobalo has presents!" the cotter squealed, planting a loud kiss on Abigail's nose. "He has brought surprising surprises!"

"Where are they?" Abigail looked around nervously. "Surprising surprises are sometimes *very* surprising," she whispered to Rufus. "Last night he brought me a live pigeon."

Bobalo sprang from Abigail's face to the table, hopping on both feet. "Behind the bookcase, so the lady with the orange hair cannot see!"

If Bobalo had brought a pigeon into the library, Rufus didn't want to miss seeing Abigail's reaction. He followed the two of them behind the shelves. There, on the floor, was a stack of several dozen books topped by a plastic ballerina doll and a man's wallet.

Abigail covered her mouth. "What *is* all this?"

"Abby-gell wanted to find out about a dancer!" Bobalo

said, his green eyes very large. "So I bring dancer books!" Despite his minuscule size, he effortlessly hoisted one in each paw. "This is book about dancer Anna Pavlova! This is book about dancer Alvin Ailey! This is about how to become dancer!" He scampered over to the wallet and pulled out a driver's license. "This man is named James Dancer, born November 14, 1976! And this is dancer doll, from a grabby little girl who cries too much."

"You *stole* somebody's wallet?" Abigail cried. "And took a child's toy? Bobalo, you have to give them back!"

"You don't like wallet?" Bobalo's furry shoulders slumped. "But it is filled with money!"

"I think I hurt his feelings again," Abigail sighed as the cotter trudged toward the door with the doll and the wallet. She turned back to the pile. "And what are we going to do about all these books?"

"Beats me," Rufus said. "Sneak out before anyone notices?"

Then one of the books caught his eye. He couldn't say why exactly—it was thin and battered and looked as if no one had checked it out for at least half a century. But it seemed familiar. He bent down and extracted it from the pile. *The Mermaid's Song and Other Poems.*

"Abigail," he said. "It's by Carson Collins."

25

THE UMBRAL'S CRY

"Rufus? Are you still here?" Footsteps echoed on the other side of the bookcase: Ms. Thorpe's Doc Martens boots. "We don't like to leave reference materials unattended."

Abigail stepped out from behind the bookcase wearing the most eager of her adult-pleasing facial expressions. "We were looking at this book of Carson Collins's poems, Ms. Thorpe! Show her, Rufus."

"The *dancer* poem!" Ms. Thorpe snatched the book from Rufus's hand and paged through it until she came to a pen-and-ink illustration of a woman in a hat and coat staring up at a lumpy, ungainly giant. Rufus's heart began to pound. He knew that giant. It was the Boulder Dude at Feylawn.

"Mind if I take a look?" he asked, trying to reclaim the book.

Ms. Thorpe held up a finger. "Listen. You get more out of poetry when you hear it aloud." She licked her lips and began to read.

"I wandered weeping through the wood
And blundered where some boulders stood.
There I sat and sobbed and sighed.
Someone close to me had died.
As I moaned and wailed and wept
The boulder-man beneath me slept.
He'd been asleep a thousand years
And yet—I woke him with my tears.
He fixed me with a flinty glance
And asked me if I'd come to dance.
He said, 'Your weeping's wasted breath.
You can dance but you can't fight death.'"

Ms. Thorpe fell silent. "If that's the dancer you were looking for, I don't think you'll find him," she said. "He's not a real person. More like a metaphor. He represents the long view, I guess. The unstoppable march of time."

Rufus took the book from her hand and looked at the drawing.

"Oh well. Thanks for helping us, Ms. Thorpe."

"Anytime, Rufus. Let me know if you need anything else."

◦◦◦◦◦

"So you're saying these boulders are the dancer in the poem?" Abigail said as they rode their bikes toward Fey-lawn.

"They have to be. I just have no idea how we're supposed to wake him."

"Tears, *obviously*," Abigail said. "Hey, look out!"

From the corner of his eye, Rufus saw a flash of blue. A
Steller's jay, wings spread in a ragged fan, swooped toward
his head. Rufus swerved, almost losing his balance. The
bird landed on a street sign, black eyes fixed on Rufus.

"Come on!" Rufus made a hard right turn onto a side
street with Abigail close behind him.

"It's following us!" she cried.

There it was, in a tree. The jay screeched, crest erect.
Rufus turned right a second time, backtracking two blocks
before turning toward Feylawn.

"I think we lost it," he panted.

But then it was there again, blue as a watching eye. It
swooped from tree to tree as they pedaled, always keeping
pace. When they turned onto the dirt road that led to Feylawn, the jay lifted over their heads with a grating cry that
was almost a shout. Then it kept going, casting a faint gray
shadow on the dirt road as it flew ahead of them, banking
left at the seven oaks, and vanishing into the green.

࿓

The farmhouse was in a state of chaotic calm. Feylings still
trooped through the living room and fluttered around the
porch, but instead of attacking, they waved as Rufus and
Abigail made their way into the kitchen. "How's the train

hunt going?" a few of them called. "Do you think you'll have it by Friday?"

Rufus hoped their confidence wasn't misplaced. Waking a stone giant wasn't going to be easy—and once it was awake, what then?

They had lunch with Grandpa Jack, who had just cooked a lasagna. "Stove's working again," he announced. "And I've been wearing the same pair of glasses since yesterday morning. Not to jinx it, but that's got to be a record!"

When they'd each eaten two helpings, Rufus pushed back his chair. "We're going to take some photos of the Boulder Dude for the website. We'll be back in an hour or so."

"I'd join you," Grandpa Jack said, "but with Feylawn so quiet, I'm going to do some work in the barn."

An inexplicable fear squeezed Rufus's chest. "I don't think you should go in there," he said. "All those holes in the floor."

"Listen to you, Nervous Nellie," Grandpa Jack said. "Don't worry—I'll watch my step. Can't do much in there with my arm in a sling, but at least I can straighten up a bit."

"You should wait," Rufus said. Something about the barn made him nervous, but he wasn't sure what. There was a gap where the memory belonged, like a missing tooth.

"Time waits for no man," Grandpa Jack said, getting to his feet. "I'm going to shave my face, change into my old dungarees, and start setting things to rights."

As Grandpa Jack climbed the stairs to his bedroom, Rufus grabbed Abigail's arm. "Come on! We have to get to the barn before he does."

"Why?"

"I can't explain it. I just know there's something dangerous in there."

"Like what kind of something?" Abigail reached to her shoulder to stroke Bobalo, whose fur had puffed up in alarm at the word *dangerous*.

"I don't *know*." Rufus shook his head as if he could rattle the memory into place. "Just trust me, okay?"

Abigail searched his face. "Okay," she said. "It's on our way to the boulders anyway, right?"

⟞⟪⟫⟝

A swampy smell assaulted their nostrils as Rufus lifted open the barn's one-hinged door. Abigail wrinkled her nose. She had left Bobalo on the path to watch for Grandpa Jack, and now she didn't seem to know what to do with her hands.

"What are we looking for?" she asked.

Rufus scanned the corners, his skin goose-pimpling. Something flapped below the floorboards, just once, like a blanket being shaken out.

"That," he said. "Whatever it is."

Abigail dropped to her knees beside the largest of a half dozen holes in the floorboards and shone her phone's flashlight into the darkness. A piercing cry rose up from below, like wind screeching over a desolate glacier. The light from the phone vanished.

"An umbral!" Abigail sat back on her heels and swiped at her screen, trying to reactivate it. "It's huge!"

Rufus felt a rush of terror—and with it, the hazy outline of a memory. "I saw it before . . . when I came in here to find something for Mump. I think I got dimpsied."

"The babies' missing mommy!" Abigail said.

"Nettle and his bunch probably lured her in here to hurt Grandpa Jack." Rufus rubbed his forehead, trying to remember what else the feylings had told them. "Quercus said umbrals make things break. Like floorboards."

"And cell phones." Abigail shoved her lifeless phone into a pocket. "We should get her out of here before Grandpa Jack arrives."

Rufus took a few careful steps closer to the hole where the umbral lurked. "But how?"

Abigail opened her mouth and made a sound like clattering icicles. The cry of the baby umbrals.

Rufus shivered. "Don't."

An answering call rose from the hole in the floor— haunting and clear, like the coldness of space. A pointed indigo tail emerged from the hole.

Rufus backed toward the door. Abigail stayed where she was, her eyes fixed on the opening in the floor. She called again, more softly now.

"This is a bad idea," Rufus said. "We're both going to

get dimpsied." It came back to him suddenly: the violet smoke ransacking his memories, pulling out the hurtful and embarrassing ones. That mocking voice. His armpits prickled with anxiety.

"She won't hurt us," Abigail said, leaning forward a little. "She's just scared."

Inch by inch, the umbral flowed up from below, spreading like oil over the floorboards. Then she lifted into the air above their heads and hovered near the ceiling.

"Why won't she just go?" Rufus said. "The door's wide open."

The mother umbral's body rippled. She turned her head and fixed them with her blank white stare. A sigh drifted from her tiny puckered mouth.

"She's afraid. Nettle and his bunch must have really scared her." Abigail moved closer to the door and imitated the baby umbrals' icy call, softly at first, and then with a note of urgency. "Come on," she called. "Go home to your babies!"

The umbral flapped once and then swooped toward them. Rufus grabbed Abigail's hand and held it, bracing for the jet of violet smoke. But the creature merely glided over them, pulling in her triangular wings as she floated through the open barn door.

Rufus dropped Abigail's hand and exhaled a shaky breath.

"She knew we were trying to help her," Abigail said.

"That's why she didn't blow smoke at us. She let us remember her."

Rufus shook his head. "I'd rather forget." He gave Abigail an admiring glance. "That cry you made though. You sounded just like them."

"Birdcalling Camp." Abigail shrugged. "I never imagined it would be so useful."

26

WAKE THE DANCER

Neither of them said anything as they walked through the woods toward the boulders. Abigail stared at her dead phone, hitting the Start button over and over.

"My dad and I usually text a lot," she said. "Now I can't even get my phone to turn on."

"I hate to say it, but it's probably bricked," Rufus said. "My watch hasn't worked since Monday, when I met the umbral the first time."

Abigail shoved the phone in her pocket and reached to her shoulder to stroke Bobalo, whose singing was reaching operatic volume. "My mom's going to kill me. *And* we need to know what time it is. I have swim practice at five."

"Ssssh." Rufus held up a finger. As Bobalo quieted under Abigail's touch, Rufus heard a kind of tuneless hum, like a bee trapped inside a radio. Then he saw where it was coming from. A small, furry goblin leaned against a tree just ahead of them, humming to herself while knitting a striped scarf. Garnet, the one they'd met by the creek.

"There you are." She smiled, revealing her pointed teeth. Her turquoise cardigan now sported a bright line of brass buttons, and she was wearing the hat with violets that Rufus had found in the barn. "I told you how to find me, but you didn't call."

"That's because we don't need you," Abigail said. On her shoulder, Bobalo coiled one of her braids around his body like a cocoon.

"You don't?" Garnet's knitting needles clacked back and forth, spilling forth a row of yellow stitches. "I wouldn't have guessed it from the way my brother's boasting around the tunnels."

Rufus started. He'd forgotten that Mr. Diggs was her brother. He looked around nervously. "Is he here? Did he send you?"

Garnet unspooled a bit more of the yellow yarn. "As it happens, I don't take orders from my brother. He's a big schemer, but he misses the details. It always made me chuckle to see Mump playing with that little tender, practically under his nose."

"I'm sure your family relationships are very interesting," Abigail said. "But we have somewhere we need to be."

Garnet looked up sharply and the hat with the violets slid backward between her ears. "Queen Queen-Anne's-Lace has a message for you. My brother has stopped visiting her and that has her worried."

She waited for a reaction. "You don't know who I'm talking about, do you?"

Rufus shook his head. "Queen-Queen?"

"Queen Queen-Anne's-Lace. Queen is her title. Queen-Anne's-Lace is her name." Garnet sighed. "I'd have thought the feylings would have mentioned her."

Rufus felt a shadow of misgiving. "Iris said their queen made a deal with the goblins to build the train."

"A raw deal, if you ask me. She married my brother. That was his price."

"Love does not care about distinctions," Bobalo squeaked from inside the coil of Abigail's braid. "A feyling can love a goblin, just like a cotter can love an Abby-gell!"

Garnet snickered. "Oh, I don't think love had much to do with it. My brother made the train willingly enough, figuring that once Queen Queen-Anne's-Lace was his wife, she'd have no choice but to help him make another one. He could do the metalwork on his own, of course, but the train would need feyling seedcraft to cross between the worlds."

"But she wouldn't help him," Rufus said.

"No." Garnet reached into a bag by her feet and took out a pair of scissors, which she used to cut her strand of yellow yarn. "She married him, but that was it. She's been sitting in a dark chamber for the past sixty-odd years holding her tongue. My brother used to visit her every day to say he would release her if she just did that one bit of seedcraft. And then suddenly, a few days ago, he stopped coming." The scissors went back into the bag. "It's not that she misses his company. Still. It's peculiar."

"Peculiar, *how*?" Abigail didn't try to hide her impatience.

Garnet shrugged. "He clearly thinks he doesn't need her. He knows you've got the engine and two of the four cars. When you have them all, he'll take them from you."

Rufus swallowed. "But why does he care so much about the train?" he asked. "What does the Green World have that's so important?"

"You mean your feyling friends haven't told you?" Garnet rolled up her knitting and tucked it into her bag. "Quite a large piece of the puzzle to leave out. But then, telling Carson didn't work out so well, did it?"

Abigail threw up her hands. "Telling her *what*?" she demanded.

Garnet played with the buttons on her cardigan, looking as coy as it was possible for someone with a fanged underbite to look. "I think I've told you enough for one day," she said. "Mump's waiting for me and he wants his supper. Queen Queen-Anne's-Lace just asked me to warn you."

She picked up her bag and began threading her way through the trees. "Oh, and if you speak to my brother," she added, turning back, "I'd rather you didn't mention this conversation. I do have to share a table with him on feast days. And we goblins have a *lot* of feast days."

⚬⚬⚬

"I don't trust that knitting fanatic," Abigail said as they cut across the meadow to the giant boulders. "Mr. Diggs probably told her to pass along that message. They're just trying to scare us."

Rufus shook his head. Abigail hadn't liked Garnet from the start, and he couldn't blame her. Still, Garnet had let them take the tender instead of giving it to Diggs. "I think she's telling the truth," he said. "I just don't understand why."

"But she's not telling the *whole* truth," Abigail said. "Why won't anyone tell us what Diggs wants with the Green World? Even Iris won't tell us."

"I know," Rufus said. A flicker of uneasiness wriggled through him. "But we're not letting him take the train, so I guess it doesn't matter why he wants it."

"Maybe not," Abigail said. She tugged on the braid that wasn't wrapped around Bobalo, her forehead creased in thought.

The Boulder Dude was just ahead, casting long shadows over the grass.

"So now we're supposed to shed tears?" he said when they'd scrambled up its shoulders. "How?"

"Think of something sad," Abigail said.

Rufus shut his eyes and imagined a FOR SALE sign posted at the entrance to Feylawn. Grandpa Jack living in some airless little apartment at Orchard Meadows.

Iris dead.

Penstemon dead.

Trillium dead.

Quercus dead.

His throat tightened. His heart sank to the bottom of his chest. But no tears—just the empty feeling that's worse than tears. He looked at Abigail.

"It's harder than I thought," she admitted. "Try pulling my hair. That always makes my eyes tear up."

She held out her braid to him. As he took it, Rufus saw a figure coming across the meadow from the farmhouse. He recognized the lanky stride and hunched posture.

"Uh-oh." These days Rufus's father never came farther into Feylawn than the house or the garden. What could he possibly want?

He scrambled down from the boulder to greet his father, the blood pounding in his ears. Abigail followed.

"I wanted to see how the project's going!" Rufus's father smiled eagerly. "Are you finding lots of photo ops?"

Abigail stared at her phone with an exaggerated expression of dismay. "This is so frustrating, Uncle Adam," she said. "The battery on my phone *just* died. I wanted to show you all the pictures we took."

"And I'd love to see them. Chrissy showed me what you

two have done on the website—it's fantastic." He clapped a hand on Rufus's shoulder. "Your enthusiasm really shows."

Rufus slid out from under his father's hand. "We'll meet you back at the house."

"I was hoping you'd give me a little tour," Rufus's father said, still smiling. "Tell me what you've been doing out here. What's so important about these rocks, for instance?"

"They were in a poem called 'The Dancer,'" Rufus said flatly.

His father nodded. "What other real-life scenery can you show me?"

"Look around," Rufus said. "It's all real-life scenery."

From the expression on her face, Rufus knew Abigail was wishing he would just play along. He could almost hear her thoughts: *Why can't you tell grown-ups what they want to hear?*

"I meant from the books." Rufus's father smoothed the waves of his hair. "I'm interested in what you've been doing, Ru."

Rufus kicked the edge of a boulder with the toe of his sneaker. "Why?" he asked. "Because you want to make sure I'm having *a turnaround summer?*"

His father winced. Abigail shifted from foot to foot, her face anxious. "Actually, Uncle Adam, the fairies in the books had a lot of their parties over there." She indicated the ravine that dropped away behind the boulders. It was rimmed with ancient oaks, their branches bearded with Spanish moss.

"No kidding!" Rufus's father surveyed the ravine as if noticing it for the first time. "Hey, Ru, is that the rope swing you made?"

The swing dangled from the thick arm of an oak at the lip of the ravine. Rufus and Grandpa Jack had made it the previous fall, scouting for the perfect spot, building the wooden seat, and then climbing high into the tree to secure the rope. He'd been trying to get his father to look at it for months.

"Can you show me how it works?" Rufus's father said now. "I'd like to see it in action."

"It's a swing," Rufus said. "It works like any other swing."

Rufus's father's smile faltered. "I'd still like to see it," he said more gently. "I know you worked hard on it."

"*I'd* like to see it," Abigail said.

Rufus could feel them both looking at him. He knew what Abigail wanted him to do. Pretend that it didn't matter that his father wanted to sell Feylawn. Pretend that everything was fine. Keep his father happy so that they could come back tomorrow and try to wake the dancer.

"Okay," he said. "Come on."

☙◈❧

The rope was bristly against his palms as he walked it up the slope of the ravine. He offered it to Abigail. "Do you want to go first?"

She looked at him doubtfully. "You go."

"It's easy." Rufus reached up the rope's length and pulled

himself onto the wooden seat. Then he was flying over the clearing, the ground falling away below. Sunlight flashed through the latticework of leaves as he reached the swing's highest arc and sailed backward through the blur of green and brown, until his feet found the dirt slope where he'd begun. He was grinning in spite of himself. The ride felt like a tonic, filling him with bubbles of laughter.

"My turn," Abigail cried. A moment later she was sweeping over the clearing, Bobalo clinging to her neck. "*Woooooo-hoooo!*"

"Nice piece of engineering," Rufus's father observed.

"It's a swing," Rufus said. "It's not *engineering*."

"You should try it, Uncle Adam," Abigail said as she landed. Her eyes sparkled. "It's *really* fun."

"You sure it'll hold me?"

"Grandpa Jack's ridden it lots of times," Rufus said.

Rufus's father wiped his palms on his trousers and took the rope from Abigail. "Wish me luck." He walked the swing a little farther up the slope of the ravine, gripped the rope, and wrapped his gangly legs around the wooden seat. With a long whoop, he sailed out into the clearing, limbs flailing. "This is *fan-tas-tic*!" he called.

It wasn't until his father was at the highest point of the swing's arc that Rufus saw the Steller's jay. It swept down into the bowl of the ravine, wings flashing blue against the green of the trees. As it glided past the rope it opened its beak in a raucous screech.

The rope snapped.

Abigail screamed. Or maybe it was Rufus. He had no sense of being in his own body. His father was falling, his legs kicking the air, the rope swirling around and under him. And then he hit the ground with a terrible thud, sending up a cloud of dirt and oak leaves that obscured his tumble into the base of the ravine.

The jay landed on the branch that had held the rope.

"All-Out!" it croaked. Its body stretched and contorted. Its legs thickened into a pair of lizard-skin pants. Its blue wings narrowed into green leaves. Its black crest became a black topknot. It was Nettle Pampaspatch, gloating.

"Death to glompers!" he shrieked, and then he was flying again, back into the woods and out of sight.

Rufus was already halfway down the slope to the spot where his father had landed.

"Be okay," he whispered as he ran. "Be okay, be okay, be okay."

His father sprawled against a sapling oak.

"Dad?" Rufus slid down to reach him, horror bringing everything into bright focus: his father's pale skin and the awkward angles of his legs, the bright drops of blood on his forehead. Abigail was just behind him, her breath coming in ragged sobs.

"Dad?" Rufus said again. "Dad?"

27

MAKE HIM DANCE

Rufus shook his father's arm gently, then harder. "Dad, wake up."

His father didn't stir.

Abigail's eyes filled with tears. "What do we do?"

Rufus couldn't answer. He pushed his face against his father's chest. Then he heard it—the faint thump of a heartbeat. He let himself listen for a moment, his own heart swelling with relief. Then he wedged his hands under his father's armpits. "Help me. Get his legs."

Abigail shook her head. "You're not supposed to move people—I learned that in first aid." She rolled up his father's pants' legs and flinched. A messy gash on his left leg was spilling a thick stream of blood. Rufus couldn't bring himself to look at it too closely.

"Give me your shirt," Abigail said. "I need to stop the bleeding. Then I'll go get Grandpa Jack."

Rufus took off his T-shirt and watched Abigail press it

tightly against the wound. "But what can *he* do? He's got a broken arm and a bruised leg and no working phone."

"He could drive into town and get a doctor. An ambulance."

Rufus looked at his father, bright blood already soaking through the T-shirt on his leg. "An ambulance can't find Feylawn. And he's bleeding a lot. I don't think we have much time."

Abigail was still pressing his shirt against his father's leg. Bobalo had wrapped himself in one of her braids and was watching her with doleful green eyes.

"We can't carry him up the ravine by ourselves," she said. "We need help. Where are all the feylings?" She shouted at the top of her lungs. "HELP! SOMEBODY! HELP US!"

After a moment, Rufus joined in. "HELP! WE NEED HELP!"

Even Bobalo was shouting now. "HELP! MY ABBY-GELL NEEDS HELP!"

They shouted until their throats were sore. Rufus was sure the feylings would come, so sure that for a moment a cloud of them seemed to be flying toward him. But it was just leaves on the branches above his head, fluttering in the wind.

He rubbed his sweaty palms across his shorts. High above them, the granite face of the Boulder Dude watched impassively. A phrase from Carson Collins's poem drifted into his head. *He'd been asleep a thousand years . . .*

"Where are you going?" Abigail swiveled to watch as he sprinted up the side of the ravine, using stray roots and rocks as handholds.

Rufus didn't answer. Dirt pushed under his fingernails and spilled over the tops of his sneakers as he climbed. Then he was at the base of the Boulder Dude, panting. He pressed his face against the coarse rock and began to cry.

It was easy this time. At the edge of the ravine, with his back to Abigail, the sorrow and fear poured out of him like warm honey. Hot tears on his face. The afternoon breeze on his bare back as it heaved with sobs. The rough, sun-baked granite beneath him.

The rock shuddered, shifted, shook.

Rufus sprang backward, his feet sliding in the loose dirt at the edge of the ravine.

The boulder gave a long groan. Then it spoke—a low rumble, like molten rock. "How long have I been asleep?"

Behind him, Abigail gave a startled cry. Rufus scrambled back down to the base of the ravine and stood next to her, his heart pounding.

"I don't know," he said. "Sixty-five years, I think."

The boulder stretched. It had the shape of a man, but a man who had been sculpted in a second-grade ceramics class by a kid who was eager to get to recess. His limbs were lumpy and half-formed, his features lopsided. He took a step closer to the edge of the ravine, thighs knocking together with the bright clang of rock against rock.

"Where's that lady?"

"What lady?" Rufus glanced at Abigail. She stood very straight, her mouth slightly open. Bobalo seemed to be trying to hide inside her T-shirt.

The Boulder Dude's forehead creased. "Short. Human. Lady. She was here."

"Well, she's gone now," Rufus said. "And we need help. My father's hurt and we need someone to carry him back to—"

"We were dancing," the Boulder Dude said. He caught sight of Abigail and leaned forward, lowering his great head over the ridge. "Are you that lady?" With a movement that combined the grace of a cat with the force of an avalanche, he leaped from the ridge, knees and elbows and skull knocking together as he tumbled into the center of the ravine.

"I'm not her," Abigail said, using her body to shield Rufus's father from the shower of debris. "Please—we were hoping—"

The granite man gave a jaw-cracking yawn and sank onto his haunches. "Sleepy," he mumbled. "Short nap."

"We don't have *time* for naps!" Rufus yelled. "My dad could *die*." The words were brambly in his throat.

"They do that," the boulder giant said. "Humans. Want to dance?"

"*No!*" Rufus felt like screaming. "He needs a doctor!"

Abigail got to her feet and took a couple of hesitant steps

toward the granite figure, smiling her politician's smile. "I *love* dancing," she said. "I take classes in ballet, tap, jazz, and hip-hop."

"Are you kidding me?" Rufus hissed. "My dad's *bleeding to death*."

"I'd like to dance with you," Abigail continued. "But first—could you carry my uncle across the meadow? Please?"

The granite man's heavy forehead bunched into a scowl. "Dance first."

"Dance *afterward*," Abigail said.

The boulder giant rubbed his eyes with his misshapen fists and yawned. He scratched a craggy hip. Then he shrugged his massive shoulders and leaned down, holding out his arms. "Carry man," he said. "Then dance."

"Are you sure this is a good idea?" Abigail whispered to Rufus.

"No," Rufus said. "I just don't know what else to do."

Together, they lifted the unconscious form of Rufus's father by the legs and shoulders and placed him on the giant's lumpy forearms. "Careful!" Rufus cried. "Don't hurt him!"

The Boulder Dude strode up the side of the ravine without answering. Rufus and Abigail scrambled after him.

They had crossed the meadow and were close to the farmhouse when Grandpa Jack came running toward them. "What on earth—?" He looked up at the giant, who had come to a halt in front of him, and then pulled off his glasses.

"Good Lord." He stared at the Boulder Dude with his mouth open. Then he gasped. "Is that my son?"

"He fell off the rope swing," Rufus said. "He's pretty badly hurt." He folded his lips between his teeth and took a shaky breath. "We have to get him to the hospital."

"Put him in the truck." Grandpa Jack beckoned to the stone giant. "Follow me."

The giant didn't move. "The girl said we would dance."

"Put my son in the truck and then you can dance your heart out," Grandpa Jack said firmly. He flinched as the giant took a step toward the farmhouse. "That way." He pointed toward the gravel road.

The giant thudded past the farmhouse until he came to Grandpa Jack's old bottle-green pickup, parked at the top of the road. "Here?"

"That's right." Grandpa Jack opened the passenger-side door. "Easy does it." His face grew pale as he got a good look at his unconscious son. "Just hold on, my boy," he murmured. "I'll get you to a doctor."

As soon as Rufus's father was in the truck, Grandpa Jack started the engine and barreled down the road, tires spitting dirt and gravel.

Halfway down, he slowed. "I'll be back as soon as I can!" he shouted out the open window. "Beeee caaareful with that giiii-ant!"

In a moment, he was out of sight.

"What do we do now?" Rufus said.

The Boulder Dude stood at the edge of the meadow. He pounded his foot on the ground in a series of hollow thuds.

"Come on," Abigail said. "We promised we'd dance."

"You go," Rufus said. He wished there had been room for him in the pickup. "I don't really feel like dancing."

Abigail blew her hair out of her eyes. "Rufus, he's the size of a house and made out of rock. Let's not make him mad."

The thuds grew louder, sending waves of vibration under their feet. Bobalo whimpered and wrapped himself more tightly in Abigail's braid. Abigail took Rufus's arm and dragged him forward. Rufus felt his legs move, but it was as if he was in a borrowed body. His feet were too big, his arms too heavy. He kept seeing the image of his father on the ground, pale and broken. Kept hearing his own voice telling his father, *I love Feylawn more than I love you.* He struggled out of Abigail's grasp.

"I need to get a shirt."

"I know you're upset." Abigail's voice was gentle. "But the Boulder Dude has the train car, remember?"

"He can keep it."

Abigail's eyes widened.

"This whole thing was a huge mistake," Rufus said. His throat was raw and tight. "If I'd just gone to summer camp like my dad wanted, none of this would have happened."

He turned to walk back to the farmhouse. The ground throbbed under his feet. *Stomp. Stomp. Stomp.*

"Rufus," Abigail said. She ran to catch up with him. "Please. Just dance with me. I don't want to do it alone."

He looked at her. Her arms were streaked with his father's blood. She looked as stunned and frightened as he felt. It wasn't her fault that he had made the ultimate Fatal Error. It was his and his alone.

"All right. Let's go."

⚬⚬⚬

"Now we dance," the Boulder Dude boomed as they approached. He strode to the center of the meadow with Rufus and Abigail following and then turned to face them. "Begin."

"There's no music," Abigail said.

The giant held up one finger. He stamped his foot, once, twice, three times, four. Then came a low rumble like summer thunder.

He was humming.

The rumble invaded their bodies, a drone that could be heard from the inside. The Boulder Dude snapped the fingers of his left hand, rock clacking against rock. He pounded his right fist against his granite chest, a jarring staccato *clonk*. Together the sounds made music—a slow, ancient, and infectious music. Without meaning to, Rufus found himself dancing.

It wasn't a happy dance. It was a dance of mourning, a dance of anger, a dance of disbelief. The steps seemed to live in the marrow of his bones: *shuffle and stamp, sway and slide*. It was as if he'd always known them. Now they were dancing in unison, the two human children and the giant rock man: *step, pivot, shake, glide*. Beneath Rufus's feet was the solid ground—the grass, and the dirt below the grass, and the rock below the dirt. He could feel it under him, layers of rock reaching all the way down to the liquid center of the Earth. The ground that was place. This place. Feylawn. Where everything had always been all right.

And then the memory of his father's plummet hit him in the chest. Rufus stopped dancing. The Boulder Dude was watching him.

"Done?" the giant asked. His arms dropped to his sides. The meadow fell silent.

"Done," Rufus said, turning away.

The Boulder Dude yawned and rubbed his eyes with his fist like a sleepy toddler. "Time to sleep, then."

"Wait!" Abigail called. "That lady you danced with before—did she give you something?"

The Boulder Dude fumbled at a crevice at his hip. As he tugged at it, it opened like a pocket. He pulled out a coach car, bright green against the gray of his lumpy hand.

"The lady asked me to keep it until she came back," he said.

"She can't come back now." Abigail reached out for the train car. "She died. A long time ago."

"She did?" The Boulder Dude's laugh was like the clatter of falling stones. "She said she wouldn't."

"Wouldn't *die?*" An icy breeze prickled Rufus's bare shoulders.

"She said if I kept it for a while, she wouldn't have to." The giant handed Abigail the coach car and resumed his heavy, plodding path across the meadow. "Humans always think they can live forever," he rumbled over his shoulder. "But they never do."

28

BETWEEN FLOORS

It was Aunt Chrissy who picked them up and took them to the hospital. But there was no news when they got there, at least nothing reassuring. "The docs are doing what they can," Grandpa Jack told them. He looked ten years older than he had that morning.

Hours trickled by. Rufus's mom was on her way back from Phoenix, but she wouldn't get there until late that night. The families and friends of other patients filed in and out of the waiting room, some jolly and talkative, others grim and quiet. Still there was no word about Rufus's father. Rufus and Abigail played a few hands of gin rummy with Grandpa Jack, but it was hard to concentrate. Finally, Rufus stretched out across two chairs and shut his eyes.

As he drifted in and out of sleep, Grandpa Jack and Aunt Chrissy spoke in low, urgent voices, sometimes right over him. They used words like *brain injury* and *organ rupture* and *compound fractures*. Troubling words, their edges shredded by sobs and indrawn breaths. *Coma. Nonrespon-sive. Transfusion. Life support.* He tried to listen, to under-stand what they were saying, but then sleep would wash over him again as if to spare him the knowledge.

When he finally came all the way awake, the waiting room was empty except for Grandpa Jack. His face looked strange, but it took Rufus a moment to realize why. He wasn't wearing glasses.

Rufus sat up. "Where is everyone?"

"Aunt Chrissy and Abigail went home to get supplies—they're staying with you tonight."

"Why?"

A long sigh. "The docs want to send your dad to a bigger hospital—it's about an hour away. I'll pick your mom up at the airport and take her there."

"Can I come?" The thought of his mom's calm presence made Rufus miss her so sharply that he felt his body might simply vanish into the distance between them.

"You'll see her in the morning. Chrissy will bring you to the hospital first thing."

"Is my dad going to die?"

Grandpa Jack took a deep breath and Rufus braced himself for what was coming. Nobody needed that much oxygen to deliver good news.

"I hope not, Ru." Grandpa Jack's eyes were moist. "They're doing what they can, but it doesn't look good."

Rufus's chest felt hollow, as if his insides had been

scooped out like a pumpkin's, leaving a thin rind that might collapse at the slightest touch. He knuckled his eyelids with his fists. Tears pushed back, but they wouldn't flow. Grandpa Jack took his hand and held it, his big thumb stroking Rufus's palm.

"What time is it?" Rufus asked at last.

Grandpa Jack checked his watch. "A little after eight." He stroked the sleeve of the oversize T-shirt Rufus was wearing. "I like your taste in clothes."

"I borrowed it from your drawer. Abigail used mine to wrap Dad's leg."

"I don't know what I was thinking, leaving you kids alone at Feylawn like that," Grandpa Jack said. "Chrissy gave me an earful, and she didn't even know about the big granite fellow."

"You were in a hurry to get Dad to the hospital," Rufus said. "And seeing the Boulder Dude must have been a shock."

"All that's true. But there's more to it. I have a habit of not looking Feylawn square in the face. It put all of us in danger." Grandpa Jack's voice quavered. "I'm so sorry."

"You couldn't have known what was going to happen."

"I knew what had happened to *me*. I could have drawn conclusions." Grandpa Jack reached to take off his glasses, but then seemed to realize they weren't there. "You know, I've been wearing glasses since I was three years old," he said. "My father took me to get 'em the day after he sent my mother to the mental hospital. I guess he noticed I was looking at things that weren't there. For years, every time he came to town he'd ask if I was seeing okay. So I convinced myself that the world I saw through spectacles was more real than the world I saw with my own eyes. I thought I'd be safer that way." His eyes, blue and watery, met Rufus's. "I couldn't have been more wrong."

It took a moment for Rufus to understand what he was saying. "You mean, you *can* see feylings? You knew they weren't moths?"

Grandpa Jack nodded. "Those creatures have been trying to knock the glasses off my face for years."

"But I *asked* you and you said it was all just stories."

Grandpa Jack dropped his gaze, then rubbed his eyes with his forefinger and thumb. "Truth is, Rufus, if you get in the habit of denying things about yourself for long enough, it just becomes second nature. Biggy and I were so scared of being locked up like our mother had been, we taught ourselves not to notice all the strange things going on around us. Even when I saw my mother dancing with that boulder fellow, right after Pop Avery died, I told myself it was an illusion."

"You *knew* the Boulder Dude was alive? And you never told me?" Rufus pulled his knees under the tent of Grandpa Jack's T-shirt. He didn't think he could take in any more news.

"You have every right to be mad," Grandpa Jack said.

"But understand: I wasn't lying to *you*, I was lying to *myself*. I knew Feylawn was peculiar, but I didn't want to face how dangerous that made it."

"We both should have listened to my dad," Rufus said. "If we had, none of this would have happened."

"Don't you dare blame yourself," Grandpa Jack said, wrapping him in his arms. "This isn't your fault."

⚶

When Aunt Chrissy and Abigail returned, Abigail invited Rufus to get dinner with her in the cafeteria. "Do you feel like talking or not talking?" she asked once they were in the elevator. "Because I borrowed my mom's computer and we could just watch funny videos and not talk about anything serious."

Rufus nodded gratefully. "That would be great."

The elevator lurched to a stop and the doors opened.

"Come on." Abigail stepped toward the door but found her way blocked by a man in a hat and overcoat who was just getting on. "Excuse me," she said, trying to step around him.

"No, no, excuse *me*," said the man, reaching out to block her path. The door slid closed behind him. "I'm afraid we haven't yet been introduced. I'm Alastair Gruen. You must be Abigail Vasquez."

Abigail gasped and backed away. On her shoulder, Bobalo's fur bristled.

Rufus darted to the control panel and stabbed the button that opened the elevator doors. Nothing happened. "Let us out," he yelled.

"Tut, tut. I only want to talk," Mr. Gruen said. The elevator heaved downward again.

"We don't *want* to talk!" Abigail spat. "Let us out of here!" She moved toward the doors as the elevator slowed to a halt and pounded on them with her fists.

Mr. Gruen put a hand on her shoulder. "Goblins are wonderful with machinery," he said in a conversational tone. "Take the electrical power system here at Good Samaritan Hospital." His hand tightened on Abigail's shoulder as he drew his face close to her ear. "One squawk from either of you, and the machines keeping Mr. Adam Collins alive might suddenly stop working."

Rufus stiffened. "What do you want from us?"

"Just a few minutes of your time," Mr. Gruen said. He seized Rufus and Abigail by the elbows as the elevator opened its doors onto a fluorescent-lit hospital corridor. "Right this way, please. *Quietly.*"

THE ANTIDOTE
TO DEATH

Two nurses chatted at the far end of the hallway, but they didn't look up as Mr. Gruen ushered Rufus and Abigail through a door that read HEALING GARDEN.

"Sit down," Mr. Gruen said, indicating a bench next to a potted maple tree.

Rufus and Abigail sat. There wasn't much hope of escape. Although open to the evening sky, the courtyard garden was enclosed on all four sides by the walls of the hospital. Gruen's goblin allies could easily be watching through the windows, ready to cut the power if either of them made a move.

"You were in this hospital once," Abigail said. "We read about it in an old newspaper clipping. They said you died."

It was still warm out, but Mr. Gruen turned up the collar of his overcoat, shoulders hunched. "I was assisting my colleague, Mr. Diggs, with a repair of the Key Station clock tower when I lost my footing," he said.

"Mr. Diggs is a goblin," Rufus interjected. "Why are you working with him?"

Mr. Gruen shrugged. "Goblins are a much-misunderstood species. I have long been privileged to assist them with their business dealings in the human realm. They have so much to offer humankind: oil, diamonds, coal. Everything that makes the world go 'round."

It was quiet in the garden, except for the steady tick of Alastair Gruen's wristwatch. Rufus got to his feet. "I don't really care why you're working with them. Just tell us what you want and let us go."

Mr. Gruen gave them a glimpse of his teeth, pulling up the corners of his mouth as if opening curtains on a stage. "What I want," he said, "is exactly what *you* want. To save your father's life."

"You tried to *kill* him!" Rufus remained standing. "Nettle was working for you! I saw him by your shop!"

"Let's focus not on the past," Gruen said, "but on our hopes for the future."

Abigail tugged the back of Rufus's shirt and he sank down onto the bench. In the twilight, he could just make out Bobalo's green eyes peering out from under the collar of her T-shirt.

"I did in fact die from the fall," Mr. Gruen said. "But Mr. Diggs is a cunning builder of mechanical creations.

He replaced my shattered bones and organs with clockwork mechanisms, restoring me to life. A miracle of engineering."

The ticking seemed to grow louder. Rufus wondered suddenly if what he was hearing was not a wristwatch after all, but the wheels and cogs inside Mr. Gruen's body.

"So you want to turn my father into a machine?" he asked. "No thanks."

"Many unpleasant things," Mr. Gruen said, "are preferable to death." He leaned against a planter filled with ornamental grasses. "Your great-grandmother thought so, anyway. She came to visit me after reading about my miraculous recovery in the paper. Her father was dying of lung cancer. She was hoping I might share the secret of my resurrection. Unfortunately for her, Mr. Diggs was not in the business of resurrecting every Tom, Dick, and Harry. Besides which, we had already discovered that the mechanisms keeping me alive have their disadvantages. It is not a warm feeling to have gears in your chest. I am always cold. My mechanisms need constant repair. I tire easily and yet I can never sleep." Mr. Gruen pushed himself off the planter and paced in front of them, suddenly restless. "But in my conversation with Mrs. Collins, I discovered that she had a solution at her fingertips that could solve both her problem and mine. Has your friend Iris ever told you why it is she will die if she doesn't get back to the Green World?"

"She just . . ." Rufus trailed off, realizing that this particular detail had never come up.

"I thought not." Mr. Gruen clasped his long hands together and made a steeple with his index fingers. "They have a tree there, in the Green World, the seeds of which might be called the seeds of life. When the feylings return to their world from ours, they use these seeds to restore their immortality. Those seeds are, in fact, the antidote to death."

Rufus felt something open in his chest, like the mouth of a hungry animal. One seed. That's all he would need to save his father.

Beside him, Abigail snorted. "So why didn't Carson ask the *feylings* to help her instead of you?"

Mr. Gruen bent down and brought his face close to Rufus. "She did. They refused. That was the moment when she understood, as you will, that feylings only care about themselves."

The animal in Rufus's chest was pacing now, like a tiger in a cage. What Mr. Gruen was saying had to be wrong. And yet—what if it wasn't? *We saw things differently*, Iris had said when he'd asked about her friendship with Carson Collins. *Humans and feylings always do in the end.*

"And that's why she cut down the Roving Tree," Rufus said slowly. "Revenge. She was angry that they wouldn't help her."

"Not revenge," Mr. Gruen said. "Leverage. We needed to bring the feylings to the bargaining table."

"Mr. Diggs offered to build the Roving Trees Railway if Queen Queen-Anne's-Lace would marry him," Abigail said, remembering what Garnet had told them. "He thought if he married her, he could make her do his bidding."

"Husbands and wives should be *partners*," Gruen corrected. "Together Mr. Diggs and his wife could build and operate a second train—one that would travel to the Green World and return with the seeds of life."

"But the queen wouldn't do it," Abigail said, eyes flashing. "She'd rather sit in the dark forever than help you with your evil plan."

Mr. Gruen stopped pacing and quirked an eyebrow at her. "Evil plan? My, my. Since when has saving lives been evil?" Once more, he leaned against the planter. "We asked Mrs. Collins to steal the train for us. We calculated that if the feylings were cut off from the Green World completely, their queen would come 'round to a reasonable position."

"Which was what?" Rufus demanded. The animal inside him was clawing at his chest. "What did you want her to do?"

"Provide the seeds of life to me and my goblin colleagues in sufficient quantities to synthesize the compound in our factories."

"Synthesize it!" Abigail repeated. "Why?"

"Goblins are men of business," Mr. Gruen said. "They know there's a market for immortality. Look at the profitable trade in face-lifts, hairpieces, and sports cars. Imagine if we could offer humans something that actually worked."

Rufus swallowed. "But the feylings still wouldn't strike a deal."

"No. And then Carson Sweete Collins left Feylawn and disappeared without a trace. We thought she had taken the train with her. At least, until a certain young man arrived at my shop a few days ago carrying the engine and tender of the Roving Trees Railway."

Rufus was barely listening. An idea had come to him, a beautiful, brilliant idea. "The feylings don't need the seeds of life to heal my father," he said. "They can do all kinds of seedcraft. I bet there are seeds at Feylawn that can help him."

Mr. Gruen laughed. "Carson Collins thought the same thing. And yet it turns out that even with all their talents, feylings have no knack for healing. Look at them now, coughing and collapsing. *Dying.* Without the seeds of life, they can't even heal themselves."

Rufus leaped to his feet, his body shot through with an anger he didn't fully understand. "We have to go. Thanks for clearing things up."

Abigail stood up as well. Mr. Gruen stayed where he was. "*Have* I clarified things for you?" he asked. "I'm glad. I did want you to understand which party is in the best position to help someone whose father is close to death. You see, we know that you have all but one of the train cars."

Abigail started to protest, but Mr. Gruen put up his hand. "I suggest you retrieve the last one without delay. The doctors have your father on life support, but I don't know how much longer he can hang on. The sooner you give us the completed train, the sooner we can retrieve the seeds from the Green World, saving his life and providing me with a far more comfortable one."

Rufus lifted his chin. "We will *never* give the train to you," he said. "If my dad needs those seeds, the feylings will get them for me."

Mr. Gruen smiled condescendingly. "Will they? I encourage you to ask them." He gestured toward the door that led back inside. "You may go," he said. "I'll be waiting for your answer."

30

A CHOICE

Rufus's house was dark and silent when he got home that night. He helped Abigail find sheets and towels, and endured Aunt Chrissy's grumbling about how much easier it would have been to stay at *her* apartment, if only her apartment wasn't filled with unpacked boxes.

When he finally went to his room, Iris was waiting for him, her eyes wide with worry. "What happened? Tell me exactly how he got hurt."

"Why don't *you* tell *me* what happened?" Rufus snapped. "The truth this time."

Iris grew very still, her wings pulled tight behind her. "What do you mean?"

"I *trusted* you," Rufus said. "You said Carson had betrayed you. You said you were the injured party. You didn't tell me you let her father die."

"Who told you that?"

"Alastair Gruen," Rufus said. "He told us why Carson

cut down the Roving Tree and took the train. He told us about the seeds of life."

Iris stared at him for a long moment. "Well, that's it, then." She lay down on the bed and curled into a fetal position, one wing cloaking her face.

"Sit up," Rufus said. "You have some explaining to do."

Iris didn't move.

"Why wouldn't you help her?" Rufus asked. "Her father was *dying*. Did you want all the seeds for yourself? You couldn't share?"

No answer. There was a knock at the door, and Abigail poked her head in. "Is it okay if I come in? My mom said we can talk for a few minutes before we go to sleep."

Rufus nodded, too angry to speak. Abigail shut the door behind her. She had Bobalo on one shoulder and her khaki backpack slung over the other. Carefully, she removed the second passenger car and placed it at the end of the train.

"Look what we found," she said to Iris. When the feyling didn't respond, she went to the bed and poked her with her finger. "We need some answers," she said. "If you knew why Carson hid the train, why not tell us?"

Iris pulled herself to a sitting position. "The seeds of life are a secret," she said in a low voice. "We aren't supposed to tell anyone who isn't a feyling."

"But somebody told Carson," Rufus said.

Iris nodded miserably. "I did." She looked up and met their eyes. "Everything that's happened is my fault. It's my fault our queen had to marry Mr. Diggs and my fault that everyone's dead or dying and my fault that something bad happened to your father. And every time I try to fix it, I make it worse!" She buried her face in her hands and sobbed, rocking back and forth until the sobs became harsh, barking coughs.

"My Abby-gell is very tired," Bobalo said. He leaped down from Abigail's shoulder and wiped Iris's face with the back of one furry paw. "Less crying, more talking now, please."

"We were best friends, Carson and I," Iris said, her voice quavering. "Like two pets in a puddle."

"Peas in a pod," Abigail said.

Iris ignored her. "She was writing her stories about Glistening Glen and I was writing my lexicon of common glomper expressions. We were always asking each other questions. When she asked me why we didn't die, I told her. I thought I could trust her. Then her father got sick."

"And she came to you for help," Rufus prompted. He felt as if the room was closing in on him. Down the hall, he could hear Aunt Chrissy in the bathroom, brushing her teeth.

"We *tried* to help, that's the thing she never remembered," Iris said. She coughed again, the sound rattly in her chest. "But we didn't know much about healing. We were immortal; we didn't need to. And it was the tobacco that was killing him—maybe if he'd been able to quit we'd have done better. But he kept on smoking. You can't save someone who won't save themselves."

"Yes, you can," Rufus said. He knelt beside the bed, staring at Iris. "You could have given him one of the seeds of life. *One* seed and none of this would have happened."

"You glompers," Iris said. "You're all the same."

"What's that supposed to mean?" Abigail demanded. "We've done everything you asked of us and more. Why didn't you just tell us the truth?"

"Because I knew what would happen once you found out about the seeds of life," Iris said. "And now it's happening." She walked to the edge of the bed and met Rufus's gaze. "Go ahead, get it over with. Ask me."

Rufus thought about the past few days—how he had been so angry that he'd hardly spoken to his father. He remembered his dad's habit of rubbing the clumps of his hair when he didn't know what to say and the way he always put on an Italian accent when he made spaghetti, and his one fancy basketball move, a fake-left shoot-right sequence that had ceased fooling Rufus about three years ago, but which his dad still tried every time they played. He thought about his father trying to teach him math, and bringing him out to look at the stars through a telescope. Everything he was about to lose.

"Just one seed," he said. "We'll find the last train car and send you to the Green World like we promised. Just bring back a seed for my father."

"No." Iris lifted her chin. "I'm sorry. But no."

Rufus slammed his fist into the mattress, his face crumpling. "Why not? It's your fault he got hurt. If I hadn't agreed to help you, none of this would have happened."

Iris flinched. "The problem with you glompers is, you can't see the fours for the threes."

"Forest for the trees," Abigail said. "It means—"

"It means you can't see the big picture—like when you're staring at a math problem and you get so distracted by the threes that you forget about the fours," Iris said. "You keep thinking about wanting your father not to die, but you're not thinking about what happens if he doesn't."

"If he doesn't die, then I have a *dad*." Rufus's voice was loud enough that Abigail brought her finger to her lips and glanced at the door. "It doesn't seem very complicated to me," he added in a quieter voice.

"But it *is* complicated," Iris said. "We feylings have to keep tasting the seeds, because every time we cross into your world, we become mortal again. But for a glomper, one seed would work forever. Not just a hundred years. Not just a thousand. Hundreds of thousands of years. Do you think your father *wants* to live that long?"

"My dad can always think of something to do," Rufus said. "He'd have his projects." He could imagine his father typing a list into a spreadsheet: *Things to Do This Century.*

"What about when everyone he knows has died?"

Rufus hesitated. "Maybe my mom could be immortal,

too." He remembered what Mr. Gruen had said about making the seeds into pills and continued, feeling more confident. "They wouldn't have to be the only ones either. We could use it as medicine—to help people."

Iris put her hands to her temples as if trying to keep her head from exploding. "You have almost eight billion glompers in your world already. What would happen if people stopped dying? How long do you think it would be before there were eighty billion people on Earth, or one hundred billion, all shoved together like pigs in a pen? Would there be a single plant or tree or animal left?"

"But we're not talking about *everyone*. We're talking about saving one person. My dad." Rufus got up and went over to the train. He wished he could climb inside and take it to the Green World to collect the seeds himself.

"The goblins will do it if you don't," he said. "If I give them the train, they can send Nettle to collect the seeds."

Iris shook her head. "I'll do whatever I can to help your father, Rufus. Except that." She coughed, a long, hard spasm that shook her entire body.

Rufus stood, his jaw set. "I don't want your help. You said it yourself—everything you do just makes things worse."

"Rufus," Abigail began. "Don't—"

"Stop!" he shouted. "Just stop. I'm *tired* of everyone telling me what to do. I'm going to save my father's life. Nothing you can say will stop me."

#GOALS

The sun was just coming up, color leaking back into the world. Rufus stood at the window. Iris, Trillium, Quercus, and Penstemon slept beside the train, using socks for sleeping bags. Below him, on the shadowy sidewalk, Gruen hunched in his gray overcoat. Waiting for his answer.

Rufus leaned his forehead against the cool glass and shut his eyes. What should he do? Betray the feylings but save his father? Or try to save the feylings and risk his father's death? He seemed incapable of doing anything but making Fatal Errors, one after another, starting with the moment he went into the barn to see what was in the icebox.

The feylings on the floor shifted and coughed in their sleep. Rufus moved away from the window. Pinned to the wall over his desk was the list of goals he and his father had made the week before, when they were planning Rufus's *turnaround summer. Goal #1: Complete a really excellent summer project. Goal #2: Finish at least three math puzzle books. Goal #3: Develop some new interests/hobbies.*

Picking up a black marker, he drew thick lines through all three of the goals. Then he wrote two new ones:

Goal #1: Keep Dad alive.

Goal #2: Keep the feylings alive.

The toolbox that held his seed collection was on the floor where he'd left it two nights before. He carried it back to his bed and sat cross-legged on the blanket to inspect the chaotic interior. Seedpods in green and brown, some flat, some curling, some spiraled, some as thick as his bottom lip, some as thin as parchment. Fat, round seeds and thin, flat seeds and seeds shaped like teardrops. Acorns, pinecones, nuts, and berries. Each of them did *something*, he knew, but could they do what he needed them to? He looked over at the sleeping feylings, debating whether he should wake them and ask for help. But then the memory of Iris's lies surged through him. No. He'd do this on his own.

He took a breath and tried greeting the seeds in his mind. *Um, hi.*

A blaze of voices ignited in response, calling, singing, whispering.

He shut his eyes. *Can you help me heal my dad?*

A strange sensation came over him, as if his body were made of summer breezes. The seeds were still chattering and clamoring, but now Rufus could somehow sort their voices in his mind. *Dark to light, eyes bright,* cooed one. *Ease the heart, please the heart,* promised another. He pictured what he knew of his father's injuries: shattered bones, ruptured organs, a bleeding brain. As he held the image in his mind, some of the seed voices faded into the background, and others grew sharper and brighter. He passed his hands over the seeds and selected first one and then another, asking a question here and there. It took a special kind of effort to stay in this place halfway between waking and dreaming, to concentrate just enough to talk without speaking and listen without hearing.

"Sticks and weeds!"

The seeds' voices faded. Trillium stood in front of him, bouncing on the balls of her feet with Smacker wrapped around her neck. "Were you just—?" She gestured at the small pile of seeds he'd chosen.

"Seed-speaking!" Iris said. She stared up at him, her eyes brimming. "You were seed-speaking, Rufus! Seed-speaking!"

"Was I?" Rufus felt himself grow solid again. The four feylings were gathered in a loose semicircle around him, their wings vibrating with excitement.

"I thought only feylings could talk to seeds," Quercus said. "How did you do it?"

Rufus swallowed. "I don't know. I just needed to do something. So my dad doesn't"—he met Iris's eyes—"die."

Iris flung herself at him, embracing his cheek. "I told

you I'd help you," she whispered in his ear. "You didn't have to do it on your own."

"Do you think it'll work?" He searched their small faces. The pile of seeds in front of him seemed so tiny and ordinary. Had he just imagined hearing them speak?

The four feylings inspected the seeds in the pile.

"Hmm," Trillium said. "We've never used seeds this way. Still, it makes a kind of sense."

"Except for these." Quercus plucked a pod from Rufus's pile. "I see what you're thinking—strengthen his bones, right? But those make you grow a tail like a monkey."

Rufus waited for the rest of them to start debating the pros and cons of different seeds the way they had when they were planning how to protect the train from the goblin. But they just looked at the seven seeds in the pile and nodded.

"But what do I do with them now?" Rufus asked.

"I'll show you when we get to the hospital," Iris said. "Bring two cups and a sharp knife." She flew back to the bed and sat down abruptly, as if dizzy. "I'm going to rest for a while. Wake me when you're ready to go."

Her eyes were half-closed and her wings were brown at the edges.

"You don't look so good," Rufus said. He couldn't stay angry with her, not when she seemed so weak. "Maybe someone else should come."

"I'm not going to waste my strength arguing with you,"

Iris said. She tipped onto her side, her eyes drifting closed. "The others need to guard the train." She opened her eyes a crack. "You're not giving it to the goblins, are you?"

Rufus shook his head, his stomach in knots.

The little pile of seeds didn't seem like much to pin his hopes on.

OPENING THE SEEDS

Leaning against the trunk of a sidewalk tree in his dark gray overcoat, Alastair Gruen almost blended into the shadows. Aunt Chrissy, talking to a client on her cell phone, didn't seem to notice him as she led Abigail and Rufus to the car. It was almost 8:00 a.m., but the sun hadn't yet burned away the clouds.

"What are you going to tell him?" Abigail whispered.

"Nothing," Rufus said. He looked down at the asphalt driveway to keep himself from looking at Alastair Gruen. The intensity of Gruen's gaze felt like fingers poking at him.

Abigail studied Rufus's face. "I knew you'd do the right thing," she said.

Rufus tried to smile, but couldn't. There was no *right thing*. Every path seemed likely to end in failure. He made himself look up and meet Gruen's eyes. Then he shook his head, just once, and got into the car.

Rufus's mom was waiting for them in the hallway outside the intensive care unit at Broadbridge Community Hospital. The skin around her eyes was red and raw and her clothes were rumpled, as if she'd slept in them. She folded Rufus into a hug without speaking. Rufus let her warmth wash over him, squeezing her as hard as he knew how.

"How's Dad?" he managed to ask at last.

"He made it through the night," his mom said, mustering a remnant of her reassuring smile. "For now, they're just trying to keep him stable—he's got so many injuries . . ." She took a ragged breath. "You can go in and see him, Rufus. Grandpa Jack's already in there—they only allow two at a time." She stroked Rufus's hair. "Don't be scared by how he looks," she whispered. "It's still him under all those tubes."

His dad slept under a thin blue blanket, linked by a variety of tubes and cords to machines that hissed and sighed and beeped like a chorus of despondent robots. Grandpa Jack sat in a chair on the far side of the bed, holding his son's hand. "Hey there, Rufus," he said, his voice gravelly. "How are you holding up?"

"Okay." Rufus stared at his father. His head was bandaged. His legs were splinted. A tube carried oxygen to his nose. He didn't look anything like the person Rufus knew—the one who always had an idea or a suggestion or a piece of information for every situation.

"Dad?" Rufus whispered. He took his father's free hand. "It's Rufus."

Iris coughed. "*This* is how you glompers keep people alive? With *machines*?"

Startled, Grandpa Jack swiveled to see who had spoken. He reached to his face for his missing glasses, then blinked as if trying to clear his eyes.

"Didn't get much sleep last night," he said. "I'm not sure if I'm—"

"You're seeing me all right," Iris snapped from her perch on Rufus's shoulder. "I'm as plain as a note on your face."

"This is Iris," Rufus said. "She's from Feylawn. She's here to help Dad get better."

Grandpa Jack opened his mouth to speak, but Iris interrupted. "You need to go," she said. "We've got work to do and I feel awful. Make sure no one comes in until Rufus comes out."

"Tell Mom I wanted a few minutes alone with Dad," Rufus said.

Grandpa Jack frowned. "I don't want anything from Feylawn getting near him."

"Iris isn't like that," Rufus said. "She won't hurt him. And she can do stuff doctors can't."

Grandpa Jack didn't move.

"Please," Rufus said. "I know it seems weird, but we have to try. What choice do we have?"

With a heavy sigh, Grandpa Jack stood. "Never thought

my son's life would be in the hands of the very creatures who've been messing up my kitchen," he said as he went to the door.

When he was gone, Iris fluttered to the bed, breathing hard. She traced a gentle pattern on Rufus's dad's cheek. "When Carson's father was dying, it seemed so strange to me. Back then, I'd never seen someone die. Now I'm almost used to it."

"He's *not* going to die." Rufus placed the bag of seeds on the bed beside her. "What do we do now?"

"Put them in a cup. Ask them to sprout."

Rufus drew a squashed paper cup from his backpack. "Ask them *how*?"

Iris took a labored breath. "With your mind. You're going to have to do it—I'm too weak."

Rufus felt a surge of panic. "I don't have magical powers like you do."

"You have *some* kind of powers or you wouldn't have been able to talk with them in the first place," Iris said. She pulled a seed out of the bag and dropped it in the cup.

Rufus shut his eyes. *Sprout*, he told it. *Sprout!*

Nothing happened. He heard voices in the hall—visitors talking in low tones, a nurse issuing instructions. How much time did he have before someone came in?

SPROUT!

He opened his eyes. The seed hadn't moved. Panic swirled through him, a blizzard of jumbled thoughts. He was an idiot to think he could do this. His father was going to die, and he couldn't save him. *Sprout, damn it! Sprout-sprout-sprout!*

"Don't shout at them," Iris said. "Just talk."

Rufus took a breath and then another, trying to quiet his mind. He let his vision blur and pulled his attention from the room. The fear receded. He imagined the seed sinking into soil like a soft bed.

Open, he said silently.

The paper cup shuddered in his hand. The seed had split in two and sent out a stream of fine white roots. An eager green shoot reached nearly to the cup's rim.

"About time," Iris said. "Try to pick up the pace, will you?"

One by one, she added more seeds to the cup. Each time, Rufus asked the seed to open and watched it split, its roots entwining with the others, green shoots braiding into a thick and tangled stalk.

"Good," Iris said when the seventh seed had opened. "Where's the knife?"

Holding the cup between his knees, Rufus fished his Swiss Army knife from his pocket and unfolded the blade. "What do I do with it?"

"Slice open my wing."

"*What?* No!"

Iris gazed at him steadily. "I'd do it, but it's awkward for me to reach back there. Just stab somewhere near the base, where it's not too withered."

"I can't. You're weak enough as it is."

"Doesn't matter. It has to be done."

She flew to his leg and turned. Her pale wings trembled. Rufus rested the point of his knife against the left one's sinewy edge. "Can't I cut myself instead?"

"No. You might have seed speech, but you're not a greenblood." Iris looked over her shoulder and opened her wing into the blade. A bead of green sap bubbled from the gash.

Rufus gasped. "Are you okay?"

"Just catch it," she cried. "In the cup, quick!"

The drop was already falling. As it landed in the cup, the clod of roots and tendrils roiled and steamed. Then they dissolved into something that looked like a translucent green raindrop.

"Pour it in his mouth," Iris said, her face ashen. "Don't let it spill."

She walked unsteadily down Rufus's leg and stepped onto the bed, her wings drooping behind her. The left one hung at an odd angle, like a door that's been left ajar.

Rufus gently parted his father's lips and tipped in the green bead. It landed on his father's tongue and vanished. He waited for his father's eyes to blink open, the color to return to his face. Now he would shake off the splints, pull out the tubes, sit up, speak.

But his father slept on, surrounded by the hiss and blip of the machines.

"Why isn't it working?" Rufus cried. "Iris? Did I do something wrong?"

Iris didn't answer. She was curled up on his father's shoulder, one withered wing cloaking her face, unconscious.

ᦔᦒᦔ

All morning, Rufus watched his father, scanning his face for a flickering eyelid, a grunt, a smile—anything that would indicate that the seedcraft was working. Nurses came in and out of the room to check the various lines and machines, periodically asking him to leave so they could perform more mysterious tasks. His mother sat beside him, holding Rufus's hand, her face creased with lines he never knew she had. Everyone spoke in low voices except Aunt Chrissy, who paced the hallway bellowing into her cell phone.

Rufus's father didn't stir. Neither did Iris, not even after Rufus gently wrapped her in a purple cabbage leaf he'd filched from the landscaping by the hospital entrance and placed her in his backpack.

At one o'clock, Abigail persuaded Rufus to join her for lunch in the cafeteria so they could work on the last clue.

> *But you cannot go vamoose.*
> *Someone has your train's caboose.*
> *The man you greet is very sweet,*
> *But here you'll meet your grave defeat.*

"Sweet," Rufus said. "What kind of man would be sweet? The owner of a candy store?"

Abigail offered Bobalo a piece of pepperoni from her slice of pizza. She had chosen a table in the far corner of the cafeteria, where they could watch the door in case Gruen or Diggs appeared.

"A baker?" she suggested. "No, I bet it's Feylawn-related." Suddenly her eyes lit up. "Pop Avery!"

"The man you greet is *Avery* Sweete," Rufus said. "Except he's dead. How are we supposed to greet a dead person?"

But even as he said it, he knew. "He's buried at Feylawn. Grandpa Jack told us when we interviewed him."

"No." Abigail shook her head vigorously. "I know what you're thinking and it's not the answer."

"But it is. Avery Sweete. *Grave* defeat. She buried it with him. It's the only thing that makes sense." He pushed away his half-eaten sandwich, suddenly nauseated.

"So we're supposed to dig up a grave?" Abigail stroked Bobalo anxiously. "How are we going to manage that?"

"Tonight. When everyone's asleep." Rufus stood and shouldered his backpack. "Grandpa Jack told us where the graveyard is—on the ridge above the woods. We'll bring the feylings and the rest of the train. If we find the caboose, they can leave tonight." He glanced at the mesh compartment where Iris slept, wrapped in her cabbage-leaf cloak. "Iris isn't going to last much longer."

"We'll find it," Abigail said. "We'll save her. We'll save all of them."

It was the least confident Rufus had ever heard her sound.

33

THE WIND'S ROAD

"I still don't understand how we're supposed to get there," Rufus whispered into the darkness.

It was a little before midnight. He and Abigail were standing in his backyard, keeping their voices low so they didn't wake Aunt Chrissy. If they did this right, no one would know they'd left the house. Rufus's mom was spending the night at the hospital. So was Grandpa Jack. A duffel bag slung over Rufus's shoulder held all four pieces of the train, along with a flashlight and a shovel. Iris slept in the pocket of his hoodie, weightless as a winter leaf.

"Horsetail." Quercus flew to a patch of ornamental plants growing along the back fence. "We'll use it to travel the Wind's Road."

Rufus and Abigail exchanged mystified glances. By the light of a streetlight, they could just make out Quercus and Trillium hovering in front of them. Each carried a green stem with a knobby growth at the end. The stems were about as thick as Rufus's thumb, and as long as his arm.

"Straddle 'em like a hobbyhorse," Penstemon instructed. "That's right. Now give 'em a good shake."

"And hold tight," Trillium said. "The change spooks them."

"*What* change?" Rufus asked. Feeling ridiculous, he planted his legs on either side of the stem and shook it vigorously. It shook back, nearly ripping itself out of his hands. Lumps of muscles rippled down the stem, fattening into flanks that pressed against his thighs.

"What the—?" he exclaimed. Hooves kicked out from the flanks, lifting him off the ground. He gripped the tossing stem and found he was digging his fingers into the mane of a snorting green horse. It reared up on its hind legs and Rufus bounced backward, flailing. The duffel crashed to the ground.

"Whoa! *Whoa!*" he cried helplessly.

"Easy, girl," Abigail said beside him. Her stem had become a horse as well, but she seemed unfazed, sitting as erect as a duchess with Bobalu on her shoulder. She caught Rufus's reins. "Hold them loosely, don't tug. Get your feet in the stirrups, heels down."

Rufus shoved the toes of his sneakers into the stirrups dangling from his saddle and gripped the reins Abigail offered him.

"Better. Her name's Grasshopper. Mine's Malachite."

"How on earth do you know their names?" Rufus asked, trying to compose himself. His horse pawed the ground, ears swiveling.

"I just named them." She swung down from her horse and grabbed the duffel, unzipping it to load the train cars into the saddlebags. "Stroke her neck, it'll calm her."

"Ready?" Penstemon asked as Abigail remounted Malachite. She nodded.

"To Feylawn, on the Wind's Road!" Penstemon cried from between Malachite's twitching ears.

"To Feylawn!" Trillium echoed from her perch on Grasshopper's forehead. The horses surged forward, straight toward the fence that separated Rufus's yard from the one next door.

"Look out!" Rufus ducked and shut his eyes, bracing for impact. Beneath him, Grasshopper's muscles tensed and stretched.

A blast of cold air hit his cheeks. He opened his eyes. The houses of his neighborhood were gone. Grasshopper's hooves churned along a foaming cloud-colored path. The horse was at full gallop, and it seemed to Rufus that the road beneath them galloped as well, sweeping them along like a river at full flood. His teeth were cold in his mouth and he realized he was grinning wildly as the night blew past him, whipping his hair back and chilling his cheeks. He leaned forward to grasp Grasshopper's neck, gripping her back with both knees. Her coat was as thick and green as the lawn at Orchard Meadows. It smelled grassy and sweet.

The feylings were laughing and shouting. Abigail tilted her head to stare at the night sky. "This is the best thing *ever*!" she called.

"Lean a bit to the right," Trillium instructed, and as Rufus leaned, Feylawn came toward them in a rush of greenery.

A three-quarters moon was just lifting above the trees. A night bird trilled softly.

"Could anyone have followed us?" Abigail whispered. Bobalo was tightly coiled in her left braid, his wide eyes reflecting the moonlight.

"Depends on whether the others have been keeping up the defenses while we were gone," Trillium said.

Silently, they nudged the horses into the woods. Branches tangled over their heads, smudging the moonlight with a leafy thumb. At last the trail leveled out and the forest faded into sparse shrubs. Before them lay a clearing bordered by a wrought-iron fence that was half-buried in climbing roses.

The graveyard.

34

THE CALL

The gate to the graveyard was so tightly bordered by climbing roses that Rufus had to use the blade of the shovel to hack it open. Inside were just two headstones, the names and dates murky in the moonlight. Abigail switched on the flashlight.

Avery Sweete 1891–1955

Carson Sweete Collins 1918–1988

A breeze whisked across the ridgetop, rustling the heavy cloak of greenery that encircled the graveyard. Rufus took a breath and drove the tip of the shovel into the grass above Avery Sweete's grave.

Abigail grimaced. "I can't believe we're doing this."

"It's better not to think about it," Rufus said. "I'll take the first turn." The ground was harder than he'd expected, and the shovel heavier. He tipped out a few shovelfuls of dirt, sweat already beading at the back of his neck. At this rate, it would take them hours. He tried not to look at the two gravestones, pearl gray in the moonlight. They reminded him of things he didn't want to think about: His father, still and quiet in his hospital bed. Iris's face when he'd tried to ask her why the seeds didn't seem to be healing him. He muscled the shovel into the ground again.

"Don't you guys have some kind of digging seeds?" he asked the feylings perched along the overgrown fence. Then he remembered the two feylings who had died conjuring the dogs that dug Grandpa Jack out from under the fallen tree. "Never mind."

The night was choppy with noises: crickets, birdcalls, bat squeaks, undefined rustling. His arms ached. The beam of Abigail's flashlight illuminated only the shallow pit in front of him and the bottom half of Avery Sweete's headstone. Below the dates, he saw, were words. He read them in a whisper: *"The call shall be heard and death shall be defeated."*

"There's the word *defeat* again," Abigail said. "Like in the rhyme—*But here you'll meet your grave defeat*. If this were a movie, we would touch the word on the headstone and it would open a secret compartment that held the caboose." She knelt down and brushed her hands over the letters. Nothing happened.

Rufus kept digging, the words on the headstone repeating in his head as he shoved the spade into the earth and dumped the dirt into a pile. *The call shall be heard*—dig. *Death shall be defeated*—dump. *The call shall be heard . . .*

He dropped the shovel, remembering something Iris had said.

"Rufus!" Abigail called as he sprinted through the cemetery gate. "Where are you going?"

He was already with the horses, fumbling with the saddlebags.

"Mind filling me in?" Iris said, poking her head from his hoodie pocket as he grabbed the engine of the Roving Trees Railway. She pulled herself up to his shoulder, her injured wing still bent and drooping.

"You told me it's a *calling bell*," Rufus said as he darted back into the graveyard. And then, before anyone had a chance to speak, he lifted the locomotive over his head and shook it.

A bright gash of sound rocked him backward. Chimes rang out in waves, sharp and clear and high. The feylings on the fence flew into the air, squeaking protests.

"*Stop!*" Abigail switched off the flashlight. "It's too loud! Gruen and Diggs will find us!"

Rufus kept shaking the bell. "Avery Sweete!" he shouted. "Avery Sweete!"

The bell's peals washed over him, drowning out his voice. Then he heard the cry, knife-sharp, jagged at the edges. The pain of it nearly split him in two. Loss, loss, unimaginable loss. Not just one death but thousands and thousands of them, each death multiplying again and again until he saw the world as nothing but a collection of deaths, every one of them a plaintive, soul-tearing cry—trees and plants, insects and animals, young and old. He gasped as the words arrowed into his heart: *There is no why. We all must die.*

And then he understood.

"It's a seed," he whispered, letting his arms fall. The peals of the bell still echoed around them. "That cry—it's a seed!"

"The Seeds of Death," Iris said in his ear. "The calling bell amplifies them, to remind us that it's time to go."

"But what are they doing in the engine?"

"Without them, the train can't pass between our world and yours. In our world nothing dies. In your world, everything does."

The bell grew silent. The feylings settled back on the fence, scanning their surroundings for movement. Below Rufus's feet, the ground shifted, like a blanket over a restless sleeper.

"Rufus? What did you just do?" Abigail whispered.

She crouched, holding the shovel like a weapon. Bobalo wriggled below the collar of her shirt. Rufus stayed where he was, the engine so heavy in his hands that it seemed to be pinning him in place. "I called Avery Sweete."

Something sprouted in a corner of Avery Sweete's grave—a knobby, white, mushroomy thing. Another poked up beside it, and then another, until the grave was silver white with them. As they grew, they toppled, falling into the dirt one by one.

"Flashlight!" Rufus whispered.

Reluctantly, Abigail set the shovel down and took the flashlight from her back pocket. When she turned a wobbly beam onto the grass, she illuminated the empty sockets of a pocked white skull.

The grave was sprouting bones.

"Oh no," Abigail said. She took a few steps back. "Rufus. This was a bad idea."

"Say his name again," Iris whispered.

Rufus's throat was very dry. "Avery Sweete!" he called in a hoarse whisper.

The bones lay in the grass, pitted and shadowed by time and dirt. Then they began to slide together, ordering themselves into legs and arms and ribs and spine. At last, the skeleton stood cautiously, as if unsure that his pieces would all stay put. As he did, the moonlight seemed to swarm to him, filling in the silvery flesh, dressing the flesh in silvery clothes, topping the head with silvery hair and the hair with a silvery hat so that at last a man stood before them, a man in whom the white bones were still visible beneath the quicksilver of his flesh.

The man looked them over. He was tall and broad-shouldered, with the confident grin that Rufus remembered from his photograph. He tapped his chest as if expecting to find something in the pocket of his jacket. "Say, you don't have a ciggy, do you?" he said. "I seem to have left mine at home."

Rufus shook his head. "I don't smoke."

"Good boy," said Avery Sweete. "Filthy habit." He looked Rufus up and down, then turned and looked at Abigail. "Kind of late for kids to be out, isn't it?" He glanced at the sky as if to check the time, then rubbed his forehead. "Can't actually remember coming up here. I wasn't sleep-walking, was I?"

"Not exactly," Rufus said.

"Where's the caboose?" Iris whispered in his ear. "Ask him!"

Avery Sweete burst into a grin. "There's a gal on your shoulder," he said to Rufus. "A small one, with wings. Like a fairy, but not as pretty."

"That's Iris," Rufus said, as Iris's wings beat against his face in irritation. "She's, uh, wondering if you've seen a little caboose."

Avery Sweete was still staring at Iris. "My daughter, Carson, writes books about fairies. I always thought she was off her nut, the way she talks about them." His eye fell on his tombstone. "What's this?"

He knelt down to read the inscription, then stood slowly and removed his hat. "Ain't that a sockdolager," he said after a moment. "Guess the ciggies got me in the end." He studied his own hands, noticing their silvery sheen and the white bones within.

"About that caboose," Rufus said. "It's just, we're in a hurry."

Sweete looked up, wearing the same confident grin he'd had when he first appeared. "Guess there's worse things to be than dead," he said, and for a moment he reminded Rufus of Grandpa Jack. "Worse places, anyway. I always loved Feylawn at night. It was good of Carsie to plant me here."

"We think she might have planted something with you," Abigail said, stepping forward. "That caboose."

"It goes with this train engine." Rufus held out the locomotive.

"Why would she bury me with a toy caboose?" Avery Sweete asked. He frowned as if trying to remember something, then knelt in the grass. "Let me check," he murmured, and plunged his hand into the earth like someone trying to pick up a pebble from the bottom of a pond.

Rufus and Abigail looked at each other, mystified. The ground looked solid, but Sweete seemed to find it as permeable as water. "Can't quite reach it." He grunted. He let his whole arm sink into the earth, then dropped his head and torso down as well. It was only after everything but his feet had disappeared that they heard a muffled cry of triumph.

"Got it!" Avery Sweete said, lifting himself back into the grass and spitting out a mouthful of dirt. "Is this what you're looking for?"

The caboose in his hands was as red as the other cars were green, its surface so shiny and crimson that it looked like it had been dipped in blood. Even from where he stood, Rufus could hear the steady drumming of the seeds inside it. Rufus handed the engine to Abigail, then took the caboose from his great-great-grandfather's shimmering hands. Quercus, Trillium, and Penstemon abandoned their posts along the wrought-iron gate, circling it like moths around a candle flame.

"Never thought I'd live to see the day," Penstemon murmured.

Iris launched herself from Rufus's shoulder and half flew, half fell onto the caboose's roof. She lay there for a moment, sprawled flat with her injured left wing bent oddly behind her, and then crawled through a window, her thin legs and sky-colored dress trailing behind.

As Rufus held the caboose, a tide of images washed over him. Flowers erupted into colors. Roots snaked beneath the ground. Vines twisted their way up the trunks of trees. And running through it all, like a great green river, was a murmur. It was birdcall and waterfall and the buzz of insects in the sticky warmth of afternoon and the cry of a newborn baby. It had no end and no beginning. It was both silence and noise. This time he knew without asking what it was. Inside the body of the caboose, the seeds pulsed and chanted: *We give breath. And conquer death.*

35

DEATH DEFYING

Abigail tugged at Rufus's arm.

"Rufus," she said. "We have it. Let's go."

He blinked, still trying to grasp what he had just heard. *The Seeds of Life were in the caboose.* Now he understood why the train had to be complete to pass between the worlds—it needed both the Seeds of Death and the Seeds of Life. Above his head, the feylings circled, chattering excitedly. All except Iris, who was still inside the caboose.

Abigail's grip on Rufus's arm tightened. "Thanks for your help, Mr. Sweete." She flashed her politest smile. "Do you need help getting back into the ground?"

"Don't see much reason to hurry." Avery Sweete stretched out on the rucked soil of his grave. "I'll lie here and watch the stars a bit."

"Good night, then." Still holding the engine, Abigail tucked the flashlight into her back pocket and gestured to Rufus to grab the shovel.

"Good night, Mr. Sweete," he said, and followed her to the graveyard gate, clutching the caboose to his chest with one hand.

"That was incredible," Abigail whispered. Bobalo emerged from her T-shirt and assumed his poetry-reciting pose. "Abby-gell the brave and mighty. Approached a grave when it was nighty . . ."

Pressed close to Rufus's heart, the Seeds of Life sang a song of their own. *We give breath. And conquer death.* His stomach clenched. How easy it would be to ride Grasshopper to Broadbridge Community Hospital and deliver them to his father.

There was a piercing shriek. "NO! THIS IS *NOT* HOW THE STORY ENDS!"

Rufus whirled around. A bright silver figure stood beside Avery Sweete. "I wrote the ending in my book!" she cried. "It says *All the finished stories will begin again.*"

Avery Sweete raised himself onto his elbows to get a better look. "Carsie? What are you squawking about?"

Carson Sweete Collins wore tapered trousers and a sweater with rolled-up sleeves. "I wrote myself a happy ending," she said. "One where we live here at Feylawn forever, and nobody dies, and nothing bad happens to us ever again."

The silver of her skin made it hard to judge her age. She seemed old enough to be a grandmother, but her eyes were as big and round as a child's. The longer Rufus looked at her, in fact, the more like a child she became. Now she wasn't a woman at all—just a little girl in a dirty white pinafore.

"If *I* don't get a happily-ever-after, *nobody* does," the little girl shouted. "If my papa has to die, so do the feylings!"

Abigail dug an elbow into Rufus's side. "Let's get out of here." They sprinted for the gate.

A long silver arm shot forward and snaked around them, drawing them backward. The feylings scattered, diving for cover in the tall grass.

"Everybody thinks I'm strange because I see fairies," the child version of Carson Sweete Collins confided as she squeezed Rufus and Abigail to her chest. She had grown quite a bit taller.

"I see fairies, too," Abigail replied, her voice choked by the ghost's chilly embrace. Bobalo whimpered from inside the collar of her shirt.

"Me too," Rufus offered as he struggled to free himself.

Carson's ghost glowed brighter. Now she was a young woman in a wool skirt and dirty boots. "I wrote a book about fairies," she boasted.

"How nice," Abigail said, trying to loosen the ghost's grip. "But we need to go, so . . ."

"It *was* nice," Carson screeched. Her silver form grew higher and brighter, like a flame feeding on dry wood. "But my husband had me locked in an asylum!"

"We got you out, Carsie." Avery Sweete stood beside his gigantic daughter, staring up at her anguished face. "You sent him away. And you published your books and had lots of fans."

"But I was lonely," Carson said. She shot up another foot, lifting Rufus and Abigail into the air. "First my mother died. Then my husband left. Then you died, Papa. Even the feylings betrayed me. I only ever asked them for one thing, but they refused."

"And I told you why!" Iris emerged from the caboose in Rufus's hands. Proximity to the Seeds of Life seemed to have restored some of her lost strength. She hoisted herself onto the car's roof and stood with her hands on her hips. "I explained until I blew up my face!"

"Turned blue in the face," Carson corrected. "You always get things wrong."

"So do you," Iris retorted. "Death is part of the logic of your world. Everybody gets a turn and then that turn is over. No do-overs."

"BUT IT'S NOT FAIR!" Carson screamed. She dropped Rufus and Abigail to the ground and swayed in front of them like a tall tree in a windstorm.

"Who said anything about fair?" Abigail burst out. She stepped forward, staring up at the towering ghost with her fists clenched by her sides. "Do you think it's fair that Rufus and I have to clean up the mess you made? Do you think it's fair that Uncle Adam's in the hospital?" She grabbed Rufus by the hand. "Come on."

They took off running, but the ghost of Carson Sweete Collins materialized in front of them, blocking their path. "I had to leave Feylawn. I had to hide from the goblin who wanted the train. But I never told him where it was. I could have, but I didn't."

"Good for you," Rufus said, trying to peer around her silvery form. The gate was so tantalizingly close. "Now let us go so he doesn't get it."

"Carsie," Avery Sweete said, striding over to join his daughter. His handsome, easygoing face was creased with concern. "You were always a live wire, kiddo, but this is bonkers. Let the children go home."

Carson's body shuddered, tugging itself in two like a dividing cell. Then it split again, and again, fanning out like a string of paper dolls, each one a tall, silver version of Carson Sweete Collins. They locked hands, forming a ring around Rufus and Abigail.

"I hid it piece by piece," the ghosts chorused. "I made up a rhyme so I could find it again. I taught the rhyme to Biggy so I wouldn't forget." The chain of Carsons locked eyes with Iris, who was still standing on the roof of the caboose in Rufus's hands. "I knew you'd come begging. I knew you'd be sick and sorry and then you'd *beg* me for the train."

"I begged you plenty of times," Iris said. "I begged you every day until you left Feylawn for good. You didn't care."

The row of enormous silver eyes filled with enormous silver tears. "You'd never lost anyone," they said. "You needed to learn how it felt."

"Well, now I know," Iris said. "Our queen is a captive. I've been to more funerals than I can count. Mine will be next."

"Not you, Iris! You were my best friend!" The chain of ghosts collapsed like a folded fan. All that was left was one silver woman with a sharp, discontented face. She turned to Avery Sweete, pressing her hands to her chest as if she'd been stabbed. "I did it all for you, Papa. I sacrificed everything to save *you*."

Avery Sweete shook his head. "I never asked you to do all that nonsense."

"Why wouldn't you stop *smoking*?" Carson wailed. "Why wouldn't you *listen* to me?"

Avery floated close to her, his expression rueful. "You can't make anyone be different than they are, Carsie. You should know that by now."

"I did it all wrong," Carson whispered. "I made a terrible, terrible mistake."

Avery put his arms around his daughter, resting his cheek on the top of her head. "I know you did," he murmured. "But the past is past. We belong in the ground, Carsie. Feeding that rich Feylawn soil." His eyes met Rufus's and he tilted his head toward the graveyard gate.

Rufus looked at Iris. She was watching him with her hands by her sides, her wings quivering. Beneath her feet, the seeds inside the caboose warbled and sighed. *We give breath. And conquer death.*

Tears pricked Rufus's eyes. "Let's get down to the Roving Tree," he said. "Before anyone changes their mind."

36

FIRE AND SMOKE

The moon was high and bright as they rode back down the path to the farmhouse. The feylings had activated the muffle and they rested on the horses' necks and rumps discussing the best way to round up all of Feylawn's feylings for an early-morning departure. Meanwhile Bobalo was reciting his poem about Abigail the Brave and Mighty. Rufus leaned over Grasshopper's neck, straining his ears for telltale footfalls or tree rustlings. But even without Bobalo's recitation he wouldn't have been able to hear anything. The muffle had them encased in their own bubble—no outside sound could penetrate.

Beside him, Abigail sighed. "I'll be glad to get out of these woods," she whispered. She tapped Malachite's flanks with her heel and the horse trotted forward. The luff-luff of hooves on leaves transformed into the clump-clump of hooves on packed earth as they moved down the path toward the farmhouse.

And then the horses were rearing and snorting, hooves pawing at a wall of netting that barred their path. Rufus tumbled from Grasshopper's back and landed painfully on his side. Above his head, Nettle and his crew of All-Outers swarmed through the air, armed now with lethal-looking metal spears instead of pencils. "All-out! All-out!" they chanted.

As he scrambled to a sitting position, Rufus heard a grunt behind him. An arm hooked around his throat, pulling him back.

"I appreciate the prompt delivery of my train," Mr. Diggs rasped in his ear. "I'll make sure to leave a five-star review."

"Let go of me," Rufus cried. He struggled to see what was happening to Abigail and the others, but the goblin tightened his grip around his throat.

"Get off " Rufus croaked. Mr. Diggs squeezed tighter, his woolly sleeve pressing, pressing, pressing against Rufus's neck.

A kaleidoscope of stars erupted behind his eyes and everything went black.

⚬ᏊᏊᎧ᎙

When he came to, he was lying in the grass with Abigail beside him. Two burly goblins with ramlike horns stood sentry above them.

"Are you okay?" Abigail whispered.

Rufus nodded, his head still spinning. "Are you?"

She gave him a rueful, upside-down smile. "So far."

"Where are the others?"

"There." Abigail gestured with her chin at two nearby goblins, one with the legs of a dog, the other with the tail of a lizard, who gripped a feyling in each fist. Her lip trembled. "But I don't know where Bobalo is. He just disappeared."

Rufus sat up and looked around. Mr. Gruen and Mr. Diggs stood beside the stump of the Roving Tree, casting gray shadows on the grass. The fully assembled train rested at their feet. Hovering in the air above them was Nettle Pampaspatch.

A surge of fury coursed through Rufus's body at the sight of the topknotted feyling. He leaned forward to listen, his teeth clenching.

"Why don't we have tracks?" Gruen was saying. "You told us the train made its own tracks from the stump to the Green World."

"I was only ever a passenger on the Roving Trees Railway." Nettle's voice had lost its habitual sneer. "Perhaps if I had a bit more time—"

"*You* built the contraption, Diggs," Gruen interrupted. He thrust his hands into the pockets of his overcoat. "Why can't you make it work?"

"I built *half* of it. My little wife made the rest." Diggs bent from the waist to glower at the train as if it were a disobedient child.

"I've tried everything I can think of," Nettle babbled. "The seedcraft is quite unusual. Very difficult, actually."

"I told you he'd be useless," Mr. Gruen sneered. "Traitors make terrible allies."

"He's served his purpose," Mr. Diggs said. "Now we have other tools at our disposal." He motioned to the goblins standing guard.

The ram-horned goblins pulled Rufus and Abigail to their feet and thrust them forward. Dog Legs and Lizard Tail strode over as well, gripping the feylings tightly.

"Let us go!" Iris hammered her fists against Dog Leg's fingers. "Let us die in peace."

"That depends on your friend Penstemon Cottonwood," Mr. Diggs said. He took Penstemon from Lizard Tail's grip and held him up at eye level. "Nettle tells me you know how to run this train. Fetch me the Seeds of Life and I'll free your friends when you return."

"I'm not a traitorous worm like Nettle Pampaspatch," Penstemon said. "You'll get no help from me."

"Don't be hasty," Mr. Diggs said. "Mr. Gruen, show our little friend your marvelous new toy."

Mr. Gruen took a thick-barreled weapon from the ram-horned goblin and pointed the muzzle skyward. A plume of flame danced into the air, hissing. Rufus felt the heat on his cheeks. His heart thudded.

"Everyone loves a cookout!" Mr. Diggs shouted. He

brought his face close to Penstemon's. "I'm going to fry your friends one by one until you agree to run my train."

Penstemon's wrinkled face went slack. He moved his lips but made no sound.

"Don't give in," Quercus yelled, thrashing in Lizard Tail's meaty grip.

"We're dying anyway," Iris called. "It doesn't matter if he speeds it up a little!"

"It might not matter to you," Mr. Gruen said. His clockwork innards ticked ominously. "But these children have their whole lives ahead of them."

The feylings stopped struggling.

"No!" Trillium shouted. "Don't you dare!"

"Leave the glompers out of it," Penstemon pleaded. "This has nothing to do with them."

"And yet they involved themselves anyway," Diggs said. "Such a pity."

Gruen raised the barrel of the flamethrower.

Rufus looked at Abigail. Her eyes were wide, her jaw set. He was so afraid that his body felt like it was already dissolving into smoke and ash. "Abigail," he said. "Call the mother."

Abigail stared at him blankly.

"Aw," Mr. Diggs sneered. "The babies want their mother."

"Yes!" Rufus said. "The babies want their mother! Call her!"

Abigail frowned. Then she raised her chin. A call

unraveled from her throat, icy and inhuman. The call of a baby umbral that wants its mother.

There was no answer. The umbrals were back in the cave by the boulders perhaps, or drinking the moon's reflections in the creek.

"What's it going to be, Penstemon?" Mr. Diggs said. "I'm going to count to three."

"Call again," Rufus said, panic whittling his voice to a whisper.

"One," said Mr. Diggs. "*Two.*"

Then a shrill, piercing cry came echoing back from the trees, followed by a swirl of smaller cries, as high and wild as the cold winds at the edge of the world. The mother umbral swooped over them, trailed by her four babies. Gruen lifted the flamethrower. The mother umbral swerved to avoid a jet of fire and spewed out a billowing cloud of violet smoke. Screeching after their mother, the babies did the same.

The smell of marsh and morning breath filled the air. Rufus bolted toward the spot by the Roving Tree where Diggs had left the train, praying he could get there before the dimpsy smoke did its work.

Already the smoke had its fingers in the pockets of his brain and was snatching out mistake after mistake. *Leaving his stuffed lion at the movie theater when he was six . . . Ordering a rocky road ice cream cone when he was eight and then discovering he hated rocky road ice cream . . . Squatting down to put the salamander in his shoe on the middle school basketball court and hearing Aidan Renks bellow, "Barefooted booby!"* . . . Rufus felt like laughing, the errors were so trivial. Had they really mattered to him once?

And there was the train, resting on the ground, close to seven feet long from end to end. Through the screeches of umbrals and the shouts of feylings and goblins, he heard the high keening of the Seeds of Death, the deep pulsing of the Seeds of Life.

Then the dimpsy smoke found what it was looking for.

His father with the rope swing in his hands. "You sure it'll hold me?"

His own sullen reply: "Grandpa Jack's ridden it lots of times."

And then. The rope snapping. His dad falling.

Falling.

Falling.

Landing, with a terrible thud, in a cloud of dust and leaves.

"No!" Rufus screamed. Was that now? Or then? His throat felt raw and shredded. He did not want to remember this. He had to run, somewhere, anywhere else. But the rope snapped again, and his dad fell again, and landed again.

And then again.

"It's all your fault," the dimpsy smoke declared. *"You didn't listen. You didn't believe your dad when he said Feylawn was dangerous. You made that swing. You told him to try it. And now look what you've done. He's going to die. And you couldn't save him."*

"I *tried*," Rufus whispered. He had to get away from the smoke. Away from the voice. "I tried to save everyone."

"*And failed*," the smoke replied, spreading out a fan of memories like a winning hand of cards: *His dad immobile in his hospital bed. Nettle screeching in triumph. The feylings caught in goblins' fists.*

"*You didn't save* anyone," the dimpsy smoke said. "*You're too dumb and too young. Now Abigail will die and you'll die and the feylings will die and your dad will die. And it will all be your fault.*"

Rufus wanted to protest, but he had no answer. There was nothing in his head but the memories of his failures and that inky, insistent voice. "*I told you so,*" it said as he blundered through the smoke. "*I told you that you would fail. I knew you couldn't do it.*"

That voice.

It was his own voice.

It was his *own voice.*

He slowed, then stopped. Still cloaked in the vile-smelling purple vapor, he made himself turn toward the train. What had the feylings told Abigail to do when she was dimpsied?

"*Nothing,*" the smoke whispered. "*There's nothing but this: the truth about who you are and what you've done.*"

Remember happy things.

The night he'd been struggling with his math homework

and his dad had brought him hot chocolate. *"Let's take a break and look at the stars—come on, it'll clear your head."*

The dimpsy smoke tried to pull the memory away, but he held on to it, feeling the warm mug in his hands, the clear, cold air, the sensation of his father's arm around his shoulders as they looked up at the night sky. They'd seen three shooting stars that night, Rufus remembered, and in between his dad had explained about meteors and meteor hunters . . .

The smoke began to thin.

Now he reached deep into the drawers of his memories.

His mom racing him down the block, laughing as they sprinted, legs pumping in unison.

Making the Museum of Interesting Things with Grandpa Jack. "Interesting's a state of mind, Ru. As long as you're interested in things, things will be interesting."

His dad smiling into his eyes as Rufus pointed out a red-shouldered hawk circling the meadow. "Tell me how you can recognize it, Rufus, I want to see what you see."

As Rufus's vision cleared, he saw a strange scene.

The feylings fluttered in all directions, some fleeing, some chasing, some fighting. Abigail was trying to wrestle the flamethrower away from Gruen, who moved slowly, jerkily, surrounded by billows of violet smoke. And there, at Rufus's feet, was the train.

He squatted down beside the locomotive. When he

touched it, it vibrated with a living energy that sent pins and needles into his palms, filling his mind with a clear, bright light. He could hear the overlapping voices of the two sets of seeds.

We give breath. And conquer death.

There is no why. We all must die.

He had to get it away from here. Hide it somewhere the goblins couldn't find it. But where?

Then Diggs lunged toward him, arms outstretched. There was nowhere to run, not with seven feet of train to carry. But Rufus held on, the pulsing energy of the train keeping his mind clear even as the violet smoke closed in again, and the all-too-familiar voice whispered, "*You failed again. You failed. You failed.*"

No, he hadn't. Not yet.

He let his mind drift away from the smoke, away from the meadow, into the place where he could hear without listening and speak without talking. The murmur of the seeds grew louder, steadying his heart, filling him with certainty.

Now, he told them. *Open the passage between the worlds.*

A beam of golden light flashed from the locomotive's head-lamp. Tracks began to unfurl before it, a glowing latticework that stretched out into the night and then beyond, into some place between dark and daylight, between here and there, somewhere that smelled of sweet berries and pine needles and sun-warmed grass, where death had never been. The engine hummed. Its pistons chugged. A puff of steam rose from its smokestack.

Mr. Diggs gave a strangled yelp and leaped in front of the train, his bird legs straddling the still-unspooling tracks.

"Stop!" he shouted. "Not now! We're not ready!"

He pursed his lips as if to whistle. The train lurched forward.

37

BREAKING UP
IS HARD TO DO

Rufus shut his eyes as Mr. Diggs threw himself in front of the train.

But there was no thud, no screech, no scream—just a loud crack, like a heavy branch breaking in the wind. When he opened his eyes, the train was motionless in front of him. Mr. Diggs was gone.

Rufus sank to his knees, wobbly with relief. The cross-hatch pattern of the tracks still glowed faintly.

What had he just done?

Shouts ricocheted around him, and the whirring of wings. Overhead, the umbrals swooped and circled, but they flew in wider arcs now, banking into the trees. A few yards away, Mr. Gruen crouched with his arms sheltering his head, motionless as a statue. Abigail had the flamethrower. She pointed it at the ram-horned goblins, who backed away, cowering.

"Run," she shouted, "before I fry you like a pair of sausages."

The goblins ran, scurrying for the safety of a hulking black vehicle they had parked in front of the farmhouse. Behind them flapped a familiar Steller's jay, his screeching voice high and shrill: "*Wait for me!*" A few All-Outers in lizard-skin suits fluttered after him.

Rufus reached Abigail just as the goblin's car peeled out, tires spitting mud and grass as it sped toward the dirt road that led downtown.

Abigail's face was wild with fear and relief. "Something happened to Gruen. It's like he's frozen—or maybe dead?" She swung around, still holding the flamethrower. "Where are the others?"

"Chasing All-Outers, I think." He turned to Mr. Gruen's motionless form. "What happened to him?"

Abigail bounced on the balls of her feet, spilling words in a giddy rush. "The umbrals—they broke everything they flew over. He's like a stopped clock!" She held up the flamethrower in her hand. "This thing, for example. If the goblins hadn't run away, I was going to have to use it as a club." She tossed the weapon aside.

Gruen's skin was chalky against the gray of his overcoat. A fine powder trickled from his sleeves onto the ground. Rufus shivered. "What *is* that?"

A breeze drifted across the moonlit meadow, stirring the powder into a spinning eddy. A look of horror passed over Abigail's face. Gruen's features were blurring, his body crumbling. His clothes sagged. The trickle of powder grew steadier, hitting the ground with a grainy hiss.

Then Mr. Gruen's body buckled. Rufus and Abigail leaped backward as a shower of clockworks tumbled from the sleeves of his overcoat. The remnants of Mr. Gruen lay at their feet: a heap of clothes and metal gears. A grinning white skull. A pile of fine white dust.

"He just disintegrated!" Abigail made a face.

Rufus backed away from the pile. "He'd been dead for so long—it must have been some kind of goblin magic holding him together."

"Hey, glompers!" Iris, Penstemon, Quercus, and Trillium swirled over their heads, all of them talking at once.

"Did you see how I took down those two All-Outers?" Quercus thrust out his chest and hitched up the pants of his silver suit.

"I saw Trillium kick Pampaspatch in the face," Iris replied. "Which *almost* made up for the experience of being manhandled by a goblin."

"But where's Diggs?" Trillium asked.

Rufus's insides twisted. "I don't know exactly. The train started up and he jumped in front of it. And then he was just *gone*."

"It slammed right into him." Quercus spoke with relish.

"*Pow!* Must have knocked him into the space between the worlds."

"The impact stopped the train in its tracks," Penstemon said. "Otherwise it might have followed him."

Rufus looked from one to the other. "I just wanted to get the train away from him," he said. "I didn't mean to *kill* him."

"I doubt he's dead," Penstemon said. "But I'd wager he's stuck between the worlds. He doesn't have the seeds he needs to cross into either one."

Wobbling awkwardly on her injured wing, Iris flew to Rufus's shoulder and wrapped her arms around his neck. "We're safe," she said. "We're safe! I have to say, I never thought you'd be able to do it. First of all, you're a glomper, and second of all, you didn't seem all that clever at the outset, and third of all, you didn't know what you were getting into, and—"

"And yet we did it," Rufus said, the realization coursing through him like a tingling river. He grinned at Abigail. "We gave the feylings back their train!"

"We did," Abigail said, laughing. "Yay, us!"

Iris cleared her throat. "Despite your many flaws, you're two of the least idiotic glompers I've ever met. I want you to know that I'm forever in your desk."

Abigail chuckled. "Debt," she said. "The expression is, *I'm forever in your debt.* Because you owe the other person a favor."

"Actually," Iris replied, "the expression is *forever in your desk*, because it's like giving them a certificate saying how grateful you are that they can keep in their desk drawer, along with other important documents that they might want to keep forever, like a book about common glomper expressions, authored by Iris Birchbattle. And if I haven't mentioned it before, you correct people too often and go to too many summer camps. On the other hand, you're much less prissy than I expected, and much, much braver, and—"

She made a strangled sound and broke off in a fit of coughing. "Oh!" She sniffed when she was done. "Penstemon, ring the calling bell! We finally get to go home!"

⁂

Rufus and Abigail stood alone beside the train. The moon had sunk low on the horizon. The feylings had scattered to pack their belongings. It felt like days had passed since they'd first snuck out of the house. Rufus ached for news of his father.

"But what about Bobalo?" Abigail said suddenly. "I don't know what could have happened to him."

"He must have escaped when the All-Outers attacked," Rufus said. "Maybe he went back to the orchard."

"But then why hasn't he come to find me?" Abigail cried. "We're *bonded*."

Rufus gave her a quizzical look. "For a minute it sounded like you actually missed him."

"I *do* miss him!" Abigail said. "What if Diggs killed him?"

At that moment, a ball of orange fur hit her smack in the face.

"I missed you, too, Abby-gell!" Bobalo squeaked as he unfurled. He plastered himself to her cheek and covered her nose with kisses. "And I thought *you* had been killed—by a bad gobby-lin."

Before Abigail could answer, a second orange ball came rolling across the meadow at breakneck speed. When it reached Abigail's feet, it scrambled up her leg with suction-cup paws and plastered itself to Bobalo.

"I *loooooooove* you!" it squealed.

"You do?" Abigail mumbled, her mouth partially covered by a double layer of cotters.

The second cotter raised its head. "Not you," it said. "I love *him*! My husband, Bobalo Fling!"

"Your *what*?" Abigail peeled the two cotters from her cheek and held them out, one in each hand.

Bobalo covered his face with his paws.

"Bobalo thought his Abby-gell was dead," he moaned. "Bobalo mourned her tragic death."

"As you can see, I'm perfectly fine," Abigail said. She dropped the two cotters to the ground and folded her arms.

Bobalo squared his fluffy shoulders. "Then Bobalo Fling still loves you!"

"And Loubella still loves Bobalo!" The second cotter tackled Bobalo and covered him with kisses.

"My Abby-gell I know so well," Bobalo shouted, his voice somewhat muffled by Loubella's kisses. "Her head is as hard as a walnut shell! At everything she does excel!"

"Of Bobalo Fling, I shout and sing!" exclaimed Loubella. "In winter, summer, fall, and spring!"

Bobalo wriggled out from under Loubella and rolled closer to Abigail's feet. "Um," he said in a low voice. "Bobalo might have accidentally gotten remarried."

"Remarried?!" Abigail exclaimed, squatting down to look at him more closely. "We were only separated for a couple of hours!"

Rufus knelt beside her. "It might be time to divorce him," he said gently. "You can't really bring him with you to summer camp anyway."

Abigail looked stricken. She lifted the cotter close to her face.

"Goodbye, Bobalo," she whispered. "Thanks for all the presents and the poems and stuff. I'm sorry it didn't work out." She kissed the top of his head before repeating the words Quercus had taught her that first day in the apricot orchard: "I cut the bond with Bobalo Fling. I cut the bond with Bobalo Fling. I cut the bond with Bobalo Fling."

Bobalo gazed at her with his green eyes very wide. "I cut the bond with you, Abby-gell," he said. "But you will always be one of my favorite wives. You have very lustrous hair." With that he leaped into Loubella's waiting arms.

"I will scream and yella—about Loubella!" he proclaimed. "Because she's my gal and I'm her fella!"

Abigail turned and walked into the meadow, clenching an unraveling braid in each fist. Rufus ran to catch up with her.

"Are you okay?" he asked.

She nodded, blinking back tears. "I just—" She brushed her chin with the end of one braid. "I just liked how much he loved me," she said. "I didn't have to win trophies, or have impressive hobbies, or anything. He just *loved* me."

Rufus wasn't sure what to say. He rubbed his hand over his hair, noticing as he did that it was a gesture he'd picked up from his father.

"I'm not going to make up poems for you or anything," he said after a moment. "But you're my cousin and kind of my best friend and you helped save the feylings and—you know. I love you just for that."

"And because I saved your life by calling the umbrals," Abigail said.

"Sure," said Rufus. "But not because you're good at everything. Kind of in spite of the fact that you're good at everything."

Abigail gave Rufus a hug. "Thanks," she said, wiping her eyes on his shoulder. "I'm glad you didn't try to make up a poem."

"Do you want to stay until the feylings leave?" Rufus asked. "Iris said they leave at sunrise."

"Of course I do. Are you kidding me? My mom won't wake up until her alarm goes off at 7."

Rufus looked at the gibbous moon, sinking low over the meadow. Two dark silhouettes grazed beside the Boulder Dude. One lifted its head and nickered softly.

"The horses!" he said. "I wondered where they'd gone!" He turned to Abigail. "Look, there's something I need to do. By myself. I'll be back as soon as I can."

38

VISITING HOURS

Grandpa Jack was asleep on a foldout chair in the hospital visitor's area, issuing whistling, teakettle snores.

Rufus put a hand on his shoulder. "It's me. Rufus."

"Huh?" Grandpa Jack startled awake and sat up, reaching to his nose for his absent glasses. "What are you doing here?"

"I came to see Dad. Is he any better?"

Grandpa Jack's shoulders relaxed. "Woke up a couple hours ago, perky as a radish after a rainstorm. The docs don't know what to make of it."

Something warm and liquid surged from Rufus's chest to his eyes. He wiped them with the back of his hand, unable to speak. "Where's Mom?" he managed finally.

"She was too tired to drive all the way back to Galosh. She booked a room at the motel across the street to get a few hours' sleep." He rubbed his chin with his good hand. "How'd *you* get here, anyway?"

"Would you believe me if I said I came on horseback?" Rufus asked.

Grandpa Jack shook his head. "I no longer know what to believe about anything," he said. "I'm not even sure I'm awake right now."

"Can I see Dad?"

"If you're quiet about it. They moved him out of the ICU. Room 426."

Rufus hugged his grandfather. "Go back to sleep, okay? I'll see you in the morning."

⁓⁓⁓

Freed from the labyrinth of tubes, his dad looked almost like himself again. He slept on his side, hands folded under his cheek, just like he did at home.

Then his eyes flickered open. "Rufus? Mom said you were home, asleep."

Instead of answering, Rufus wrapped his arms around his dad and squeezed as hard as he knew how.

His dad kissed the top of his head and rocked him from side to side. "I'm awfully glad to see you," he said. "You smell like the great outdoors."

"I've never heard you call the outdoors *great* before." Rufus peered into his dad's face. "How are you?"

His dad ran his hands over his own face and arms.

"Pretty good!" he said. "A little stiff. I guess I had a big fall. At Feylawn, right?"

"Yeah." Rufus shut his eyes against the memory of his dad tumbling into the ravine. "I'm sorry. There was a kind of war going on, and you just happened to get caught in it."

His dad smiled, a smile that said he knew Rufus was talking nonsense but didn't mind because he was happy just to hear him talk. "I think there's probably a simpler explanation," he said. "I shouldn't have jumped on that swing without testing it to see if it could hold my weight."

"It's going to be better at Feylawn now," Rufus said. "Remember that train Grandpa Jack found in the barn? Abigail and I found all the pieces. It was really hard and I was afraid we wouldn't be able to do it, but we did."

His dad wrapped his arms around Rufus and drew him close. "Then you achieved your goal," he said. "That's a successful summer project."

❦

The sun was peeking over the horizon as Grasshopper touched back down at Feylawn. The air filled with trills and rivulets of birdsong. Swarms of feylings drifted across the meadow, singing traveling songs and talking in high, excited tones.

"Well done, glomper!" they called as Rufus walked to the farmhouse. "Abundantly well done!"

He found Abigail sitting in the grass near the stump of the Roving Tree, surrounded by milling, chattering feylings. They circled her head like tourists on a helicopter excursion.

"That's one of the glompers that found it," one of them remarked. "I pinched her once—before she was anybody."

The train rested on the ground by the stump, its paint shimmering. Inside the cab, Trillium and Penstemon were working furiously, adjusting valves, gauges, and dials and shoveling sticks into the boiler. The engine thrummed. Clouds of white steam huffed from the smokestack.

"She's ready to run!" Penstemon called. As he spoke, two thin strands of tracks glided over the grass like quicksilver.

Quercus stood by the passenger cars. "Now boarding at platform 1," he called, "the Roving Trees Railway, express service to the Green World!"

Feylings pressed forward, jostling one another in their eagerness to get on board. Faces appeared in the windows of the coaches.

"Where's Iris?" Abigail asked. Rufus looked around and finally sighted her dragging an oversize suitcase across the lawn, her injured wing quivering with the strain.

He ran to join her. "Can I help you with that?"

She looked up, her black hair damp and curly with sweat, her sky-blue dress tattered and stained. "Would you?" she said, alighting on his shoulder. "I don't want to miss the train."

Overhead, a Steller's jay circled, bright blue in the early-morning twilight. It landed in front of Rufus with a brittle squawk, trailed by a dozen bedraggled All-Outers.

"Get away from us!" Rufus ordered, his hands balling into fists.

"Please!" the jay screeched. His black crest drooped. "Please! Let me go home."

The feylings who were waiting to board the train watched warily.

"You're outnumbered, Nettle!" some of them shouted. "You'd better scram while we're still deciding what to do with you!"

"We're not armed," pleaded one of the All-Outers. "Just let us on the train and we'll do whatever you say."

Peeking out of the cab, Trillium snorted. Quercus hitched up his pants.

"We can wall them in with brambles," he said. "Or bind them in tanglevine. Turn 'em into trouts and leave 'em gasping on the grass."

"They abundantly deserve it," Trillium burst out. "They could have killed us all."

"I'm done fighting," Iris said. She fluttered down to stand in front of the disheveled jay.

"Are you too cowardly to take your true form, Nettle?"

"I can't do it," the bird squawked. "I'm too tired."

"Not as tired as you're going to be," Iris said. "Take it from somebody who's made a few terrible mistakes. It can take years to put things right. Sometimes it feels like you never will."

"I just want to go home," the jay screeched. "Please let me aboard!"

Iris shook her head. "We'll take your followers if they want to come. But not you. Not until you make amends for all the harm you've caused."

Nettle's crest flared indignantly. "You can't leave me among the glompers." The All-Outers had already skulked into the shrinking line of passengers, leaving the jay alone in the grass.

"Where you go next is up to you," Iris said. "I suggest you stay at Feylawn to help the glompers care for it," Iris said. She reached into her pouch and drew out a reddish seedpod.

Rufus and Abigail exchanged glances. "I don't *want* him helping us," Rufus said. What he wanted was to never see Nettle again.

Iris sighed. "You two are less ignorant than you were when I met you, but that's not saying much. It's going to take a while for the rest of us to be well enough to return, and Feylawn needs constant care. There's a lot to do. I left you a list."

"A *list?*" Rufus said. "Are you kidding me?"

Iris extended the seedpod to Nettle. "By tasting blue-black peony seed, you pledge your service in word and deed."

Nettle danced from side to side on his skinny legs, but finally bowed his head and pecked up a single seed, wincing as he swallowed.

Iris turned to Rufus and Abigail. "He can't harm you now," she said. "Hand me my suitcase, will you?"

The train shimmered, a green streak on the green grass. Everyone else had climbed aboard. Rufus placed Iris's bag inside the last coach. Iris climbed in after it.

"AAAAAAALLLLL ABOOOOOOAAAARD!" Quercus called.

"Try not to mess things up too terribly while we're gone," Iris said.

"But without mistakes, there wouldn't be stories," Rufus said. At that moment, with the sun warming the back of his neck and his nose filled with the scent of wet grass, he was less afraid of making Fatal Errors than he had ever been in his life.

Standing beside him, Abigail squeezed his hand. Together, they watched the train chug along its silver tracks and vanish into the place between the worlds.

ACKNOWLEDGMENTS

I am grateful to so many people.

First and foremost, my parents, who gave me a childhood filled with stories and the time and freedom to explore magical places. My mother's unquestioning support for this manuscript when nobody was allowed to read it is a major reason it finally ended up between two covers. How grateful I am to have been born into a family of writers!

Alisha Niehaus Berger encouraged me to write this book when it was just "something I'm playing around with," and her brilliance and pixie dust guided it all the way to the end. By sheer magic she became part of the team of midwives we called the Cliffhangers, alongside Deborah Davis, Rachel Rodriguez, Elizabeth Scarpelli, and Marsha Diane Arnold. My deepest gratitude to each of you for your detailed and thoughtful critiques.

To my extraordinary agent, Erin Murphy, who makes everything possible. To you and to everyone in the incredible EMLA community, I'm grateful to be able to say, *I'm yours*.

Bottomless thanks to my dream editor, Joy Peskin,

whose mind meld made this book what it was trying to be. And to all the people at Farrar Straus Giroux and MCPG who work tirelessly to create beautiful books and launch them into the world, thank you!

Thanks also to Suzan Goodman and Sophia Caressa, who answered my medical questions (but are not to be blamed for the liberties I took with their answers), and to the kind folks at the late lamented Tin Plate Junction in Oakland, whose wonderful store inspired Galosh's much darker version.

Most of all, thanks to Cliff and Milo, with whom I first set out on this railway journey. You are everywhere in these pages. How lucky I am to have you.